A FRENCH AFFAIR

JENNIFER BOHNET

Boldwood

First published in Great Britain in 2020 by Boldwood Books Ltd.

A CIP catalogue record for this book is available from the British Library.

Paperback ISBN 978-1-80048-315-6

Large Print ISBN 978-1-83889-118-3

Ebook ISBN 978-1-83889-119-0

Kindle ISBN 978-1-83889-120-6

Audio CD ISBN 978-1-80048-312-5

MP3 CD ISBN 978-1-83889-231-9

Digital audio download ISBN 978-1-80048-313-2

Boldwood Books Ltd
23 Bowerdean Street

London SW6 3TN

www.boldwoodbooks.com

This one is for my sister, Beverley, with love.

1

It was late afternoon on the last Friday before Christmas and Belinda Marshall, roving manager and chief troubleshooter for the Milton chain of Devonshire-based hotels had just been given some bombshell news from Nigel and Molly Milton, her employers. She'd been wondering why she'd been called into the inner sanctum so late in the day. Now she knew.

'You've bought a new business in France? We're finally expanding into Europe? That's great news. I know you had a couple of holidays in France this year, but I thought they were just that – holidays for you both. You didn't mention you were even looking at places,' Belinda said, leaning against the filing cabinet as she accepted the champagne Nigel had insisted on pouring. 'Cheers.'

'It came up unexpectedly,' Molly said. 'In truth it's all been a bit impulsive.'

'Anyway, we both know the place and we're thrilled with it,' Nigel interrupted. 'Molly can't wait to spend time there when it's all been rejuvenated. Bit run-down at the moment. Which is where you come in, of course.'

Belinda sipped her champagne before saying, 'So come on, you two, put me out of my misery. Where is our new hotel? Which particular part of France? Biarritz? St-Tropez? Paris?'

Nigel laughed. 'I know we run a successful company, Belinda, but prices for places like that are way out of our league. No, Camping dans La Fôret is in—'

'Hang on – did you just say, Camping dans La Fôret?' Alarm bells began to ring in Belinda's head. 'That's a funny name for a hotel.'

'It's not a hotel. It's a boutique campsite in Brittany, Northern France. Finistère, to be precise. Huge potential, but we're going to need your expertise to drag it into the twenty-first century. Bring it up to standard so that more people can enjoy the Milton Hotel experience,' Molly said.

Belinda looked from Nigel to Molly and back at Nigel again, stunned. 'But we're in the hotel business not camping, not even glamping.' It had taken her three years of studying and hard work to be awarded her 2.1 in Hotel Hospitality Management. Not once had running a campsite, even a boutique one, ever crossed her path. Let alone one in Brittany.

'Camping has just become our business,' Nigel said. 'It's all the hospitality business. All about people. Making sure guests enjoy the experience of staying in a Milton hotel – and now a campsite. No difference really.'

'But Finistère – isn't it always raining there? Who in their right mind would want to camp in the damp? Morbihan maybe, but not Finistère. Not surprised it's run-down.'

'Don't exaggerate. It's an urban myth it's always raining there,' Nigel said. 'And with global warming and the movement of the jet stream, the weather is improving there every year. It could soon be The Breton Riviera!'

'We had lovely weather the couple of times we were there,'

Molly chimed in. 'It's only run-down because our friends who owned it found it all too much to keep on top of. It's in a beautiful spot – just needs some TLC to turn it back into a real paradise.'

Belinda looked at them both as the news penetrated her brain. 'So let me get this straight. You've bought a run-down campsite called Camping dans La Fôret in Finistère and you want me to help you transform the place and fill it literally with happy campers.' This was nightmarish news to her, but she couldn't say that to Nigel and Molly. She took a deep breath. 'Okay. Is there a website I can look at? Start to get some ideas flowing. As it's only a campsite, I won't really need to visit. I can do it over the internet.'

'No, no. We're sending you to France ASAP in the New Year,' Nigel interrupted. 'You'll have two months – maybe three – to sort out the site and get it ready to fill with those proverbial happy campers this summer.'

Belinda felt a cold shiver run through her body. This couldn't be happening. There was no way she could disappear off to France for weeks on end. There was Chloe and the twins to consider. Not exactly dependent on her, but they needed her to be around. And what about BB, her dog?

It was Molly who broke the silence that had fallen. 'We know it's a lot to ask of you,' she hesitated. 'Especially given you and your mum's circumstances, but we're sure it's something you'll enjoy doing. It's always quiet in the hotels after New Year, so it's a good time for you to go.'

With a grin, Nigel raised his glass in her direction for a toast. 'Here's to Camping dans La Fôret. We have every faith in you, don't we, Molls? You'll soon have the place up to scratch. You and Alain, the manager, who is already on site.'

'He's already on site? Surely he can oversee things then?' Belinda asked quickly.

'Needs a woman's touch,' Molly said. 'And, in particular, your touch. You've always been good at seeing things differently and coming up with fresh ideas.'

Speechless, Belinda could only clink her glass with theirs. Nigel and Molly might have every faith in her, but there was no way she wanted to go and live in Finistère. Whenever the possibility of going to Brittany had come up in the past, she'd vehemently vetoed it. As for spending two or three months there, well, she couldn't do it, however much Nigel and Molly insisted. She'd have to resign. Find another job with another hotel chain. Either that or find a way of persuading Nigel and Molly to send someone else. Someone who didn't get heart palpitations at the thought of returning to Brittany.

* * *

For the next ten days, Belinda pushed all thoughts of Brittany to the back of her mind, which was surprisingly easy during the day as the hotels filled with customers getting into the festive mood, leaving little time for her to think about Nigel and Molly's bombshell, let alone make any contingency plans.

All the hotels had some regular 'Christmas' clients returning and there was lots of laughter and fun everywhere. Some of the regular holidaymakers even brought presents for Belinda and other staff members, thanking them for always making their holidays so happy.

The Christmas decorations Belinda had organised for all three hotels had included several real fir trees hung with bands of simple silver lights. A large tree was placed in each foyer and small ones in every available space throughout the hotels. The effect, with every window and polished surface reflecting a myriad of twinkling lights, was magical. The oohs and ahhs from guests as they arrived made Belinda smile.

The busy days took her mind off things, but the nights were something else. Night after sleepless night, Belinda wrestled with her conscience. There was no way she wanted to let Nigel and Molly down after they'd given her this second chance in the hotel industry.

Four years ago, when her life had fallen apart and she'd been in desperate need of a job, every other hotel she'd approached had turned her away, saying her college diplomas obtained in her twenties were way out of date and she had no recent hotel industry experience. Milton Hotels Ltd had been the only business willing to take a chance on her. Not only had they thrown her a lifeline with a job but also a new home after the house she'd shared with Peter, her husband of twenty years, had been sold. She'd suspected in the beginning that it was because Molly had been good friends with her mum, Joan, and felt sorry for her. But she'd quickly proved herself more than capable of doing the job and the three of them had soon settled down into a good working relationship.

They were like a second family to her now and seeing her ideas being put into practice in the hotels was a great feeling. The variety between the three Milton hotels made the job interesting. One was in historic Tavistock, another was on the quay in Dartmouth where she lived and the third was a real seaside hotel in Torquay with clients who returned year after year with their families for the acres of golden beach across the road. All different and all providing different challenges in the clientele they attracted and the way they were run. The thought of leaving, even for a few weeks, and managing a campsite didn't appeal. Especially one that was in Brittany.

Belinda had almost everything back in place that she'd

dreamed of having while growing up. Her plan for surviving life after divorce had, once she'd woken up and realised she needed a plan, succeeded. She'd successfully climbed out of the second black hole in her life and was in a happy place. A place where she wanted to remain. She was happier with her current lifestyle than she'd ever expected to be after the cruel way Peter had left her the day after Chloe's wedding. She loved her tiny penthouse flat at the top of the old hotel in Dartmouth, her evenings with Jane, her best friend, shopping in Torquay and walking BB, her dog.

Three years ago, when she was wallowing in the depths of despair after the divorce, followed nine months later by her mother's death, Chloe had found a little wriggling grey and white puppy, huddled under the hull of one of the boats laid up for winter in a nearby riverside park. Despite asking around, no one claimed him and Chloe had brought him home to Belinda, insisting it was meant to be.

'You need each other, Mum,' she'd said. 'He'll be your Best Buddy.' She was right. Belinda and the dog had quickly bonded and became inseparable. The vet pronounced him to be a Tibetan terrier when they took him to be checked out and vaccinated. 'Best Buddy' quickly became shortened to BB and he'd become a familiar sight, padding along at her side as she strode through the hotels. There was no way she could leave him behind.

* * *

Belinda and BB spent Christmas Day with Chloe, Max and the twins, Aimee and Charlie. With the twins nearly three years old, it was the right age to turn the day into a real family celebration. It wasn't until the twins were tucked up in bed and the adults had collapsed in the sitting room that Belinda told Chloe and Max about Nigel's latest acquisition and how he wanted her involved.

'He wants me to go and stay over there for possibly three months.'

'Brittany?' Chloe said, looking at Belinda concerned. 'Are you going?'

Belinda shrugged. 'I don't want to. I'll miss you all. It'll be like putting my life here on hold.'

'Brittany is lovely, especially in the spring,' Max said. 'I remember family holidays there growing up. We'll bring the twins to see you once you've sorted the place out.'

Belinda smiled at him. 'That would be something to look forward to,' she said. 'If I go.'

2

Once Christmas and the New Year festivities were over, Belinda tried at every opportunity to get Nigel and Molly to change their minds about her overseeing the rejuvenation of the campsite in Brittany. Both of them insisted, together, and individually when she cornered them separately, that she was the one they wanted to head up the makeover of the campsite and drag it into the twenty-first century. According to them, it was the perfect project for her and they really didn't understand her reluctance to accept it. They showed her pictures and a short video they'd taken on their phone.

'It's got everything families could want for a holiday in unspoilt countryside,' Nigel said.

Belinda had to agree. The place, with its log cabins scattered higgledy-piggledy around the site rather than in regimented rows and the long low stone building down by the river that served as the restaurant-cum-café for the site, looked to be picturesque, if in need of some tender loving care.

When Nigel insisted she'd have to stay in Finistère for most of the time to oversee the workmen, she *had* almost resigned.

'But what about the hotels here? I visit them all at least twice a week. Sometimes more. And the weekly accounts? I know I can do most things remotely, but surely I need to come home at least once every ten days?'

Molly had said she and Nigel would manage everything between them. 'Be like the old days for us, before you came into our lives.'

Even trying to get Nigel to believe that her French wasn't good enough didn't work.

'You forget I've heard you in action with French tourists. Your language skills are better than most and using it every day you'll soon be word-perfect.'

Her final argument was BB. 'There is no way I'm leaving BB,' she said. 'That is non-negotiable.'

'Completely understand that,' Nigel said. 'Take him. I'll even pay for his pet passport.'

Belinda sighed, sensing that nothing was going to change their minds and she was limited to the two choices. Go or resign. Neither of which she wanted to do.

Talking to Jane, her best friend, was no help.

'It's a challenge,' Jane said.

'I like to set my own challenges,' Belinda said. 'Besides, there's a difference between a challenge and an unwanted surprise. And you know how much I hate surprises and change.' Changes in her life had always tended to be unexpected and more than catastrophic.

'You'll be so busy, time will fly by. Nigel and Molly wouldn't be insisting you go to France if they didn't think you could do it. And let's face it, nothing much ever happens here until spring. The hotels aren't exactly busy – oh, except for Easter of course, which is late this year anyway. Being surrounded by all those hunky Frenchmen will be a bonus,' Jane added with an innocent look on her face, which induced a resigned laugh from Belinda.

'At least you won't be there trying to matchmake,' Belinda said. She and Jane had met at a book club three years ago when Belinda was struggling to cope after her unexpected divorce. Jane had been on a mission ever since to find Belinda a replacement husband, determined her new friend wouldn't sink into a lonely middle age.

Several friends of Jane's husband, Brett, had duly been introduced to Belinda at supper parties, but sadly not one of them had come up to Belinda's new, exacting, requirements. Certainly none had given her even a tiny frisson of excitement when she met them. Jane had declared only last week that Belinda was impossible to please. She wasn't really, she was just determined never to be hurt in the way Peter had hurt her ever again.

'We're talking northern Brittany here, not the Côte d'Azur, which, as we all know, is where all the hunky Frenchmen hang out. If Nigel had bought a campsite in Cannes or Antibes, I'd have gone like a shot. All that sunshine and je ne sais quoi, mmm.' Belinda glanced at Jane. 'Guess that makes me somewhat shallow?'

'Just a bit. I don't understand why you're so upset at the thought of spending time in France. You've had holidays over there and loved it. You adore Paris and you've had several holidays in Nice. Paris and the Riviera aren't the sum total of France, you know. Besides it's not forever. You'll be back before you know it.' Jane looked at Belinda. 'Anyway, you haven't come up with a real reason yet for not going.'

'I do know there's more to France than the major tourist destinations, but Brittany is not somewhere I've ever longed to visit.' Belinda shrugged. 'I don't like being out of my comfort zone these days. And, honestly, what do I know about campsites? I've never stayed in one. I like five-star hotels,' was the only excuse she could think of without lying to her friend.

How could she admit to Jane the real reason behind her reluctance to go to Brittany? About that promise she'd made her mother when she was so ill? That she would go back to Brittany, lay the ghosts to rest. But it was a promise made under duress. Since her mum's death, Belinda had guiltily pushed it to the back of her mind. After all, her mother would never know if she kept or broke the promise. Briefly, she toyed with the idea of telling Jane the real reason why she was fighting going to Brittany, but there were things in her past she'd never talked about to anyone outside of the family. Even Peter had only known the sketchiest outline of her previous life before she met him.

Belinda sighed. Jane was right. It wasn't forever. She'd agree to go, keep her head down, concentrate on work, stay on site and ignore everything else. If the opportunity came up, maybe she would try and do something about those ghosts. And the good thing was she'd be back home ready to pick up her normal routine with the hotels in time for high season and summer.

To Belinda's unspoken relief, her departure for France was delayed until late February by two things. The first was the fact that the Plymouth–Roscoff ferry was out of service in the New Year for six weeks of maintenance. The second was the organising of BB's pet passport with all the necessary vaccinations and form filling.

As soon as she had a definite date for leaving, Belinda googled the nearest village to the campsite and booked herself in for a couple of nights at the Auberge de Campagne. That way she could check out the state of the cabins before living on the site. No way was she in the mood for slumming it in less than ideal conditions.

Despite the hotels being quiet in the first few weeks of the New Year, the days at work were busy for Belinda. Determined to leave everything in order for Nigel and Molly to deal with while she was away, she spent hours on the computer organising things.

In the evenings of the week leading up to departure day, she cleaned the flat until every surface shone, emptied the fridge of its meagre contents and washed every shelf before switching it off. Anything to take her mind off the impending situation.

Her clothes were washed, ironed and folded ready to be put in the suitcase. Before she could reach the large suitcase that she'd stored in the understairs cupboard the day she'd moved into the flat, she had to practically empty the cupboard of stuff she'd shoved in there – out of sight out of mind, for the most part: vacuum cleaner, ironing board, wellington boots, a small fan heater and a large cardboard storage box with a lid.

She'd found the box in the bottom of her mum's wardrobe two years ago when she was emptying her house ready for sale. A brief look inside then had told Belinda it was just a collection of letters, photos, old passports, official letters and the odd keepsake from her childhood, so she'd put it to one side for when she had a moment to go through it. The moment had never arrived.

Pulling out the suitcase, she pushed the box to the back of the cupboard and replaced everything else in front of it, promising herself that she'd finally go through it all when she returned from Brittany.

Belinda placed the suitcase on the bed and began to systematically place things in it. BB whined and jumped up onto the bed and sat on the open lid, regarding her reproachfully. Picking him up, she cuddled him. 'Don't worry, darling BB, you're coming with me.' The dog licked her hand and didn't protest when she set him down on the floor.

* * *

Two evenings before she left, Nigel and Molly joined her for dinner in the Dartmouth hotel, to introduce her to Alain Salvin, the campsite manager, via a video call. Despite her apprehension about the whole campsite business, Belinda couldn't help but be curious about the man who would be her co-worker in Brittany.

'What qualifications does this Alain Salvin have? Is he an experienced campsite manager?'

Nigel shrugged. 'I didn't ask. Our friends' recommendation was enough for us.'

Belinda stared at him. That was most unlike Nigel.

'He's local, so he knows the area, he speaks some English and he's a capable outdoor type, good in an emergency, according to them. You can ask him yourself later.'

But Belinda, determined to do just that, never had the chance.

Once dinner was over, tablets were produced, numbers tapped in and they waited for the French connection to join them.

Alain Salvin, when he appeared on the screen, was not the young man she'd been expecting. This man to whom Nigel was introducing her was in his late fifties with a certain roguish Gaelic look about him.

'Hello, Alain. I'm looking forward to joining you in Camping dans La Fôret later this week,' Belinda said, trying to strike the right note before she began questioning him.

'Bonjour.'

With that, Alain disappeared from the screen and the connection was lost. Nigel swore under his breath and spent several moments trying to regain a connection before throwing his hands up in the air in disgust and muttering something rude about technology.

A frustrated Belinda could only sigh. At least she could now put a face to the name Alain Salvin. Finding out about him would have to keep until she was on site.

A day later, the last weekend in February, it was time to leave. But not before first dropping in on Chloe, Max and the twins.

Belinda read several bedtime stories to the twins and kissed them goodnight after promising to bring them a present each back from France. She made her way downstairs and enjoyed an early supper with Chloe and Max before hugging them both and leaving to drive to Plymouth to catch the cross-Channel ferry for an overnight sailing to Roscoff.

Thankfully, the crossing was calm, but sleep eluded her and she tossed and turned the night away. Even knowing that she'd be returning for a week to help out over the Easter holiday when the hotels were busy didn't help. She had to survive until then, first.

4

Sitting in her car the next morning waiting for the queue of cars in front of her to start leaving the ferry, Belinda set the satnav for 'Camping dans La Fôret, Finistère'.

A feeble sun in the grey sky failed to break through to clear the early-morning mist that hung over the countryside as she left Roscoff behind her. Belinda took her time driving along, enjoying the surprisingly traffic-free roads taking her past field after field that would soon contain the artichokes and the renowned onions of the area. Trees with their bare branches stood tall alongside roadside hedges that were half the height of the Devon ones she was used to. Later, on the windswept Parc d'Armorique, as she reached the top of a hill, Belinda had a misty glimpse of a view that on a clear day would stretch for miles and miles away into the distance.

When BB whined at her from his seat alongside her, she pulled into a lay-by at the top of one of those hills, unclipped his seat belt harness and slipped his lead on before getting out of the car. Once the little dog had sniffed the new smells and peed, Belinda put him back in the car. She sat for a few moments looking out at the wild open moorland in front of her. Strangely familiar and yet new and unseen.

Not one hundred per cent comfortable with driving her beloved Mazda MX5 on the 'wrong' side of the road, she'd set the satnav to find the quietest route. Now, obeying its directions and leaving the wide-open space of the moor, Belinda found herself driving down quiet side roads taking her deeper into the heart of Finistère close to the border of Morbihan.

Driving through in some cases deserted villages and small hamlets, she experienced several unexpected feelings of déjà vu. Feelings she pushed firmly away, but her sense of unease grew as her destination drew closer. Long shut-down memories began to surface despite her attempts to keep them buried. She really didn't want to be here in Brittany. To remember. She couldn't – wouldn't – allow herself to think about the past.

A quick glance at the satnav display on the dashboard indicated that she was nearly at the end of her journey. The next village with its 'Welcome' sign on the verge confirmed the fact that the time to change her mind and carry on driving until she was far away was running out. She barely registered the school or the church as she approached the main street. The aroma of freshly baked bread from the boulangerie drifted past her nostrils as she reached the centre of the village and her stomach rumbled, reminding her about her decision not to eat breakfast on the ferry. Another hundred metres and the village was behind her and she was approaching a T-junction.

Belinda gripped the steering wheel, her knuckles white as she fought the desire to turn round and go back to England. To tell Nigel and Molly that she couldn't do it and resign, like she should have done in the very beginning. She was experienced enough now to get another job.

Seconds before the satnav announced 'In twenty yards turn

left', Belinda saw the 'Camping dans La Fôret' sign on the verge, pointing down a narrow tree-lined track. She stretched out her left hand and turned the satnav off. This was it. The point of no return. If she turned onto the lane, she would be committed to stay and do the job Nigel expected her to do.

Sitting there, her foot on the brake, Belinda mentally gave herself a good talking-to. She was a grown-up for goodness' sake, no longer an impressionable teenager. That person had put the past behind her years ago and got on with life, never dreaming that one day she would be forced to once again come face to face with it. But maybe she was overreacting? After all, it had happened thirty-five years ago. Times were different. People were different. *She* was different.

Determinedly, Belinda lifted her foot off the brake and pressed the accelerator, turning the steering wheel slowly as the car moved forward onto the lane.

The gate at the campsite entrance was hanging off at a drunken angle to one side, a weather-beaten 'Fermé' sign pinned to the top bar. The first thing to put on her to-do list. Belinda forced herself to drive slowly, zigzagging the car up the potholed driveway that seemed to go on forever. The second thing to go on her to-do list. Finally, she pulled up in front of two tired-looking wooden buildings. One had the word 'Shop' above its doorway and sun-faded posters advertising bread, drinks and ice creams. The other had a shallow flight of steps leading to the door and the words 'Reception – Accueil' in faded paint across the top of the door.

Her heart thumping, Belinda parked the car alongside an ancient mud-splattered 2CV, picked up her laptop bag from the passenger seat, got out, promised BB she'd let him out again soon, slammed the door and looked around.

What on earth had Nigel and Molly been thinking about? The photos they'd shown her hadn't looked like this. The place was so run-down, it was a joke. Like most campsites in France, Camping dans La Fôret had closed over the winter – if indeed it had even been open last summer. Looking at the sorry state of things, Belinda doubted that there had been many customers even if it had been open. She sighed. Without even having seen the complete site yet, she doubted that June next year was a realistic date, let alone June this year – a mere twelve weeks away.

She opened the laptop bag and pulled out the folder Nigel had given her with the details, plans and a few out-of-focus pictures that she'd slipped inside. With no website to study, the folder contained minimal information. Alain Salvin, would be there to greet her when she arrived Nigel had said and he would give her all the information and help she needed.

Presumably the old 2CV was his car and the light was on in reception. Surely he must have heard her arrive? Why hadn't he appeared to greet her? It wasn't as if there were hordes of cars or people descending on the place. It would have been good manners for him to come out and greet her. They were, after all, going to be working together. It was hardly the most promising of starts and Alain Salvin had lost a number of brownie points, as far as she was concerned.

Belinda took a deep breath, straightened her shoulders, pulled her five foot three inch body up to its full height and climbed the steps to the reception. She didn't bother to knock before she opened the door and walked in. 'Bonjour.'

A large ginger cat curled up on the desk asleep opened its eyes briefly and looked at her, but the man concentrating on the computer screen in front of it didn't even design to look up before saying, 'I'll be with you in a moment.'

Belinda, recognising Alain Salvin from the brief look she'd had of him the night of the supposed video call, could feel her anger rising as he continued to ignore her. A course in front-of-house etiquette wouldn't go amiss. Belinda tapped her foot, decided to count to ten slowly and then, if he was still engrossed on his computer, she'd leave and start to explore outside by herself.

She'd reached nine and was about to turn and leave when the man looked up and stared at her for several seconds with an unfathomable expression on his face. When he finally spoke, his voice was hard.

'Bonjour. I don't say welcome to Camping dans La Fôret because I sure as 'ell don't need or want a troubleshooter 'ere.'

His rudeness took her breath away. Talk about a frosty reception. Belinda took a deep breath. 'Well, Mr Salvin, that makes two of us then. Because, to quote you, I sure as hell don't want to be here,' and Belinda glared at him before turning on her heels, marching out and slamming the door as hard as she could behind her.

Shaking, she got in the car and sat with her bowed head resting on the centre of the steering wheel for a moment, trying to pull herself together. BB, sensing she was upset, gave her a gentle nudge with his nose, while guilt crowded in on Belinda. She shouldn't have reacted like that. Totally unprofessional of her. But who exactly did Alain Salvin think he was? Nigel had never said a word about the manager being a man with a serious attitude problem. And how exactly was she going to deal with him?

Sitting there Belinda inwardly berated herself. 'You're here to do a job. A job you know you're good at. Take notes, make plans and draw up a working campaign and then get Nigel to employ someone else to see it all to fruition.'

Before that happened though, she'd talk to Nigel and tell him exactly what she thought of his new manager. Monsieur Salvin had shown her he was the sort of person who couldn't deal with authority and to whom compromise was a dirty word. The hospitality industry didn't need rude employees like him and the quicker Nigel sacked him, the better.

5

Sitting in the car, Belinda struggled to stop her hands shaking as she took her mobile out of her bag and tried to compose her thoughts. The text she'd promised to send Nigel was brief and to the point:

Arrived. Talk later.

She switched her phone to voice message, knowing that Nigel was likely to ring her back immediately, demanding to know what she thought of the campsite and, right now, she was incapable of talking to him coherently. Besides she'd not seen anything yet apart from the tatty reception cabin and the rudest man she'd encountered in a while. Even if she marched straight back in and demanded that Alain Salvin gave her an immediate guided tour of the place, she doubted he'd oblige. Which meant she needed to revise her original plans for the rest of the day.

She scrolled through to the notes app on her phone and read the list of the things she'd planned for this first day. Site visit. Take photos. Make notes. Start to formulate a campaign of improvement. Check-in at the auberge. Belinda glanced at her watch. Midday. Right, time for Plan B. Go to the village, explore what was on offer, maybe have a coffee if there was a café. Buy a ham and cheese baguette from the boulangerie for lunch. Find the auberge. Return to the campsite and explore by herself. She didn't need a guided tour. In fact, it was probably better to be alone to uncover the horrors that she suspected would be lurking everywhere.

She picked up her tote and Buddy's lead. She'd leave the car here and walk back into the village. The exercise would do her good and the fresh air would clear her head. Maybe even give her some idea on how to deal with Alain Salvin.

'Come on, BB. Time for your first walk in France.' The dog wagged his tail as she clipped his lead on and licked her hand.

Belinda took her time walking to the village. It was good to stretch her legs and BB was beside himself with all the strange smells he discovered in the grass-covered verges. The absence of traffic allowed Belinda to look around at the surrounding countryside. Too early in the year for any crops to be growing, but she could see several tractors in the fields, spreading the muck she could smell and spraying fertiliser over the earth. Smoke was rising out of a nearby farmhouse chimney and a cluster of wind turbines in the distance were turning.

The boulangerie, when she reached it, was closed for lunch. The village shop too had the shutters pulled down, the cardboard clock sign on the door pointing to 2.30 for reopening. Belinda sighed. She'd forgotten about the irritating French habit of shutting up shop for a couple of hours in the middle of the day.

Outside 'Yann's Place', opposite the church, four cars were parked in a row and Belinda made her way over the square towards it. Hopefully it would be a bar-cum-restaurant and she'd be able to at least buy a sandwich and coffee.

A short silence greeted her entrance as she pushed the door open and walked in, as people glanced up and gave her a brief stare before dropping their gaze.

The man behind the counter called out a welcoming 'Bonjour' as Belinda made her way towards an empty table in the corner.

'Bonjour,' Belinda replied politely as she settled BB at her feet under the table. 'Une café au lait, s'il vous plaît.'

Waiting for her coffee, Belinda studied the blackboards fixed to the wall advertising cassoulet as the 'plat du jour' and other meals and snacks, including savoury crêpes. A crêpe and a glass of rosé for lunch would be perfect. She wasn't that hungry.

'You like to eat?' the man asked, placing her coffee on the table.

Belinda hid a smile. Her accent had clearly given her away as English. Good. The locals probably wouldn't be eager to engage her in conversation now. She certainly didn't intend to get involved in the local community or make friends with anyone while she was here.

'Please,' and pointing to the end blackboard, Belinda ordered a ham and egg crêpe and a glass of rosé.

'Bien. Five minutes.'

The man returned to behind the bar and called her order through to someone in the kitchen.

Sitting there sipping her coffee, Belinda looked around. It wasn't a big bar, but it had a welcoming vibe to it, which the wood burner burning away in the chimney recess at the end of the room enforced. She could imagine the place filled with locals on a winter's weekend evening happily warming themselves by the fire and enjoying a glass or two of Brittany cider. Perhaps the bagpipes currently lying on a table near the fire would be picked up and traditional Breton songs would be sung.

A gust of cold air blew in as the door opened and a chorus of 'Bonjours' went back and forth as a group of young men entered and made for the stools around the bar. Watching as the barman served them bottles of beer as he took their food orders, Belinda smiled to herself as she heard the words 'beaucoup des frites' several times. Briefly she wondered whether the campsite café had been a 'chips with everything' sort of place.

The crêpe, when the barman placed it and her glass of wine on the table, looked delicious and he wished her 'Bon appétit' before turning away to collect glasses from a nearby table.

As she ate her lunch, Belinda heard some of the muted conversations around her. The words 'anglaise' and 'étrangère' caught her attention and she guessed they were talking and wondering about the unknown Englishwoman. Inwardly she shrugged. They'd find out soon enough – village grapevines were the same the world over.

When the barman came to take her empty plate away and asked if there was anything else she'd like, she shook her head. 'Non merci,' but knowing the man had at least some English, she asked, 'Could you give me directions to the Auberge de Campagne, s'il vous plaît?'

'Rue du Moulin. Left by the cemetery.'

'Merci.'

Belinda paid the bill, gathered her things together and, holding BB's lead tightly, left the bar. Rue du Moulin, a single-track road, was easy to find and Belinda found the 'Auberge de Campagne' about two hundred metres along on the right-hand side. Larger than the surrounding houses, it was set back from the road with a short drive lined with some well-pruned bushes leading to the shallow flight of steps up to its front door. A large ship's captain-type brass bell was fixed to the wall near the door.

Smiling at the 'We speak English here' sign, Belinda climbed the steps and pulled the cord.

The woman who opened the door several seconds later was about her own age and gave Belinda a friendly smile.

'Bonjour. I'm Belinda Marshall and I have a room booked with you for a couple of nights.'

'Hello and welcome. I'm Fern LeRoy. Come on in and I'll show you all six and you can take your pick. Not many tourists around at this time of year,' and she held out her hand.

'You're English?' Belinda said, shaking the offered hand.

'Yes,' and Fern bent down to stroke BB. 'Aren't you the beautiful one? I hope you like Lady, my girl.' She glanced up at Belinda. 'I've got a West Highland White terrier. Come on, let's introduce them. She's in the boot room.'

'BB usually loves other dogs, particularly bitches,' Belinda said. 'Shouldn't be a problem.'

It wasn't. Within minutes, the two dogs were playing happily together and Fern took Belinda upstairs to choose a bedroom. She chose the second room she saw – a large room at the back of the house overlooking a beautiful garden and the countryside.

'You have a lovely auberge here. Bigger than I was expecting.'

'It's an old maison de maître,' Fern explained. 'Built in the nineteenth century for a prosperous businessman, when there were such people in rural Finistère.'

Belinda detected a strained note in the short laugh that followed the explanation before Fern spoke again.

'Would you like a cup of tea? Or are you dashing off somewhere?'

Belinda knew she should return to the campsite to start assessing things, but the more time she could spend away from the place and the inevitable confrontation with Alain Salvin, the better right now.

'Tea would be wonderful,' she said. 'I'm guessing you'll be stocked up with English tea, which somehow the French never seem to make properly.'

Belinda followed Fern back down the unexpected wide staircase with its gentle curve at the bottom. The huge kitchen with its La Cornue range, two shabby-chic old-fashioned dressers laden with crockery, an American-style double fridge and a large wood-burning stove in the granite fireplace at the far end, was a mix of traditional and new melded together in a homely way. Shiny copper pots hung above the cooking area and a refectory table with half a dozen chairs placed around it was in the centre of the room.

Fern filled the kettle and switched it on before busying herself getting mugs and biscuits ready.

'Your kitchen is amazing. I'm no cook, but even I could be tempted to try my hand here,' Belinda said. 'Did you design it?'

Fern nodded. 'I've always longed for a large, heart-of-the-home-type kitchen, and I finally got my dream here. A bit late in life as the kids are all independent these days so family meals rarely happen.' She shrugged and changed the subject. 'Milk and sugar?'

Belinda shook her head. 'Just a dash of milk, please.'

Fern poured two cups and passed one to Belinda.

'What about luggage? No offence, but you don't seem the type to travel without a change of clothes, but I didn't see a car outside.'

'My car's the other side of the village.' For some reason, Belinda hesitated saying where it actually was. 'I had lunch in the bar and they gave me directions here. BB needed a walk too,' Belinda smiled. 'Talking of lunch, do you do evening meals? Can I eat here tonight? I don't need anything fancy – an omelette would be fine.'

'I can do better than that,' Fern said, hesitating. 'I do have an official dining room, but do you fancy a kitchen supper with just the two of us? Unless you'd prefer to eat alone?'

'Kitchen supper for two sounds ideal,' Belinda answered. Company and a friendly face would probably be more than welcome after the next few hours at the campsite. 'I've got some business things I need to sort this afternoon, not least collecting my car. I'll be back around six, if that's okay?'

Fern nodded. 'Supper at seven then.'

Belinda, relieved that Fern didn't ask any questions, quickly finished her tea before snapping BB's lead on. 'Bye for now then. I'll see you later.'

* * *

Fern closed the front door behind Belinda and, already planning the meal she'd cook for the two of them, returned to the kitchen, Lady trotting at her heels. It was good to have someone to cook for again. Christmas, when the girls were home, had been the last time she'd done any proper cooking. This evening she fancied cooking chicken in red wine – her version of the French classic coq au vin, followed by a cheeseboard in true French style. She had a rather nice gorgonzola and a wedge of Cantal in the fridge. If Belinda wanted something sweet afterwards, there was a chocolate cake which would go well with coffee. There, that was supper sorted.

Opening the freezer drawer and taking out a couple of chicken breasts, Fern couldn't stop wondering what Belinda was actually doing here in Brittany, particularly at this time of the year. Not many people chose to come before winter was completely over. Maybe she had business in the area? She'd said she had a few things to sort out this afternoon, but the village didn't even boast a small 'zone industrielle' – the French equivalent of an out-of-town shopping and small industry centre. There were a couple of local artists and a writer tucked away in their own cottages busy creating, while down on a secluded stretch of the river a young couple had recently started a trout business, but that was the extent of business in the area – apart from the bar tabac, the village shop and boulangerie of course.

Preparing the veg to go with the chicken, Fern thought about the run-down campsite on the other side of the village and dismissed the thought instantly. No way could she see Belinda being involved with that. Belinda struck Fern as someone who liked her home comforts. She knew without asking that Belinda would detest the idea of shower blocks and rows of communal toilets.

Maybe Belinda was house hunting? There were so many places currently on the market, she'd be spoilt for choice. She was too young to retire, so perhaps she fancied a holiday home? Pulling the cork on a bottle of red Bordeaux, Fern poured it thoughtfully over the chicken she'd placed in the Le Creuset casserole dish. If she was looking to buy somewhere, would a friendly warning about the pitfalls of buying a property in the heart of the French countryside from a stranger be welcome? Until you'd experienced these pitfalls, you'd never know they even existed. And Fern was now an expert in dealing with the unexpected problems that living in France threw up. If she hadn't had Laurent smoothing the way in the beginning when she first arrived, she doubted she'd have coped.

'I'll have to wait and see, won't I?' Fern said, glancing across at Lady snuggled in her basket. 'Maybe Belinda will open up a bit over supper. Anyway, whatever she's here for, it will be nice to have company for a change this evening. And a new friend for you too, if only for a few nights.'

6

On the walk back to the campsite, Belinda's thoughts darted here, there and everywhere. One minute she was mentally remaking a list in her head of things she needed to check out, the next she was stopping to admire the view and enjoy the fresh air. The countryside here was truly beautiful.

She turned off the road onto the campsite lane and, stepping around the potholes, made her way up towards the reception chalet. There was no sign of the 2CV she'd parked alongside earlier and when she climbed the steps to try it, the chalet door was locked. Part of her was relieved that Alain Salvin had taken himself off goodness only knew where, but another part was cross that he hadn't stayed around. A relief in one way as she could now have a good nose around without him being there. Explore by herself, take some up-to-date photographs to show Nigel the current state of the place and try to start outlining a few basic plans for improvement. At the very least, get some ideas flowing around her brain.

Standing on the steps with her back towards the reception door, looking around, Belinda realised the main access path splintered into several routes, most of which appeared to disappear under a canopy of trees or out-of-control shrubs. Overgrown foliage on either side of one of the paths, though, had been cut back recently. Belinda screwed up her eyes in an effort to read a dilapidated sun-bleached wooden sign in desperate need of a fresh coat of paint that was pinned to a tall tree. It was impossible to make any letters out, but as it seemed a reasonably clear path, she'd start her exploration along it and see where it led.

BB whined at her and shook his head; his own inimitable way of saying, 'Unclip the lead, I want to explore'.

'Sorry, BB, you're on the lead for now. I don't want you getting lost,' Belinda said, bending down and stroking him. 'Come on, let's brave the jungle.'

The path she'd chosen as her starting point led her deep into the campsite. Nigel had told her it was spread over roughly six acres and in its day had won awards for its spacious layout and beautiful unspoilt setting. Wandering along the path, Belinda struggled to imagine how the neglected site had looked in the past. It was going to take a lot of work before it recovered the way Nigel insisted it would.

As she wandered around, Belinda realised all the paths on the site looked to be interconnected to a path that went around the circumference of the place. Pushing her way along one of the paths, knocking flowers off the overgrown flowering camellia shrubs that crowded in, she stopped short. In front of her was a large paved area with several wooden picnic benches piled up around the edge and a brick-built barbecue and pizza oven. The entertainment area. To one side of it was a long stone building with 'Café' painted above the boarded-up entrance that Nigel had shown her a photo of. She rubbed some grime off the window and peered inside, but it was too dark to make anything out.

Walking past the building to where the path joined the main

one that circumnavigated the site, Belinda stopped and looked over the hydrangea bush hedge and caught her breath as she saw the river and its path a mere fifteen metres away. Looking along the hedge, she saw what appeared to be a gap and moved towards it. To her delight, she found a wooden gate set into the space, which yielded when she pushed it and opened enough for her to squeeze through. A few yards down the path on the right, there was a backless wooden bench in desperate need of painting, but Belinda sank down onto it, grateful for its presence.

A small dinghy, moored close to the bank, was moving gently on the water. Belinda sat there for several moments, mesmerised as she watched a trio of ducks take flight. A heron landed gracefully upstream in the gently flowing water and an animal that moved too quickly in the water for her to be sure but was very otter-like in its movements swam before her. She'd forgotten how beautiful Brittany was, even on an overcast winter afternoon.

As that treacherous thought struck her, she returned to the gate and started to walk along the main path before veering off left and walking back into the centre of the site along another path.

Along this path, several individual wooden chalets were spaced a good distance from each other in a higgledy-piggledy manner. Each had its own terrace for al fresco eating and hard-standing for a car.

Belinda, though, was surprised to see one was tidier and better maintained than the others. Even the flower bed in front was weed-free and spring bulbs were flowering. A bicycle with a basket fixed to its handlebars was leant up against the side of the chalet. If she didn't know better, she'd say someone was staying there, maybe even living there permanently.

Belinda climbed the shallow steps onto the decking area in front of the cabin and knocked on the door. Silence. No sign of life. Thoughtfully, Belinda walked back to the path and took a photograph.

This part of the site felt a little bit spooky, with too many trees and overgrown bushes making it dark. Glimpsing two buildings further over, she discovered they were the shower block and toilets. The outsides of both were in need of a good power wash and a fresh coat of paint. The insides were also in definite need of a good clean. Belinda took several photographs before she continued to make her way back to the main reception area.

To her surprise, as she walked, ideas about updating and improving the site began to filter into her mind, and she spoke into her phone recorder, making notes. As she neared what she recognised as the back of the office chalet, she saw another building hidden amongst the trees. Walking over to it, she realised it was a house. A faded notice on the door said 'Private. Interdit. Staff'.

When Belinda tried the door, she wasn't surprised to find it was locked. To one side of the house was a large hangar with maintenance vehicles and other machinery in it, including a golf buggy, tractor, quad bike and chainsaws. Most of the equipment looked in need of a good clean and overhaul but hopefully would be usable.

Overcome by a sudden shiver of cold, Belinda realised the sky was clouding over and she was getting cold. Time to get in the car and put the heater on to warm up while she tried to put her notes in order and waited for Alain Salvin to return.

A quarter of an hour later, a noisy car exhaust alerted her to the fact that someone was coming. Alain Salvin. His 2CV might be a classic, but if he didn't give it some loving care and attention soon, it would end up in the scrapyard. Belinda watched him get out of the car and waited for him to acknowledge her. Instead, he ignored her and began walking towards the office steps. What was his problem?

Furious, she wound her window down.

'A moment, Mr Salvin.'

She registered the shrug of his shoulders and the deep sigh he made before he turned and stared at her. She returned his stare before speaking.

'Breakfast meeting here tomorrow morning at 8 a.m. Make sure you have the keys to everything. Do *not* be late. Have a good evening.' She threw a false smile at him before revving the engine and driving away.

7

An hour or so later, after a reviving shower and half an hour working on her laptop back at the auberge, Belinda decided there was time before dinner to make a couple of Skype calls, one to Chloe and one to Nigel.

She rang Chloe first because of the twins' bedtime. Closing the connection afterwards, Belinda sighed. Although relieved to hear they were all well, she was missing them already and she'd only just arrived.

Afterwards, she rang Nigel. As soon as they'd exchanged the normal pleasantries, she dived straight in. 'Did you actually walk around the site before you bought it?'

'Most of it,' Nigel said.

'I'm sending you a file of photographs and a provisional incomplete list of what needs to be done, as well as a list of the equipment we need to buy. Bringing this place up to our usual Milton Hotels standard in the timescale you've given me will be difficult.'

'Getting the place up to scratch will be a challenge, I grant you, but we always thought you liked a challenge.'

'This campsite is more than just a challenge, although it does have potential. There's a couple of run-down buildings on the site that need demolishing. The long traditional mas on the far edge laughingly called a café... that, though, is a gem.' Personally Belinda thought that particular mas could be the key to making the campsite a success in and out of the season.

'It is?'

'Fully restored, it would be a wonderful venue for weddings and other large functions. A basic café needs to be nearer the entrance.'

'So, finally, there is something you like about the place.'

Belinda decided to ignore the amusement she could hear in Nigel's voice.

'You also need to know I'm probably going to stay at the auberge in the village for an indefinite period. There is nowhere on site where I would consider sleeping currently, although I haven't yet had a chance to check out the staff cottage.'

'Stay at the auberge for as long as you need to. Anything else?'

'One major problem, your so-called manager, he's got a real attitude problem. Either that or he hates the English. Or maybe he hates women. Not sure I can work with him. Can you sack him?' Belinda could have sworn she heard Nigel smother a laugh.

'That's priceless. He wants me to sack you. Says he can't work with you.'

'What? He's had the nerve to ring you and complain about me?' Belinda couldn't believe what she was hearing. 'On what grounds?'

'He doesn't need an uptight bossy female undermining what he's already doing.'

'I haven't been here eight hours yet! We've barely spoken to each other and there is absolutely no evidence of him doing any actual work, apart from maybe pruning and cutting back a few bushes.'

'Anyway, I told him what I'm telling you. I'm not sacking either of you, I need the two of you to work together.'

Belinda was silent.

'Come on. You're normally so good with people. Always diplomatic and kind. Don't let Alain get to you. He's French, he can't help having attitude, it's in their DNA. But he's a good bloke really.'

Belinda ignored his words. 'How about if I resign? I can be on the morning ferry and come home.'

She heard Nigel sigh. 'Don't be silly. You've only just arrived. Give it a couple of weeks and see if things improve between you. If not, I promise we'll think again,' and Nigel ended the call.

Belinda was still seething five minutes later as she made her way downstairs to the auberge kitchen.

Fern took one look at her and handed her a glass of wine. 'You look a bit uptight. Everything okay?'

Belinda nodded before taking a drink. 'Thanks. Just a work problem.'

She laughed as she caught sight of BB, who had deserted her the moment she'd arrived back at the auberge, making a beeline for Lady, his new friend, and the warmth of the kitchen. He was now curled up with Lady in her basket, looking completely at home.

'That's a bit of a tight squeeze, BB. Mind you don't squash Lady.'

Half an hour later, Belinda placed her knife and fork on her empty dinner plate. 'That was delicious. I'd ask you for the recipe, but I rarely cook these days and I know I'd never be able to produce a meal like that.'

Fern shrugged away her praise. 'I enjoy cooking.' She stood

up and cleared the plates before putting the cheeseboard on the table. 'So, if you don't cook, what do you eat? Ready meals?'

'I work for a small chain of three hotels, so I can always find a proper meal if I want it. If there's time to stop for lunch, I eat in whichever hotel I'm working at, and in the evening at home, I'll have a bowl of soup or a sandwich of some sort. If I'm really hungry, I can always have dinner in the hotel restaurant.'

'What d'you do in these hotels – obviously nothing kitchen-related.' Fern smiled.

'I've been known to get stuck into the washing-up when the dishwasher breaks down, but that's about it.' Belinda laughed. 'Nigel, my boss, defines my role as a troubleshooter. Basically means that I oversee the smooth running of everything. If there's a problem, I have to solve it. I do the website and the accounts for each of the hotels every week too. I interview the staff with Nigel and Molly, his wife. And because I have a flair for interior design, I also help with that when any of the hotels are given a makeover.'

Fern stared at her wide-eyed. 'Are there enough hours in the day for you to do all that? I feel positively lazy listening to you.'

Belinda laughed. 'It is a bit full on, I admit. But it saved me from going loopy after my divorce. I'm just hoping Nigel and Molly manage to keep on top of everything while I'm over here to sort out their latest acquisition.'

Fern looked at her, puzzled. 'And where is that? The nearest hotel is at least fifteen kilometres away.'

'They've branched out,' Belinda said. 'Not sure now I've seen the place, which is just the other side of the village, whether they are completely in their right minds, but,' she shrugged, 'they're very determined.'

'They've bought the campsite, haven't they?' Fern said as the truth dawned on her. 'I knew it was up for sale. You'll have your work cut out with that place.'

'I know.' Belinda nodded ruefully. 'And I've got approximately two, possibly three, months to get it up and running.' She swirled the wine round in her glass. 'A task I wasn't sure I wanted or was even up to before I arrived. Now, having seen the site and met the resident attitude-riddled Frenchman currently employed as an on-site manager, I know for sure. I wish I was still in Devon.' She fell silent for several seconds. 'But, hey, I'm a troubleshooter. Alain Salvin is trouble, so I could always shoot him, couldn't I? End of problem.' She drained her glass and replaced it on the table and saw the look on Fern's face. 'Don't worry, I won't really shoot him, as much as I'd like to,' she muttered under her breath. 'Haven't got a gun handy.'

'But Alain is a lovely man,' Fern said. 'I've met him once or twice since he returned. Lady adores him. I didn't realise he was still involved with the site.'

Belinda stared at her. She was the second person this evening to defend Alain. As if a dog liking him was proof of a good human being!

'Hmm. The jury is out on that, I'm afraid.' She looked at Fern expectantly. 'What do you mean, though, still involved with the site?'

'Your Nigel would have bought the place from Alain's parents.'

'He did say something about old friends being involved.' Belinda nodded thoughtfully. No wonder Nigel was reluctant to sack him. 'Right, enough about me. How did you end up here in deepest Brittany?'

'Long story short: I got married, had two children, got divorced and became a single mum for about ten years. Once the girls were independent, I knew I needed to do something for me, so I enrolled on a Prue Leith catering course, thinking I'd open a seaside B&B or a café somewhere in the West Country when I qualified.' Fern smiled. 'Fate decreed otherwise. I met a sexy Frenchman on the course and plans changed. I got married again instead.'

'Gosh, that sounds romantic,' Belinda said.

Fern nodded. 'It was and totally unexpected. I wasn't looking for a new relationship but...' Fern shrugged. 'Laurent was very persuasive, with his tales of how much I'd love living in Brittany with him. We'd been married three years when he inherited this place from his grandmother, which gave him the opportunity to open his own place.' Fern took a sip of her wine. 'Mind you, I couldn't believe it the first time I saw it. Talk about back in the dark ages, and that was just the furniture. Electrics, plumbing, decorating – so much had to be redone.'

'How long did it take you to renovate?'

'Fourteen months of hard work,' Fern said. 'It's five years now since we opened.'

'When do I get to meet your husband?'

Fern bit her bottom lip and blinked hard before she answered. 'Eighteen months ago, a drunk driver on the N164 near Châteauneuf-du-Faou changed my life again.'

Belinda looked at her, stunned. 'I'm so sorry. I can't imagine how you must feel.'

Fern shook her head. 'Numb is the only way to describe it. Some days the numbness lifts a fraction, other days...' She shrugged. 'Other days it doesn't. C'est la vie – or rather it's not,' she added with a break in her voice.

8

The next morning, Belinda refused breakfast but enjoyed a cup of coffee with Fern before leaving for the campsite and her early meeting with Alain.

'Wish me luck,' she said. 'I've got a feeling your "lovely" Mr Salvin is going to try and make my life as difficult as possible.'

'Kitchen supper again tonight,' Fern said. 'And you can tell me all about it.'

'Thanks – already looking forward to it,' and Belinda, with BB at her heels, headed down the front steps to her car.

It was a lovely, spring-like morning. There was a light mist hanging over the valley and as Belinda drove into the village, the sun's early rays were colouring the sky behind the hill in a pinkish frenzy. Had it been anywhere but Brittany, Belinda knew she'd be thinking how beautiful it was. The bakery was open and even with the car windows closed, Belinda caught the tantalising smell of freshly baked bread. Maybe a warm pain au chocolat would bribe Alain into being, if not nice to her, at least civil? Worth a try.

Five minutes later, she was driving out of the village, a bag of delicious croissants on the dashboard, out of reach of BB sitting beside her and sniffing the air.

Ten to eight and there was no sign of Alain's car outside the office, so Belinda parked but kept the engine running for some heat, before taking out her notebook and reading the notes she'd made for this meeting. She was determined to make Alain realise that Nigel had high standards for all his hotels and wanted the same for this new venture. Alain Salvin needed to know there was going to be no cutting of corners or shoddy workmanship in order to get the site ready for the season. She hoped he realised they were both in for a lot of hard work in the next few weeks and months.

It was one minute to eight when BB pricked his ears at the sound of an approaching car. At least he was on time, Belinda thought. By the time Alain had parked, Belinda, with BB on his lead, was standing waiting for him by the office steps, holding her tote and the bag of croissants. She'd decided a friendly 'hail-fellow-well-met' approach was worth a try.

'Good morning,' she said. 'I thought a cup of coffee and a croissant before we start? We need to get an action plan put together, so after coffee perhaps we could start with a walk around the place and discuss what needs doing. Then we can decide what is the most urgent.'

'I 'ave a plan worked out – I know exactly what it is that needs doing,' Alain said. He walked past her and unlocked the office door.

Belinda bit her tongue and followed him inside, trying to contain the rising anger she felt at his rudeness. Somehow she had to get him onside, losing her temper and being rude back was not the way, however much she was tempted. She took a deep breath.

'Well, perhaps you'd care to share this plan of yours with me and we can talk about it.'

He ignored her and she watched as he switched on the computer before moving to a worktop with a kettle, a couple of mugs and a jar of instant coffee. He switched the kettle on before glaring across at her.

'I told Nigel I don't need his troubleshooter 'ere, I can sort the site alone. I know the place, I'm local, I actually speak the language, I 'ave the contacts, and I don't mind getting my 'ands dirty with physical work when necessary.' He looked her up and down. 'Which is something I doubt you'd do even if you were capable.'

Belinda, sensing she was staring at him in open-mouthed astonishment, quickly closed her mouth, wishing she could think of a crushing reply that would put Alain Salvin in his place once and for all. But he was speaking again.

'How about we 'ave a truce? You deal with the paperwork, tidy the office, look pretty for visitors, make the coffee, and moi? I do the rest. D'accord? Black for me. No sugar,' he added, nodding towards the kettle, before he moved across to the computer.

Knowing she was likely to tell Alain exactly what she thought of him if she wasn't careful and that wouldn't help matters, Belinda took her time unclipping BB from his lead so he could explore the office, before walking slowly towards the coffee making utensils. To her annoyance, BB made a beeline for Alain, who bent down to stroke him. Watching him stroke BB, Belinda remembered Fern's comment that he was a lovely man, and that Lady liked him. Maybe it was just her who rubbed him up the wrong way? Whatever the cause she needed to sort it out.

'That's an awful lot of assumptions you've made about me, Mr Salvin, and my role here,' Belinda said as she put three big heaped spoonfuls of coffee granules into a small mug, her back towards Alain. The friendly approach hadn't worked so it was his own fault if she made her point another way. 'So I'm sure you won't mind me telling you that I think you're an arrogant and pompous Frenchman with a serious attitude problem. Two things you need to remember though before treating me like the office dogsbody: one, I'm Nigel's representative here and in charge of the purse strings. And two, we have to work together.' She might desperately want to walk away but she'd told Nigel she'd give it a week and she would. Letting Alain walk all over her though was not an option.

The kettle switched itself off while she was speaking and she carefully poured water into the mug and stirred the contents. Good and strong like the French drank it. Belinda toyed with the idea of adding sugar but dismissed it as too childish. She was a troubleshooter for goodness' sake – she could handle this situation without losing her cool.

She picked up the mug of coffee and turned round to look at Alain's back as he stood concentrating on the computer screen. How the hell was she going to make this work? She certainly wasn't going to kowtow to him by backing down.

She stifled a sigh before moving forward to stand at his side.

'Coffee.' She placed the mug carefully on the desk. Opening the bag of croissants, she offered it to him.

'Non merci.' Alain kept his attention on the computer.

Belinda took a quick look at the screen. 'Is that an aerial photo of the campsite? How old is it? The bit you've zoomed in on looks far too well maintained for it to be a recent shot.'

'Eight years ago. Before everything started to fall apart.'

'Could you scroll around a bit and show me more? I saw the café when I walked around yesterday. I'm interested to see how it looked then.'

Alain let out a sigh and moved the cursor, quickly giving her a brief glimpse of the building before moving it back to the area he'd been studying.

Belinda drummed her fingers on the desk. 'Right. Earlier you suggested your version of a truce,' she said. 'Well, here's my version. Basically, it involves you stopping being such a male chauvinist, with an attitude that dates back to the 1950s. You give me the guided tour. We discuss what you think needs doing. I tell you what I think. And then we discuss it.' She stopped to draw breath. 'I'll be taking over the organisation of things, so I need the password for the computer. I also need keys to the office and any other buildings that are locked. You give me access to everything I need and we will work together to achieve what Nigel wants. And you need to realise I'm not going away. I'm here to do a job for Nigel – the new owner of this site – and I will.'

Ignoring her words, Alain reached out and picked up his mug of coffee and took a long drink. Belinda watched his face change as he swallowed and realised how awful the coffee was. She half expected him to spit the drink everywhere and silently awarded him full marks when he didn't.

'Sorry, did I make it too strong for you? Don't expect you'll tell me to make the coffee again, will you?' and she smiled sweetly at him. 'Have a croissant to take the taste away.'

This time, he took one out of the bag she held out.

'For the record – I'm not bossy or uptight, but I will not be spoken to rudely or treated like an idiot. I admit I'm a bit of a perfectionist, though, when it comes to getting things done properly. Something which Nigel appreciates.'

Alain glanced at her as he swallowed a piece of croissant but didn't acknowledge that she knew about him phoning Nigel.

'I make my own coffee in future,' Alain said and walked over to the small sink to throw the remains of his coffee away. 'As for the rest of it, I don't 'ave a choice, so truce it is.' He looked at

Belinda and sighed. 'Peut-être I owe you an apology. I'm not normally rude and chauvinistic, not intentionally anyway, so I apologise for my behaviour. No excuse, but I 'ave a lot on my mind at the moment.' He held his hand out. 'Mais, I can't promise to agree with everything you say or do.'

Belinda shook his hand. 'Apology accepted.' Inwardly, she breathed a sigh of relief. Thank goodness for that, a truce. Hopefully it would last. 'Your English is very good by the way.'

She gave into temptation and took a croissant out of the bag. All the aggro had given her an appetite.

'Did Nigel outline his plans for the campsite to you when he was over here?' she asked before biting into the flaky patisserie.

'No. We 'ave a brief telephone conversation when he offer me the job, but we've not yet met face to face to discuss things. Basically after I'd accepted, he told me to do what was necessary to get the site back up and running in the shortest time span possible, but nothing significant was mentioned,' Alain said. 'Other than warning me he was sending his right hand woman over to assist.'

Belinda let the interesting fact that Nigel and Alain had not met up to discuss things slip into the back of her mind. 'Okay. The brief he gave me was to go upmarket. He wants to get into the glamping business.'

'What the 'ell is glamping?'

'Seriously? I can't believe you haven't heard of glamping. Where have you been for the last few years? Outer Mongolia?'

'Africa,' Alain muttered.

'Oh. Anyway, I liken glamping to camping with attitude,' Belinda said, wondering what he'd been doing over there. Working for Médecins Sans Frontières? Possible, although his bedside manner would have needed some tuition. He was fit enough to have been a mercenary in some war-torn state. But whatever had taken him to Africa was none of her business. 'Permanent tents with modern-day equipment, self-contained facilities and comfortable beds,' she continued. 'A couple of modern luxury pods.'

'Is he serious?' Alain raised his eyebrows as he looked at her.

'Oh yes. He reckons that's the way to go – aspirational and upmarket.'

'I don't—' Alain stopped. 'The campsite does not need pods. The site, it 'as always been a family-friendly one, nothing upmarket about it. A place for families to relax. Kids to be carefree and run wild.'

Belinda looked at him, waiting for him to add the phrase 'when my parents ran the place', but he didn't. Briefly she wondered why? Time to let him know she knew.

'How long did your parents own the site for?'

'About fifteen years.' The look Alain gave her was defiant. 'They bought it when they retired and enjoyed running it.'

'Must be difficult for you, seeing how run-down it is now. Did it all just become too much for them?'

Alain nodded. 'The fact I wasn't around for some years made it worse. The so-called manager they employed basically took the money for five years and ran. To say they were pleased when Nigel offered to 'elp—' He shrugged.

'The thing is, these days most people have homes full of stuff: TVs, computers, dishwashers, power showers, fridges, hot tubs, everything on tap. The idea of coming away on holiday and roughing it—' Belinda shrugged. 'Well, that appeals to some people, but there is definitely a market for more comfortable holidays. For being at one with nature in comfort. It'll still be a great family holiday destination when we've updated it – only better,' Belinda said.

'It's going to cost tens of thousands of euros,' Alain said. 'Not to mention months of work. Much longer than the agreed agenda.'

'Is that a problem for you?'

For no longer than a split second, a look of discomfort flitted across Alain's face, gone so quickly that afterwards Belinda wondered if she'd imagined it.

Alain nodded. 'Yes. We 'ave to open as quickly as possible. Said that's why he was sending you over, to speed things up.'

'Nigel is a businessman, he knows it takes time to recuperate an investment. I doubt that he's expecting this place to turn any sort of profit for at least three to five years. With the amount of money we're going to spend on new equipment and facilities, personally I'd say it's probably going to be even longer.'

Alain muttered something under his breath that Belinda didn't quite catch, before forcing a smile on his face. 'You 'ave details in that folder of yours?'

'Yes. Is your plan on the computer?'

Alain nodded.

'Let's print it out and then we can take both of them with us when we do a site inspection,' Belinda said, relieved when Alain opened up the plan on the computer and pressed the print button without grumbling at her.

Before they started to walk the site, Belinda insisted Alain show her the house she'd seen yesterday. 'Manager's house? Is it habitable?'

Alain nodded. 'Yes. Needs a damn good clean though.' He pulled a bunch of keys out of his pocket and inserted one in the lock.

The house, a typical Breton conversion from an old farm building many years ago, was basic, but Belinda could see its potential. Downstairs, there was a kitchen and a large sitting room with a wood burner. A steep open wooden staircase led upstairs, where there were two double bedrooms, a single bedroom and a bathroom with a big old-fashioned bath and overhead shower. *Get the house cleaned ready to live in*, was the first thing that went on Belinda's list.

'We'll get this place cleaned up ready for you to move in.'

Alain shook his head. 'I 'ave no plans to move in until the season starts.'

'Well, somebody needs to be living on site soon and if it's not you, it will have to be me. Once it's clean, I'll move in while I'm out here,' Belinda said. It wouldn't be as cosy as the auberge but at least it would save Nigel some money.

* * *

Three hours later, as they made their way back to the office, Belinda's head was reeling with the knowledge of just how much she needed to organise. Alain had shown her the tent pitching area of the campsite, which was in desperate need of being mown otherwise they'd be making silage there very soon. The area for visiting camper vans and caravans was almost as bad. She'd learnt that the leases on all the cabins had reverted back to the campsite, including the one she'd seen with a bicycle and flowers.

'Why does that one look as if it's lived in?'

'Because it is,' Alain admitted. 'Bernie moved in there a while ago when he had a row with his father. Dad told him he could stay there for as long as he liked. To treat it as his 'ome.'

'Who's Bernie?'

'A villager who needed somewhere to live.'

'Time to move him out,' Belinda said briskly, making a note.

'He's not doing any 'arm living there,' Alain said quietly. 'We can leave him there for a bit. He's got nowhere to go.'

Belinda looked at him. 'Nowhere? His parents won't take him back?'

Alain shook his head. 'They're both dead now.'

'Does he work?'

Alain shook his head again. 'He's not the most reliable – unless it involves animals. Then he's dedicated to their care.'

'Okay, he can stay for a bit, we'll work around him,' Belinda said. Evicting this Bernie wasn't at the top of her priority list right now. 'I'll need to meet him though. Maybe we can get him involved with the grounds here? The patch of ground around his cabin is very tidy and well looked after.'

'Peut-être.' Alain shrugged.

At least she and Alain had managed to reach a compromise on certain things, although there had been several fierce arguments during the course of the morning when they'd disagreed over what Nigel would want and what was needed. Including one about not only where the three glamping pods were going to be positioned but the kind of pod to install. But Belinda was content to wait until she had enough information to enable her to win the argument.

There was one thing they were both in total agreement on, however – the whole place needed clearing of all the overgrown shrubs, trees and grass.

'We need to get a team in,' Belinda said. 'Too much work here for you to carry out alone. Do you know of a local company? Or should we employ a couple of men and you supervise? We're going to need a permanent groundsman once it's sorted as well.'

Alain nodded. 'Already organised a team to come in. Now the weather is improving, they'll 'ave it sorted within a week. The machinery in the hangar is old but most of it works, just needs cleaning and oiling. I'll let Yann in the bar know and he'll spread the word about job vacancies. And we can notify the Pôle Emploi that we are looking for seasonal staff.'

'Is that what I'd call the job centre?' Belinda asked.

Alain nodded.

'I'll write out a list of jobs, both immediate and seasonal, like receptionist, cleaners, gardeners. I'll check with Nigel about whether he wants to rent out the café when it's ready or whether he wants to employ staff for it.'

Alain glanced at his watch. 'I need some food. We go for lunch in the village?'

Belinda shook her head. 'No thanks. I'll work through. I'll grab a cup of coffee and there's a croissant left if I need it. I need to phone my daughter too.'

'That decision marks you out as a true Englishwoman. Breaking off work for lunch is sacrosanct round here. No self-respecting French person would even consider taking less than an hour for lunch.'

'And that's what's wrong with the French.' Belinda shrugged. 'I'd rather get the work done and finish the day early. Too long a lunch makes people lethargic. I'll spend the time on the computer. Get familiar with the programs you have on there. See if the bookings and payment app is modern enough to cope. I take it the internet connection is good?'

'It's good,' Alain said. 'For rural Brittany. I'll see you later.'

Belinda registered the speculative look he gave her as he went to say something before changing his mind and closing the door behind him.

She made herself a cup of coffee and gave BB a drink before settling herself in front of the computer. It was then she realised what was behind Alain's look. Everything on the computer was in French and he didn't expect her to understand any of it. Monsieur Salvin had made another mistake there!

9

After Belinda had left for the campsite and her anticipated diffi-cult morning with Alain Salvin, Fern did her usual out-of-season housework routine, making sure the auberge was spick and span for any passing tourists.

It didn't take long and by ten o'clock she was in the kitchen, making her morning coffee and writing a list for her planned visit to the supermarché, fifteen kilometres away. Since Laurent's death she'd taken to shopping at the LeClerc at Gourin as she rarely saw anyone she knew there and in those early, strangely, detached-from-reality months, she couldn't face the kind platitudes people expressed. It was easier to shop amongst strangers. Now it was a habit. A habit that included walking Lady in the nearby park of Tronjoly before heading for the supermarché.

Half an hour later, Fern pulled into the car park attached to the Chateau Tronjoly. Getting out of the car, she walked to the back to lift the hatchback door for Lady to jump out. Before she could clip the lead on, Lady ran towards the only car parked nearby. A tall, distinguished-looking man who reminded Fern of someone she couldn't quite put a name to was standing next to a 4 x 4, looking around him.

'Viens ici, Lady,' Fern called out quickly.

The man glanced across at Fern before bending down to pet Lady. 'Pas de problème.'

'Désolé,' Fern said, quickly clipping the lead on Lady.

'N'est-ce pas un bel endroit?'

Fern nodded. His accent was different and she guessed French wasn't his native language.

'Yes, it is very beautiful,' she answered in English. 'Are you American? Your accent is...'

The man laughed. 'That bad? That's not good. Yep, I'm American. Scott Kergoëts.' He held out his hand. 'Pleased to meet you, ma'am.'

'Fern LeRoy.' She shook his hand, surprised by how firm his shake was.

'Now that's a French surname,' Scott said, looking at her. 'But you're not French, are you?'

She smiled. 'No, I'm English. I married a Frenchman.'

'And who's this?' Scott asked, crouching down to stroke Lady again, who immediately sat and looked at him.

'Lady. Whom I'm about to walk around the park.'

Fern sensed his hesitation before he asked. 'Maybe I could walk with you? I sure could do with some company.'

'Why not. I usually go this way,' and Fern set off down the path that led past the chateau and around the lake. This was a public place and there were other people around and although this man was a random stranger, she didn't think for one moment that he was a threat to her. She'd learnt to sum people up at a glance and to be a good judge of character running the auberge and had been known to turn people away that she instinctively didn't trust. 'How long are you here for?' she asked.

Scott shrugged. 'For as long as I want really. My ticket is open-ended. I retired a few months ago and there's nothing urgent back home waiting for my attention.'

'Where is home?'

'New York City. I'm really here to check out how your Statue of Liberty compares with our Liberty Island one,' Scott answered.

Fern laughed. 'It's a miniature version, that's for sure.'

Scott flashed her a disarming smile. 'At least I can stand up close without having to pay.'

'Are you staying in Gourin?'

'Not at the moment. I've rented a gîte on the outskirts, but, to be honest, it's a bit isolated and I think I'd prefer to have company nearby. I'll probably find a hotel, maybe even an Airbnb in town, when my jet lag finally clears. I only landed three days ago and it's taking time to wear off.'

Fern nodded sympathetically.

'You live locally I guess?' Scott said.

Fern shook her head. 'Not really. I'm fifteen kilometres away. Carhaix–Plouguer direction. I run an auberge.'

They continued to walk in companionable silence for a while before the front of the restored chateau came into view.

'Wow. I wasn't expecting it to be quite so splendid,' Scott said, stopping in the middle of the path. 'I've seen paintings and photos of the place, but...' He shook his head. 'Seeing it in the flesh, so to speak, it's completely taken me by surprise.'

Fern, standing at his side, had to admit the old chateau was looking particularly beautiful in the sunshine, with the spring daffodils, primroses and the many camellia shrubs in flower.

Scott appeared to be transfixed by the scene. When Lady pulled on her lead wanting to move, Fern broke into his reverie.

'It is rather splendid. Easy to imagine how lovely it must have been to actually live in it. Scott, I'm sorry, but I'm going to have to walk – Lady is getting impatient. It's been lovely meeting you and I hope you enjoy your stay in Brittany,' and she began to walk away.

'Sorry, I was miles away there,' Scott apologised and he fell into step alongside her once again. 'Is there anywhere here I can buy you a coffee?'

'Thank you, but I don't think there is a café here – maybe in the summer but not right now,' Fern said, thinking it would have been nice to have stopped for a coffee. 'And I have to get to the supermarché.'

Scott looked disappointed but didn't argue as they walked back to the car park in silence.

Fern pressed the remote lock on her car and quickly bundled Lady into her basket in the back. When she straightened up, Scott had opened the driver's door and smiled at her as she slipped into her seat. 'Thank you.'

'Would you and your husband like to join me for dinner one evening?' Scott asked. 'A bit of *entente cordiale*?'

Fern froze. She hadn't been expecting that. She should have remembered how hospitable some Americans were. She shook her head. She had to get away. Scott was a nice man and she didn't want to upset him by bursting into tears because he'd unwittingly mentioned her husband.

'Not possible, I'm afraid. Laurent, my husband, died in an accident eighteen months ago.' She stared out over the dashboard of the car rather than look at him as she spoke. She switched the car engine on and prepared to drive away.

'I'm so sorry. I didn't mean to upset you,' Scott said, instantly contrite. 'You take care – have a nice day.' To Fern's relief, he closed the car door and moved back.

Driving out of the car park, Fern glanced in her rear-view mirror to see him standing there watching her leave. At least she'd managed to keep the tears that were now coursing down her cheeks at bay in front of him. Tears were never very far away when she had to share her story with strangers, even after all these months.

She stayed in the car for several moments once she reached the supermarché, taking deep breaths and generally calming down. She managed to repair her make-up, add another slick of lipstick, comb her hair and give herself a quick squirt of perfume.

And berate herself for being so frightened at the thought of having dinner with a man on her own.

* * *

That evening, as she and Belinda enjoyed the poached salmon, new potatoes and early tender asparagus she'd cooked, Fern looked at Belinda as she handed her the hollandaise sauce. Could she tell Belinda about her reaction to Scott's invitation? Having a girlfriend she could talk to in her own language and know she would understand was something that Fern had missed in the last few years. Both she and Laurent had made new French friends here in Brittany but she'd slowly lost contact with her old friends in the UK. After Laurent died she'd started to avoid their mutual friends, wanting to spare them the embarrassment of facing a grieving widow. She and Belinda might have only met recently, but she sensed that they were going to be good friends.

'I met an American today, Scott Kergoëts, while I was walking Lady.'

'And?' Belinda looked at her. 'Was he a nice American?'

'I got the feeling that he was a real gentleman. Obviously well educated. Easy to talk to.' Fern picked up her wine glass and took a sip before saying quietly, 'He asked if "my husband and I" would have dinner with him one evening.' She glanced at

Belinda. 'I told him Laurent was dead and then basically ran away, fast. I feel so stupid. I'm fifty-four years old, my kids behave more grown-up than I do.' Fern gave a heavy sigh.

'Ah,' Belinda answered, a thoughtful tone to her voice. 'Moving on is hard, isn't it? I found it difficult being alone after my husband left me and I couldn't shake the apathy off for months. Nigel and Molly giving me a job was my saving. I had to get out of the house and go to work. It must be even harder after a bereavement to pull yourself back into the world.'

'True. My first marriage, which ended in divorce, was different. It was my decision. I did the right thing for me and the children and I got on with life. But I never expected to lose Laurent like I did.' Fern bit her lip knowing tears were dangerously close again.

'Do you like running the auberge on your own?'

'Honestly? Laurent and I were a team. It was fun opening our home and entertaining people. We really enjoyed it.' She sighed. 'On my own, it's different. Harder. I love it when I'm busy in the summer with guests, cooking and gardening, but I've learnt that the majority of holidaymakers prefer to drive south in search of the sun. It's rare all six rooms are filled. And, as you can see, from November to April, it's dead around here.'

'Does the auberge give you a good life?' Belinda asked.

'Yes, but being solely responsible for everything, with no one to talk through problems with is a drain. I rather fancy working for someone else and not being the person in overall charge.'

'And how's the social life around here? How many times this winter have you been out for lunch or dinner with friends?'

'I have lunch once a month with my brother-in-law,' she said. 'And Laurent's son, Fabian, comes for dinner occasionally. That's about it.' She shrugged. 'I walk Lady a lot. So plenty of fresh air.'

'No girly natters with friends? No Ladies Wot Lunch around here?'

Fern laughed. 'If there are, I've never met them.'

Belinda regarded her thoughtfully. 'Speaking as a very new friend, you've got to get to grips with life again. Would you consider selling this place and starting somewhere new? Or does it hold too many happy memories for you to leave?'

'It's complicated and not that easy to sell up,' Fern said. 'This place has been in the LeRoy family forever. When Laurent and I married, I sold my house in the UK and we used the capital to do up this place. We were in our forever home, where we were going to grow old together. And that's the problem now. Under French inheritance laws, as Laurent's widow, I can live here until I die, but in reality it is Fabian's inheritance. It's an arrangement which gives me a home but no access to capital. Or the ability to move,' she added quietly. 'Without an income, I can't afford to even rent somewhere.'

'Can Fabian buy you out? Or agree to sell it? Does he want to live here? Run the auberge?'

'I think Fabian and his family will eventually live here. Whether they will run the place as an auberge, I don't know. Fabian doesn't have any money and couldn't afford a mortgage large enough to pay me back. There have been a few hints about me closing the auberge and letting them move in with me.' Fern shook her head. 'As fond as I am of Fabian and his wife, that arrangement would be a disaster. Selling the place is out of the question, the extended family would be horrified at the thought. It's such a large part of their heritage.'

'Difficult,' Belinda said. 'I hadn't realised French inheritance laws were so complex. Would you like to return to the UK?'

Fern shrugged. 'To be honest, I don't know any more what I do want. I do know things have to change though. Bumping into

Scott today has made me think a bit more about the future. Oh.'
She looked at Belinda. 'I've realised who he reminded me of –
Richard Gere.'

'Shame you ran away from him then.' Belinda smiled. 'Dinner
with a Richard Gere lookalike could have been your first step into
a new life.'

10

The next week at the campsite sped past as Belinda got to grips with a mountain of things. One of the first things she did, unbeknown to Alain, was to save everything on the office computer to a memory stick and download it onto her laptop. That way, there were no arguments when Alain wanted to work on the computer. It also had the added benefit too that she could work from the comfort of her own room at the auberge of an evening before wandering downstairs to enjoy a nightcap with Fern.

The amount of work that needed organising threatened to overwhelm her a few times, there was so much. Her to-do list was endless: organise five or six local women to clean the cabins, the café and the manager's house; a team of men to pressure-wash the shower and toilet blocks before painting. Alain took over the job of organising the outdoor teams of workers, leaving Belinda to deal with the teams working inside. In addition, there was the website to bring up to date, pods for the glamping area to source, lots of new equipment to order, not to mention finding staff for the season.

A routine established itself over the course of that week and the days continued to fly by. Every morning, she left the auberge just before eight o'clock, stopped in the village for a couple of croissants and a salad baguette for her lunch. Fern had lent her a cafetière and she'd stocked up on ground coffee from the village shop, instant coffee being one of her personal bêtes noires. By the time Alain strolled in at about ten past eight the coffee was ready. Over a quick coffee and croissant, they caught each other up on how things were progressing and what their individual plans were for the day. At midday Alain disappeared for lunch, leaving Belinda to eat her baguette and deal with her emails. The afternoons followed a similar pattern with them both concentrating on their allotted tasks. Belinda shut down her laptop around four thirty most days, said goodbye to Alain and made her way back to the auberge.

Although there was so much to do, the campsite was definitely beginning to respond to all of the noisy cutting down, pruning back and mowing work that had happened over the last few days.

One lunchtime after everyone including Alain had disappeared for an hour or two, Belinda decided to eat outside in the sunshine. The only noise she heard as she made her way along the path towards the river was the tweeting of various birds. Belinda recognised the call of a blackbird, pigeons cooing away in the tall pines and a chaffinch singing perched amongst the burgeoning branches of an oak tree before hearing a noise that stopped her in her tracks. The whrrr-tapping sound of a nearby woodpecker. A sound she hadn't heard in years. A sound that took her right back to her childhood home, where it had been a noise that was taken for granted in the background of life.

A picture of the old stone mas that had been home for so long floated, unbidden, into her mind as she walked. A simple two-storey building, it hadn't been a prestigious place, shambolic described it better. A shelter built long ago by a Breton farmer to house various animals and his family. Down the years, it had been enlarged and converted in a haphazard manner, the cows moved into a separate shelter and their previous accommodation had become the kitchen of the house. Belinda smiled, remembering how her father had done the final conversion and turned the old milking parlour at the back of the house into her bedroom. She'd loved that room, with its view out over the countryside and the field shelter for Lucky.

Lucky. That had been the hardest part of that awful day when her life had fallen apart. Knowing she was leaving the pony. Inconsolable, she'd cried for hours until her mother snapped at her. 'For God's sake, Belinda, shut up. I feel like crying too, but it won't solve anything. Lucky will go to a good home. Your dad will make sure of that.'

Belinda did stop crying eventually, but only because she didn't have any tears left to spill. Years later, she'd realised her difficult relationship with her mother had started its downward spiral that day with her lack of empathy over leaving Lucky. It was a breach of the mother–daughter bond that had never completely healed. Jean's refusal to allow Belinda to even mention, let alone contact, her father ensured the fracture remained. Belinda was convinced her mother's barely audible last words, '*I'm so* sorry' and the deathbed promise to '*Go and lay the ghosts*' she'd been coerced into making had been her mother's final plea for forgiveness.

Belinda came out of her reverie with a start as BB gave a short sharp bark before racing off, heading for the cabin where Bernie lived. She hadn't had a chance to question Alain about Bernie, they'd both been so busy. Perhaps this was her chance to get to know him. As she hurried to catch BB up, she saw a man weeding the small patch of garden that surrounded the cabin. The ginger cat was curled up fast asleep in the basket of the bicycle that was propped once again against the fence.

'Bonjour,' she said when she reached the man and held out her hand. 'I'm Belinda Marshall. I was hoping to see Bernie.'

The man patted BB before he straightened up and shook her hand.

'Demat. Bernie.' He prodded his chest with a finger.

The two words caught Belinda by surprise. Not so much the word demat, which was the Breton word for hello and one of the few words she remembered in her very limited Breton vocabulary. The real surprise was the man himself. For some reason, she'd been expecting Bernie to be in his teens or early twenties maybe. This man had to be in his late thirties or even possibly early forties.

'You're Bernie?' she said, looking at him. 'Do you speak French or English?'

He smiled and shook his head before saying something rapidly in Breton.

Belinda frantically tried to remember the few words of Breton her grandmother had taught her so long ago. She knew a lot of the older generation still railed against the use of French and tried to stop what they regarded as their true language from dying out. She suspected Bernie had been force-fed the old language from an early age.

She smiled at him and raised her hands in defeat. 'Desolé.' A conversation was obviously not an option. Not knowing what else to do or say, she waved her right hand in farewell before saying, 'Bye-bye, à demain,' trusting that he would know and understand the phrase, and calling BB to heel, Belinda walked on down the path.

Five minutes later, sitting on the bench overlooking the river, she took a bite of her baguette and thought about Bernie. When

Alain had told her Bernie's father had thrown him out, she'd immediately thought of a troublesome teenager, not a full-grown man. Bernie gave her the impression of being a gentle soul who liked a simple life. The fact he only understood Breton though must be a problem for him. Not many people these days spoke the old language, so meeting people and making friends must be difficult. And what was she going to do about him living in the cabin? Having met the man, she felt sorry for him and disinclined to move him on, although that would be the sensible course of action. If he remained, would it upset people? What would holidaymakers think of him when he didn't reply to them? She'd talk to Alain again about Bernie before she spoke to Nigel to explain the situation and ask what he wanted her to do.

Belinda watched as a trio of ducks performed a fly-past before settling on the river. She sighed. It really was a beautiful spot. There was even a small sandy beach further along. It was easy to imagine families enjoying holidays on the campsite when it was fully operational again. If it wasn't for the fact that it was in Brittany, she might even be tempted herself.

Pulling a small piece of ham out of the baguette, she gave it to BB before finishing the rest and getting to her feet. 'Cup of coffee back at the office for me, water for you, and then it's work again.'

There was no sign of Bernie as they walked back past the cabin and the bike had gone too.

Once she'd made her coffee, Belinda sat down and emailed Nigel and Molly with an update of the progress so far and querying the delivery for the new equipment Nigel was sending over from England. She also asked whether a decision had been made about running or leasing out the café. There was a lot of work to be done to get it up to the necessary hygiene requirements, but some of the expense of buying new catering equipment could be passed on to a tenant if they leased it out.

Around mid-afternoon she went across to the manager's house to see how the team she'd organised to clean it were getting on. They'd started on the bedrooms and the bathroom that morning and everything upstairs was sparkling. Now they were working their magic downstairs. The sitting room and the small sunroom looked far more inviting than when she'd first seen it. In the kitchen, the loose covers from the small settee were whirling around in the washing machine, whilst the vigorous use of steel wool on the oven was getting rid of seasons of grease.

Thanking everyone for their hard work, Belinda returned to the office, deep in thought. A few more days and she'd be able to leave the auberge and move into the house. Leaving Fern and the auberge would be a real wrench though. The two of them had become firm friends and Belinda worried about leaving her alone. The campsite house would be basic accommodation, nowhere near as comfortable as the auberge, but living on site had always been the intention. At least there was a usable bathroom and the kitchen was adequate for her needs. Belinda sighed. She'd talk to Fern tonight about moving out and also insist that they went out for lunch one Sunday, her treat. Maybe they could meet up at least once a week while she was in France.

Alain was in the office when she pushed open the door, staring intently at the computer and muttering under his breath. Belinda hesitated, before moving to his side. Relations between them had been less strained recently but she was still wary of upsetting him and opening herself up to more rude comments.

'Problem?' she asked.

'For me, not you,' Alain answered, closing the email programme he had open on the screen. 'I 'ave to deal with something this weekend in the UK. I'll see you Monday morning peut-être.' He picked up his jacket from the chair, looked at her, went to say something, changed his mind and walked out.

Belinda stared after him. What the hell? He couldn't just walk away with no explanation, even if it was a personal matter. Maybe she could have helped, if only he'd told her. Belinda took a deep breath. Over the past week or two she'd realised that Alain Salvin didn't confide in people or ask for help. But it was that 'perhaps' at the end of his last sentence that stayed in her mind and worried her.

* * *

Back at the auberge that evening while they ate dinner, Belinda told Fern she'd be moving out – probably at the end of the next week.

'The cleaners have worked really hard on the manager's house and I always intended to live on site as soon as possible. Just waiting for the bedding and other stuff from Nigel to arrive.'

Fern's face fell. 'I'm going to miss you.'

'Not half as much as I'm going to miss you and your delicious food,' Belinda said. 'I'm only up the road, a nice afternoon walk for Lady. Once I'm settled in, I'll make you cheese on toast one evening.' She finished the last mouthful of rich chocolate mousse that Fern had made and replaced her spoon. 'That was delicious.' She glanced at Fern, who was still looking downcast. 'Cheer up. The tourists will be arriving soon and you'll be buzzing. I've got Sunday off and thought we could go out for lunch? My treat. You'll know the best place to go. Book a table and we'll be ladies who lunch, okay?' Belinda smiled when Fern nodded her agreement. If only there was something tangible she could do to help ease the lingering grief in her friend's life.

11

Belinda and Fern loaded the two dogs into Fern's car mid-morning on Sunday in preparation for a walk alongside the river that was close to the restaurant where Fern had booked a table. Fern had insisted on driving, saying it was easier as she knew the roads.

'My car has got satnav, you know,' Belinda teased her.

It was when they'd been driving away from the village for ten minutes that a sense of déjà vu flooded Belinda's body and she shivered with the intensity of it. She recognised the direction they were travelling in. A direction she'd deliberately avoided ever since she'd arrived. Why oh why hadn't she asked Fern where they were going so that she could have mentally prepared herself for the journey. Although, even if she had known, she wouldn't have anticipated the route.

Fern was steering the car down quiet country roads. Roads Belinda had travelled many times in the past. Roads she'd never expected to drive along again. As the car tyres swished over roads still damp in places from an early-morning shower, unwanted memories were surfacing in her mind. Haphazard recollections:

the school bus; Amelie, her best friend; a cottage; Lucky spooking at a tractor. Belinda squeezed her eyes to shut out the passing scenery in an effort to stop the memories coming, and wished the journey over. In that moment, it came to her in an intuitive flash what Fern was doing.

'You're avoiding the N164, aren't you?' Belinda said quietly, opening her eyes and glancing across at her friend.

'Yep. Can't drive on it. Always go the scenic route these days.' Fern's over-bright voice masked the grief that lay behind the decision.

'Fair enough,' Belinda said. She'd rather put up with a few of her own unwanted memories than have an unhappy Fern drive on the busy dual carriageway when she was still feeling so raw. Belinda knew only too well that while life itself could change in a heartbreaking instant, the collective tsunami of the events it triggered in that nanosecond of time lingered for years. Seemingly forever in some cases.

The rest of the journey continued in silence as Belinda resolutely dismissed her memories and thought about the campsite while Fern concentrated on driving.

Five minutes later, Fern parked alongside the river and Belinda smothered a sigh of relief as they got out of the car.

'That's the restaurant we're having lunch in,' Fern said, pointing to a complex on the other side of the river, approached by a bridge. 'Come on, let's walk the dogs and build up an appetite.'

With both dogs on leads, happily showing them the way, the two of them strolled along. Other people were out and about, enjoying the spring-like morning and several polite 'Bonjours' were exchanged as they passed. Fishermen were setting up their rods and little encampments of seats, picnic boxes and fishing nets at various points along the river.

'I wonder if fishermen used to come to the campsite? We have the fishing rights on the river for about a kilometre,' Belinda said, watching as one man showed a small boy how to cast his line. 'Do you think fishing holidays would prove popular?'

'Years ago, Alain's parents used to organise an annual fishing festival. Laurent went the last year it was held. About thirty men and their families turned up for the weekend.'

'I must talk to Alain about it,' Belinda said. They continued to walk in companionable silence until it was time to return to the car.

Thirty minutes later, they were driving over the bridge and parking in the restaurant car park.

'The dogs will be okay in the car?' Belinda asked.

'This place is dog-friendly. They'll have a drink and then lay under our table. At least Lady will.' Fern looked at Belinda.

'BB will too,' Belinda hastened to assure her, but crossed her fingers as she spoke. Lady was far better behaved than BB.

'Mrs LeRoy and Lady, how lovely to see you both again and to meet your friends,' the receptionist greeted them as they entered. They were shown straight to their table by a window overlooking the river and, thankfully, BB followed Lady's lead and obediently lay down under the table.

Belinda smothered a laugh as she looked around. 'Nearly every table has a dog under it.'

Fern smiled. 'It's good business. So many people walk the river path every day with their dog and stop off here for a coffee or lunch, they'd be silly to ban dogs. Besides, the French have never had a problem allowing dogs into their cafés and restaurants. I remember when I first came over, people used to put them in their supermarché trolley and push them around whilst they did their shopping. Brussels put a stop to that a few years back.'

Belinda smiled, a memory of going shopping with her mum and seeing just that in the nearest supermarché to home coming to mind. At the time it hadn't seemed strange, just a normal thing to do.

A waitress appeared with a bread basket, a menu for each of them and the wine list which she handed to Fern as she spoke to her in French.

Listening to the two of them, there was something vaguely familiar about the woman that Belinda couldn't quite pin down. It wasn't until the waitress turned to include Belinda in the discussion about which wine they would like to accompany their meal that the name on the neat badge she wore pinned to her pristine black blouse leapt out at her. Sandrine.

Belinda quickly put her head down and studied the menu.

'Sorry I don't speak or understand French.' She gave an apologetic shrug. 'I'm English. Whatever my friend chooses will be fine by me.' Rather than acknowledge the stare she sensed Fern was sending in her direction, Belinda reached out for the water carafe and poured herself a glass.

The waitress turned back to Fern, with her pencil poised.

Fern placed their order of two green salads for starters and two roast beef main courses, explaining that as she was driving, a half carafe of the house Bordeaux between them would be fine. 'Merci,' and Fern handed back the menus.

Once the waitress was out of earshot, she looked across at Belinda, her eyebrows raised.

'I know you speak French, so what was that all about?'

Belinda leant across the table and whispered, 'She was my bête noir at school. I'll tell you more later. Right now I need a glass of that wine you ordered.' She took a bread roll from the basket and, breaking a piece off, chewed it thoughtfully, registering as she did so Fern's shocked look at her words.

Would Sandrine recognise her? If it hadn't been for her name badge, Belinda probably wouldn't have realised the woman was Sandrine, she'd changed so much. Yes, there had been something vaguely familiar about her, but the slim blonde she'd known had matured into a middle-aged woman with henna-red hair.

When Sandrine reappeared with their wine, Belinda kept her head averted and looked out of the window.

Fern poured a glass of the wine and pushed it across the table to Belinda. 'Here you go. I'm intrigued about how you know Sandrine from school, but if you don't want to talk about it, you don't have to.'

Belinda picked up her glass and gently swirled the wine around, wondering whether to tell Fern the truth.

'I'm hoping that she won't recognise me and dump my lunch in my lap.' She took a mouthful of her drink and decided the best thing to do would be to tell Fern a shortened, sanitised, version of the truth about how she knew Sandrine. 'I grew up not a million miles from this place,' Belinda said. 'On the way here, we drove down lanes that I used to know every bend and pothole on. I saw cottages that people I knew lived in.' She took another sip of wine. 'I should have realised that sooner or later I would come face to face with someone from my past. Shame it turned out to be, not an old enemy exactly, but certainly someone who made my teenage years difficult.' Belinda bit back on a smile. 'But then I don't suppose hers were trouble-free either.'

Fern poured a small amount of wine into her own glass. 'How come you went to school in France?'

'I was born in England, but my dad was French.'

'When did you leave? And why?'

Belinda gave a rueful smile. 'The day of my last Baccalauréat. As for why...' She saw Sandrine coming towards them with their starters and fell silent as she reached their table, trying hard to ignore the scrutinising look Sandrine gave her as she placed the salad in front of her. Maybe she did recognise her.

'Bon appétit,' the waitress wished them both before walking away.

'I have to admit I'm surprised Sandrine still lives in the area,' Belinda said quietly. 'She was always moaning about the place, saying she couldn't wait to leave and get a proper life.' She smothered the thought that she, on the other hand, had never envisaged leaving, she'd loved living in Brittany – before that life had been snatched away from her.

'She was working here the first time Laurent brought me and that was a good few years ago now,' Fern said.

Belinda, realising she hadn't answered Fern's last question, decided a change of conversation was needed, otherwise her lunch was going to be ruined by ghosts from the past and the presence of waitresses in the present.

'I've been meaning to ask, do you know anything about Bernie? He appears to be a permanent fixture on the campsite.'

Fern nodded. 'Everyone in the village knows Bernie's story. He was a surprise menopause baby. His two older brothers had left home before he was born and his parents, particularly his father, were resentful that they were back in the throes of bringing up another child that they didn't particularly want.' Fern sighed. 'And when it was discovered that he had a bit of a problem mentally, they were, let's say, bitter about it. You know the saying – it takes a village to raise a child – well, that's what happened here in a way. Everyone used to look out for him and when his father threw him out about six years ago after his mother died, the village rallied around to make sure Bernie always had somewhere to go and something to eat. I think he's been living on the site for about five years now, since his father died anyway. He's a very kind, gentle man and absolutely marvellous with animals.'

'So if I were to insist he has to find somewhere else to live and leave Camping dans La Fôret, I'd be labelled the big bad newcomer. Great.' Belinda sighed. 'He only speaks Breton though. How do people communicate with him?'

Fern gave a wry smile. 'More people than you'd expect still speak Breton around here. And, between you and me, I think he understands basic French. He always seems to understand anything I say to him anyway. I'm pretty sure too that Alain speaks a little Breton.'

'It doesn't sound as though his continued presence is likely to cause problems,' Belinda said. 'And if it does, I'll leave Alain to sort it out.' She looked at Fern and hesitated. 'I don't suppose you've heard anything on the village grapevine about Alain? About why he's gone to the UK this weekend?'

Fern shook her head. 'No, sorry, I've not heard a thing. Not that I hear much anyway.'

Ten minutes later after they'd both enjoyed their first course a young girl appeared to clear their starter plates, followed by Sandrine, who placed their roast beef main courses in front of them.

Conversation between them ceased for several moments as they both tucked in to their meals. When they both muttered 'Delicious' at the same time, Belinda laughed before whispering, 'Not the same without a Yorkshire pud though, is it? I bet you make wonderful Yorkshire puds.'

'I do,' Fern said. 'I'm renowned for my Yorkshire puds.'

'Did you ever go to the café on the campsite? I'm curious about what sort of food they offered there. Chips with everything or something more upmarket?' Belinda asked.

'I don't think it even opened in the last two years,' Fern answered. 'Campers used Yann's Bar and occasionally I got a few evening reservations for dinner. What sort of food are you planning?' She sighed. 'It's the kind of place that years ago I would have loved to have taken on. So much potential there.'

'I'd like to go more restaurant-type food rather than café. It's such a wonderful setting for functions too. But the site will need a more basic café too.' Belinda shrugged. 'We'll see. Whatever I suggest, Alain is sure to argue against.'

'You two still not getting on?'

'We've established a fragile truce. Not sure how long it will last, to be honest,' Belinda said. 'I'm beginning to feel there's something under the surface ready to explode, but I have no idea what.' One thing she did know though was that as an expert in keeping secrets, she could always second guess when someone else was hiding something.

12

The ginger cat was sitting on the top step by the door and mewed at her hopefully as Belinda unlocked the office door early Monday morning. She'd made her way to the campsite at the usual time, stopping in the village to pick up croissants and her lunchtime baguette on the way. If Alain didn't turn up, she'd share the plain croissant with BB and the ducks down on the river.

'Morning, Ging,' Belinda said, bending down to give the cat a stroke. She really must ask Alain what the cat's proper name was.

Ging followed her into the office, jumped onto the desk and curled up in his usual position out of BB's way. The two of them had settled down well together, even played sometimes, but BB was liable to get overexcited and would receive a sharp tap on his nose when he upset Ging.

While the computer booted up, Belinda made herself a coffee and found herself thinking about the last couple of weeks. The days had gone so quickly, it was hard to believe that this would be her third week at Camping dans La Fôret. Another two and she would be heading home for the Easter holiday rush in the hotels and spending time with Chloe and the twins. She knew Alain was planning on having some of the caravan places and tent pitches open for the holidays as a trial run before the official opening on the first of June. Part of her was disappointed that she'd be missing the arrival of these first visitors, but Belinda was longing to see the family again, even if only for a week. Skype calls just weren't the same.

Outside, she could hear voices and car doors slamming as the men working outside and the cleaners arrived. Today, the men were pressure-washing the area down by the café and the cleaners were going to start on the last of the cabins. She'd give both teams half an hour and then wander down and see how they were all doing, make sure they had all the tools they needed as Alain wasn't here.

The morning passed quickly as Belinda did admin jobs on the computer, checked out a couple of suppliers and did some more work updating the website. She was about to start researching the location of the nearest makers and distributors of pods and tree houses when BB pricked his ears and she heard a car door slam. Alain was back.

But it was a stranger who opened the office door and gave her a cheerful 'Bonjour' as he walked in. He held out his hand for her to shake. 'Hervé Bois.'

'Belinda Marshall. Bonjour,' Belinda answered, wondering if she was supposed to know who this smartly dressed and good-looking Frenchman was.

'Alain out on the site?' Hervé asked.

'No. Was he expecting you?'

'I said I'd pop in sometime to discuss something with him. Any idea when he'll be here?'

Belinda shook her head. 'Afraid not. Was it something to do

with the campsite you wanted to discuss or something personal? If it's about the site, maybe I can help.'

'Has Alain employed you to help run the place?' Hervé asked.

Belinda gave him a 'we're not amused by that remark' look straight out of her French grandmother's repertoire. 'Alain and I are joint managers for the new owners. So, is it business or personal? If it's personal, then I'm sorry I can't help, so I'll say goodbye.' Her voice sounded sharper than she intended, but she needed to dispel the man's notion that Alain was in charge here and that she was merely his employee.

'Desolé. I didn't realise,' Hervé apologised. 'It's about the vide-grenier we've held here in the past in aid of a few of the local charities. Hoping that we can have one again this year now that Alain is back... now that the place is up and running again,' he amended hastily.

Belinda, having been to many a vide-grenier in the past, knew that they were France's equivalent of a car boot sale.

'We?' she queried.

'Yann's Gang. The bar in the village?' Hervé added by way of explanation. 'A few of us help him organise a couple of things throughout the year – a village run, lotto night, music evenings, the vide-grenier, that kind of thing, all in aid of charity.'

Belinda opened the computer diary. 'I'm sure we can help, but I'm going to need more information. Presumably people pay you for a pitch? Do you pay us for the use of the site? Or is it regarded as a charitable contribution from us? How many stallholders usually? That sort of thing.' She paused. 'Do you have a date in mind?'

'First Sunday in May. Ten o'clock until six.'

'How many people usually come? And, this is a crucial question, how disruptive is it likely to be to holidaymakers staying on site? I'll provisionally pencil the date in, but I need you to come back with answers to my questions – and anything else you think we need to be aware of – before we agree. It's early in the season and I have to warn you that there may well be renovation work still going on around the place.' Belinda glanced across at Hervé and was surprised to find him staring at her, a look of amazement on his face. 'What? Why are you looking at me like that?'

'Are you always like this? Efficiently bossy?' The words were accompanied by a smile that somehow took any suggestion of criticism away. Despite herself, Belinda smiled back at him.

'In a word, yes, I'm afraid I am. I try to anticipate problems and prevent them happening.'

'Will you please come and work for me?'

Belinda laughed. 'No. Once this place is up and running, I shall happily return to my normal job in the UK.'

Hervé looked disappointed for a second. 'Mais, you are here for a few weeks yet? Peut-être you and I—'

Belinda held up her hand and cut him off in mid-sentence, anticipating what he was about to say. 'I'll certainly be here long enough for you to give me the answers to the questions I've asked you and a decision to be taken about the vide-grenier,' she said, her voice cool and her face emotionless as she stared at him. As attractive as Hervé Bois might be, she had no intention of having anything but a business relationship with him. She could count on the fingers of one hand the number of men she'd dated since her divorce and she wasn't about to add to them with Hervé. A relationship was the last thing she needed.

He returned her stare before giving a slight nod. 'Okay. I'll see you later in the week with the answers you need. Merci. Au revoir.'

'If you let us know when you're coming, I'll make sure Alain is here too,' Belinda said as he opened the door. 'Au revoir,' she added, but the door had already closed behind him.

Hearing voices and car doors slamming as the workers left for lunch, Belinda realised the time.

Alain still hadn't shown up when Belinda locked up that evening and returned to the auberge. Fern made her a cup of tea and pushed a plate of shortbread biscuits towards her.

'What's up?'

'Alain's not returned and I don't know what to do about it,' Belinda said. 'I can't even phone him as he's never given me his mobile number.' She made a mental note to insist when he got back that he gave it to her. 'I can't phone Nigel to ask if he's been in touch, as I suspect Nigel doesn't know he's taking time off for personal reasons.'

'Maybe the weather has delayed the ferry? And don't forget, there's still the "gilets jaunes" blocking roads and holding things up without warning. I'm sure he'll turn up for work tomorrow.'

'Hope you're right.' Belinda swallowed a bite of her biscuit. 'I met someone called Hervé Bois this morning. Wants to organise a vide-grenier on the campsite. Do you know him?'

'He was a friend of Laurent's.' Fern looked at Belinda. 'I've met him a few times. Divorced. Two grown-up daughters. Successful businessman. He's good company.'

'I'm sure he is,' Belinda admitted.

'He does have a bit of a reputation as a ladies' man so not a long-term prospect but could be fun while you're over here,' Fern said thoughtfully.

Belinda shook her head. 'Nope. Not interested even in a short-term relationship. I'm sure he was going to ask me out, but I managed to stop him before he could voice the words. I'm hoping he got the message.' Talking to Hervé Bois about the vide-grenier was definitely something that she planned on leaving to Alain. Presuming he intended on returning.

13

Alain was already in the office when Belinda arrived the next morning. BB greeted him enthusiastically, Belinda less so.

'Twenty-four hours late, but you're back,' she said, stating the obvious. 'Your weekend in the UK go okay?' If she thought Alain was going to explain and apologise for his absence, she was wrong.

'Yes thanks,' Alain said and carried on reading his emails.

Belinda busied herself spooning coffee into the cafetière and making the coffee. Alain took the mug she handed him a minute or two later.

'Thanks. No croissant?'

'Didn't bother to buy any. The ducks enjoyed yours yesterday,' Belinda said, sipping her coffee. 'Incidentally, we should exchange mobile numbers in case of emergency.'

'No problems 'ere while I was away?'

'None that didn't exist before. The cleaning and clearing has virtually finished, you need to organise people to paint the shower block and the toilets. The cleaners are making a start on the cabins.

Oh, and your friend Hervé called in to ask about holding a vide-grenier. He's coming back with full details. Also, there's a campsite between Brest and Roscoff that we need to visit together. Apparently they have a couple of pods. We can see how they fit in and ask their advice on which to go for before we order any for here.'

Alain pulled a face. 'You know 'ow I feel about that. I don't want to get involved with them. You go.'

Belinda looked at him exacerbated. 'You have to be involved. You're going to be the one managing them when the camp opens and I'm back in the UK.'

Alain shrugged. 'I will worry about it when – *if* – we get any bookings for them.'

'We'll get bookings.' Belinda stared at him and reached a decision. 'Right. I'll ask Nigel to book a night ferry, I'll meet him at Roscoff, we'll spend the day sorting Pods out and he can go back on the evening ferry.'

Before Alain could answer, the office door opened and a delivery man stood there, electronic signing device in his hand.

'Three parcels for Marshall,' he said, holding the device out. 'Where do you want them?'

'Manager's cottage,' Belinda said, scrawling a signature with her finger before following the man out. 'I'll show you.'

At least unpacking parcels would take her mind off Alain's stubborn refusal to have anything to do with the pods. She didn't, of course, have any intention of dragging Nigel over here when she was quite capable of making a decision herself. She'd only suggested it in the hope that Alain would change his mind. But she could really do with a second opinion before she committed to spending a large sum of Nigel's money. She'd been hoping that Alain would agree to accompany her and she'd be able to change his opinion about the pods. She'd see if Fern would like to go with her instead, they could make a day of it, have lunch up on the coast.

It took Belinda a couple of hours to unpack and put the contents of two of the boxes away in the cottage. Knowing that the hotels back in the UK all had surplus equipment stacked away, it had made sense to make use of it rather than buy new. Bed linen, towels, pillows, cushions, cutlery, electric kettle, crockery – Nigel had sent everything she'd itemised to make the cottage as comfortable as possible.

She smiled as she unpacked the third box, a bean-to-cup coffee machine that was surplus to requirements in one of the hotels. She'd enjoy using that while she was living here.

She was up in the bedroom at the front of the house making up the bed when she heard footsteps on the stairs.

'Who's this for?' Alain asked, appearing in the doorway.

'Me. I told you that as soon as the place was clean and user-friendly I intended to move in. More convenient to be on site and it saves Nigel some money.' Expertly she did the last hospital corner on the bottom sheet before reaching for the duvet cover and shaking it out flat on the bed. 'While you're here, you can give me a hand putting this on.' Not giving him the chance to refuse, she handed him a corner of the duvet and began to push the opposite corner up into the cover with its pretty red poppy design.

Without a word, Alain did as she asked, although she could almost feel the tension emitting from him as he worked. It was a strangely intimate thing to be doing with a man she barely knew, she realised, before pushing the errant thought away.

'Thanks,' she said, reaching for a pillow and slipping it into a pillowcase. 'Did you want me for something?'

'I come with you to look at the pods. Let me know which day.'

Belinda looked at him, surprised. 'You've changed your mind?

Okay. I'll ring the site and book an appointment,' Belinda said, longing to ask him why he'd changed his mind, but Alain had already turned away and was going downstairs.

Making her way downstairs, Belinda glanced in the small sitting room, which was cosy and inviting now the clean loose covers were in place on the settee and the armchairs grouped around a coffee table in front of the clean log burner.

Her mobile buzzed. Nigel. Just the person she wanted to talk to.

'Hi. Thanks for the delivery. Planning to move into the house this week. Everything all right your end?' she asked, but Nigel's words drove everything she needed to say out of her mind.

'Need to give you the heads-up about a change of plan,' Nigel said. 'Reckon you can finish getting things ready for Easter over there in the next few days and come back here a week early?'

'Honestly? There's still so much to organise – staff to find, the café to organise, the cabins to refurnish, the small shop has to be stocked. And I haven't sourced any pods yet. Why?'

'I might need you to stay back here for a bit after Easter. Maybe indefinitely. Alain's going to have to cope on his own. Molly's not well.' Nigel's voice was gruff. 'Got to have an operation before Easter and then several weeks convalescence.'

Belinda took a deep breath. 'Oh, poor Molly. Okay. I'll work on getting the site ticking over for camper vans and tents but put everything else on hold until later in the season. I doubt there will be much business around before June anyway. Give my love to Molly.'

Belinda made her way back to the office, deep in thought and worrying about Molly. Whatever was wrong with her Belinda prayed it was nothing too serious. A flash of disappointment that she was having to leave early surprised her. She'd got so used to living in Brittany and working at the campsite that it would be an unexpected wrench leaving. Alain was nowhere to be seen and she guessed that he was out on the site checking on the workers. She sat down at the desk, opened her laptop and started to make notes about the jobs that had suddenly become urgent. Finding staff was definitely top of the list. Half an hour later, when Alain appeared, she had a plan of action in place.

'Our day of sourcing pods is off, I'm afraid. Nigel phoned earlier,' she said, looking up at him. 'Molly is ill and he wants me back early. Might even want me to stay on indefinitely.' She pressed a key on the laptop and the office printer sprang into life. 'I've worked out the essentials that need to be in place here before I leave in five days' time.' She got up and crossed over to the printer and picked up a sheet of paper and handed it to Alain. 'Emergency action plan. I was going to move into the cottage tomorrow, but I think I'll stay on at the auberge now. You'll have to move in once the site opens and I'm away. At least the bed's made.'

Alain looked up from the paper. 'I can see why Nigel calls you his wonder woman. You're good.'

Belinda shrugged. 'It's my job. I've buzzed the cleaners, asking them to call in here before they leave. I'm hoping that one or two of them will want some part-time work other than cleaning. We need a receptionist, a general help and a groundsperson/handyman – all to start before Easter. We'll need more people once the season gets underway, but that should get you over the Easter hump. Any of the men looking for a seasonal position as groundsman?'

'I do it with Bernie,' Alain said.

'You've spoken to him about staying on site and helping out?'

'Not yet, but I will.'

'I'm going to call in on the village shop tonight on my way to the auberge. Talk to them about stocking the shop with the basics and maybe even running it. It's doubtful that the café will be organised and in a fit state to open for Easter, so it can just stay closed,' Belinda continued. 'We won't make any announcement about the campsite being open, we'll just settle for any passing trade. You'll have to make sure, though, you explain about the lack of facilities to any hopeful campers. Camper vans and caravans are usually self-sufficient for cooking, any visitors in tents who pitch up without a camping stove will have to go to Yann's to eat.'

'Stop worrying, pas un problem,' Alain said.

Belinda hoped he was right. Hopefully she'd covered everything but in truth there was still so much to do she wasn't sure they'd be ready by summer let alone Easter.

* * *

Later that day, Belinda told Fern about her change of plans and checked it was all right for her to stay at the auberge until she returned to Devon.

'You don't need my room for a booking?' she asked. 'It will make my life easier not having to cater for myself on top of everything else I have to do before I leave.'

'No bookings until Easter, then it's only one double for three nights. Although I did have a phone call this afternoon from Carhaix tourist office, asking if I had a vacancy for the next few days. But I haven't heard anything more, so I guess they've found somewhere.' Fern looked at Belinda anxiously. 'Does this mean you won't be coming back?'

'No idea really what's going to happen,' Belinda said, surprised at the feeling of sadness that swept through her at the thought of not returning to Brittany and cementing her friendship with Fern.

14

Thursday morning when Belinda left for the campsite Fern decided to visit her mother-in-law, Anouk. Laurent's father had died some twenty years before and Anouk had lived alone ever since in the Huelgoat house she'd moved into the day of her marriage. Fern had always got on well with Anouk and Laurent's death had served to bring them closer.

Overlooking the lake at Huelgoat, the house was too big for her now, but Anouk seemed determined to stay in it, saying she couldn't imagine living anywhere else. Fern knew that Fabian felt the time was coming when his grandmother would have to accept that the upkeep of the place was beyond her and move into something smaller, more manageable. Ninety next birthday, Anouk might manage a 1K walk every day, but the huge garden was becoming a burden despite Fabian doing the heavy digging and the mowing. Fern understood all too well though how the tug of happy memories kept you connected to the home you'd shared with a loved one.

Before she left home, Fern telephoned Anouk to say that she was planning to visit.

'I thought as it's market day we could do a bit of shopping and then have a coffee in the main square.'

To Fern's surprise, Anouk sounded subdued when she agreed.

'Are you okay?' Fern asked, concerned.

'I'm as fine as I can be at my age,' Anouk replied. 'A walk around the market and some company sounds great.'

'See you in about half an hour then.' Fern switched off her phone pensively. It was unlike Anouk to mention her age. She hoped Fabian hadn't been on at her again about moving.

* * *

After a stroll around the market, buying a few bits and pieces and stopping to chat with various stallholder friends, they made their way to the café next door to the small supermarché at the end of the square. Fern settled Anouk at one of the pavement tables, leaving her with Lady and the few bags of shopping, while she went in to choose the cakes to go with their coffee. When she returned, Fabian was chatting to his grandmother.

'Bonjour, Fern. Ça va? I was passing and saw grand-mère. It is good of you to bring her out like this.' He hesitated and glanced at his grandmother. 'She has perhaps told you our news?'

Anouk gave an imperceptible shake of her head.

'Carole and I we 'ave a new baby on the way. Une petite sister for Jean-Marc.'

'Congratulations, please give my love to Carole,' Fern said. 'I'm so pleased for you both.' She genuinely was, despite the sinking feeling in the pit of her tummy. She suspected she knew what was about to come.

'Maybe we come, Carole and me, talk to you about the house again?'

Fern sighed. 'Fabian, you know the only way I can leave is for you to buy me out. I have to buy somewhere to live and all my capital has been invested in the auberge. Has something changed? Have you found a mortgage?'

Fabian shook his head. 'No. C'est pas possible. But I own half the maison and want to live in it with my family.' His voice had steadily risen and people were glancing their way.

Anouk patted him gently on the arm.

'I'm sorry, but this isn't the place to discuss a private family matter,' Fern said.

Fabian took a breath and exhaled deeply. 'I'm sorry also. But Carole, she wants a proper family home and I get so frustrated about the impossibility of it all.'

'I know it's difficult, but the harsh truth is if your father was still alive, you wouldn't even be entertaining these thoughts.'

'But he's not alive, is he? And you are living in a house that rightfully belongs to me as his son.'

'It is also a house that needed a lot of work doing to it when Laurent inherited it from his grandmother – work that you will reap the benefit of when you inherit. It was that money, my children's inheritance, that paid for those renovations. Money that I am trying to replace and pay the overheads by continuing to run it as an auberge. You can hardly deny my children have a right to an inheritance from me.' Fern rubbed her face. 'I don't like the situation any more than you do, but, hopefully, in a couple more years, I'll have recuperated enough to move out.'

An unhappy Fabian sighed. 'I 'ave to go. We need a proper family conference to sort something out. There are two possible solutions we haven't talked about yet. Au revoir,' and he kissed his grandmother goodbye before hesitantly turning to Fern and kissing her cheek too. 'Desolé,' he muttered and walked away.

Anouk sighed. 'One of the solutions he suggests if you won't move out is that he, Carole and the children move in with me.'

'How do you feel about that?' Fern asked. 'Would it work? You'd have someone on hand to keep an eye on you.'

'I think it would be less my home than theirs. Selfish, I know, but I've lived alone for so long now,' Anouk shrugged, 'it would be like an invasion of my private space.'

Fern hesitated. 'Do you know what he's thinking of as the second possible solution?'

'I 'ardly like to tell you.' Anouk paused. 'You and I should move in together into one of the houses. He's not fussy which but would prefer for you to move in with me.'

Fern stared at her, open-mouthed. She could see from Fabian's point of view that that idea made perfect sense.

'I can see you no like that idea any more than I do,' Anouk said. She pushed the coffee cup in front of her away. 'Sometimes I feel I've lived too long. Fabian knows my house will be his when I die, he's just going to 'ave to wait.'

'Oh, Anouk.' Fern reached out and held the older woman's hand, sensing her distress. 'Please don't talk like that. I know Fabian doesn't wish you dead. If he wishes anyone dead, it's probably me.' Right now, though, she could cheerfully murder Fabian and his wife for their selfishness and lack of compassion towards his grandmother.

* * *

An hour later, driving back to the auberge, having taken Anouk home, Fern felt despondent and unsettled. She'd thought she was beginning to recover from the loss of Laurent, but the events of the morning had shaken her. The pressure Fabian was putting on her to move out of the auberge made her feel guilty, when she truly had nothing to feel guilty about Laurent's death. It was French inheritance laws that were at the root of the problem.

Fabian would get his inheritance in due course, but her girls would get significantly less if she simply walked away from the auberge.

She had Laurent's insurance money tucked away for the girls as a safety net, but she'd been banking on the auberge earning money and being able to recuperate at least some of the money they'd spent on renovations. The inescapable fact, though, was wherever she lived she needed a steady income of some sort. Jobs were notoriously difficult to come by in this part of France, put a middle-aged English female into the equation and it became damn near impossible.

Maybe she should think about Fabian's second suggestion of she and Anouk moving in together. Not in the Huelgoat house, but in the auberge. With Anouk installed in one of the bedrooms, there would still be five bedrooms to let out. Anouk was becoming increasingly frail and as much as she might hate the idea of leaving her beloved family home, it was inevitable. At least she wouldn't end up in an old folks' home if she moved in with her.

Fern's grip on the steering wheel tightened. 'Bloody drunken driver,' she cursed under her breath. 'You annihilated more than Laurent's life when you killed him – you stole my happiness and created turmoil in his family.'

15

The remaining days before Belinda returned to the UK passed in a whirl of activity. The village shop owners had jumped at the opportunity to run the campsite shop rent-free over the Easter holiday period, even though Belinda had stressed there were unlikely to be many customers. They'd also indicated they'd be interested in a proper rent-paying lease for the summer months once the campsite was up and running.

Which meant that one morning, Belinda joined everyone in cleaning the shop, whilst Alain checked out the freezers and the electricity with one of the men.

When everyone disappeared for lunch, Alain ignored her protests and insisted that she joined him for a snack at Yann's.

'A crêpe and a glass of wine, an hour at the most,' he said. 'You'll be back working before you realise it.'

'I was going to do some admin over the lunch hour,' Belinda answered, surprised by his offer. 'Besides, I'm dirty from all the scrubbing.' She glanced down at her grubby jeans and sweatshirt.

'It's a village bar. People, they go from work.'

Belinda sighed. She was hungry. 'An hour, no longer. There's still so much to do before I leave.'

'We go in my car,' Alain said. 'Come on BB. Time to find you a sausage.'

Belinda couldn't summon the energy to argue and followed him out to the 2CV. She bit back on the memory of a long ago yellow 2CV as BB jumped onto her lap for the short drive to the village and she gave him a tight hug.

Most of their current workforce had opted for lunch in the bar and smiled at her and Alain as they walked in. After asking her what she would like – 'Ham and egg crêpe and a glass of white wine please' – Alain went straight to the bar while Belinda found an empty table near the window and settled BB under it.

'Five minutes for food,' Alain said, joining her with the wine she'd asked for and a beer for himself. 'Santé.'

'Santé,' Belinda echoed as they clinked glasses. 'Hope it is only five minutes for the food. I can't believe I let you talk me into coming here. I should be back at the office doing stuff I didn't get to do this morning.'

Alain looked at her but didn't say anything.

'Why are you looking at me like that?' Belinda demanded.

'I think if you ever relax. Ever stop thinking about work. Have fun.'

'Yes, of course I do, but right now I need to stay on top of things here before I return to England.'

'So what is it you do, when you are on top of things?'

'I... I walk BB, read, talk with friends, meet up with my daughter and my grandchildren. All the usual things.' Belinda took a sip of her drink, before throwing the question back at Alain. 'What do you do?'

'I like to walk in the countryside, cook delicious meals for my friends. Your grandchildren? How many 'ave you?'

Belinda kept the thought that Alain's own list of two things wasn't exactly fun-filled either to herself, and answered his question about her grandchildren. 'Two. A boy and a girl – they're twins. They'll be three later this year. Do you have any?'

Alain nodded, a wry look on his face. 'I 'ave a son, but no grandchildren yet.'

The arrival of their food at that moment stopped Belinda asking him about his son and for several moments they were silent as they both tucked into their crêpes. Once her initial hunger had been satisfied Belinda looked at Alain.

'I've a couple of women coming in tomorrow at two o'clock about the receptionist job. Can you be around to meet them?'

'Are they local? I might already know them.'

Belinda glanced around the bar. 'One of them is sat over there with Bernie. The woman with the blonde hair tied back. She's been helping around the site and asked me if we'd consider her. She's never done a receptionist job before, so we'd have to train her from the ground up. Says she's computer-literate, though, which is a bonus point.'

'That's Marie,' Alain answered. 'She'd make a good receptionist. She's personable and good with people. She's got my vote. So don't waste your time, cancel the other interview. Would you like another drink?'

Belinda laughed and shook her head. 'I can't do that. No more wine, thanks, but I'd like a coffee please and then we'd better get back.'

Alain ordered the coffees as an assistant cleared their plates. 'You see your daughter and her family while you're in the UK?'

Belinda nodded happily. 'Yes, she lives in the same town. I've missed her while I've been here, but we don't see an awful lot of each other anyway. We're both so busy. I do get to babysit once a week while she and her husband have a "date night".

And we have Sunday lunch together once a month in one of the hotels.'

When the waiter brought their coffees, he placed the bill on the table and Belinda reached for her purse to pay her share. Alain stopped her.

'I pay for lunch,' he said.

'No, I'll pay my share,' Belinda said.

'Please, I insist. Take it as an apology for my behaviour when you arrived.'

Belinda looked at him, a half-smile on her face. 'You've already apologised for that, but thank you,' and she put her purse away.

'Can I ask you something?' Alain said.

'You can, but I reserve the right to remain silent.' Belinda looked at him as he carefully replaced his coffee cup on its saucer.

'Do you remember that first day when you arrived and I told you I didn't want you 'ere and you stormed off saying you, and I quote, "sure as 'ell" didn't want to be 'ere. Why was that?'

'As I remember it, I quoted your own words back at you. So I could ask you the same question.' Belinda closed her eyes and sighed. 'It's personal and, actually,' she opened her eyes as she spoke and looked at him, 'I'd really rather not talk about it right now, especially in a public place.'

'Fair enough,' Alain said. 'I was just curious.' He stood up. 'Let's go. I pay the bill and see you by the car.'

A gentle rain was falling as Belinda waited outside for Alain under the shelter of a nearby tree. She glanced at her watch. Lunch had taken less than an hour. There was time to do something she'd been putting off ever since she'd arrived for one reason or another. And if she didn't come back, would she ever have the chance again? Could she ask Alain to take her somewhere, no questions asked?

As he appeared and they got in the car, Belinda took a deep breath. 'I'm sorry if I was rude back there. Would it be possible to take a short detour? There's something I've been meaning to do for weeks, ever since I got here in fact.'

Alain glanced at her, curious. 'You going to tell me why?'

'When we get there I will,' Belinda said quietly.

'Okay. Where are we going?'

'Huelgoat direction via the scenic route, not the N164, for about five kilometres.'

Sitting in the car listening to the mesmeric swish of the windscreen wipers swiping rhythmically across the screen, Belinda wondered if she was doing the right thing. She should have done this journey alone, not dragged a man who knew nothing about her past life along because she didn't want to go alone. Alain wasn't a total stranger, but it wasn't fair on him. On the other hand, it was because of the question he'd asked that she'd impulsively decided to go. It would have been far more sensible to have asked Fern to have taken a detour when they'd met on Sunday for lunch.

'Oh,' she said, realising the crossroads they needed were approaching. 'Turn left here.'

The narrow road twisted and turned, a tall church spire guiding them into a small village.

'If we can park near the church,' Belinda said quietly.

Alain parked, turned the engine off and turned to her. 'And now?' he asked, his voice gentle, his attitude concerned.

Belinda gripped the door handle and pressed it down, ready to push it open before answering.

'My paternal grandmother lived in this village. I lived on a smallholding a few kilometres away from here from the age of one until I was seventeen when... when I left.' Belinda pushed open the car door and got out, relieved the rain had stopped.

Without waiting for Alain, she walked towards the open gates of the churchyard and immediately turned left along a path. When he caught up with her, she said, 'It's strange, isn't it, the things you remember? I haven't been in this churchyard for nearly forty years, but I know exactly where the old family grave is.'

A minute later she stopped in front of a gravel-filled plot with a carved granite angel standing at its head. Of the names carved on the lichen-covered headstone, it was just possible to make out part of the names and the dates from the eighteenth century. The last name was still clearly visible: Martha Odette Rochelle Belrose. 1915–1979.

'I was twelve when she died and missed her so much,' Belinda said quietly. 'I spent a lot of time with her. She'd have been spinning in her grave if she'd known what was going to happen five years later.' Belinda stopped speaking and blinked rapidly.

'You okay?' Alain asked.

Belinda nodded. 'Thank you.'

'You like a few minutes alone? I see you back at the car,' Alain offered.

Belinda shook her head. 'I've been wanting to come and pay my respects for a long time. I just couldn't face it alone,' Belinda said. 'When – if – I get back after Easter, I'll come with flowers. Thank you for bringing me today.' She gave Alain a wobbly smile. 'We'd better get back.'

She was relieved when Alain turned and began to walk back to the car and didn't press her for details on what had happened five years after her grandmother had died.

'Your turn,' she said as they drove out of the village.

'My turn?'

Belinda nodded. 'Yes. You know a little now of why I didn't want to be here, but why didn't you want me here?'

'That, I'm afraid, I'm not going to tell you today. As you said earlier, it's personal and I don't wish to discuss it.'

Belinda opened her mouth to protest and closed it again. If Alain didn't want to tell her, she couldn't make him. She hadn't told him the full story surrounding her grandmother either. Some things were better kept private.

16

It was a subdued Belinda who arrived back at the auberge that evening. She said a quick 'Hi' to Fern who was in the kitchen preparing dinner, before declining to join her for their usual cup of tea and going straight to her room instead. When she went downstairs ready for dinner at seven o'clock, she made a concentrated effort to try and push all thoughts of her grandmother out of her mind.

'You're quiet tonight. Bad day at the office?' Fern joked as she placed their starters and wine on the table.

'So-so,' Belinda said. 'Been a funny day really.' She took a forkful of the green salad that accompanied the walnut and onion tart Fern had made. 'I had lunch at Yann's with Alain – which was unusual in itself. Afterwards, he took me to see my grandmother's grave.'

Fern stared at her, guessing that this had been an emotional visit, and waited for her to continue.

'I have nothing but good memories of my mami. I loved spending time with her – I learnt a lot from her. Sitting out in the garden on summer evenings with a book in her hand, reading until the light had gone, was her idea of a good time. She loved gardening and reading.' Belinda smiled. 'She taught me how to make lace too. She was one of the last women in the village to make the traditional Breton lace coiffe. She wore hers with pride every single day. Hers was a simple head covering, not for mami the ridiculously tall hats that still come out for fetes and festivals these days.' Belinda took a sip of the wine Fern had poured her earlier. 'I can still probably make a lace collar but, sadly, her cooking skills didn't rub off on me.'

'Tch – how many people can say they can make a lace collar?' Fern said. 'At least you've got happy memories of your grandmother.'

Belinda nodded. 'True.' She was quiet for a moment or two, concentrating on eating her starter. 'Delicious as per usual,' she said, placing her knife and fork down on the plate. 'The problem is negative memories tend to overshadow everything else if you're not careful. I've been guilty of letting certain unhappy memories do that for a very long time.'

'Is this to do with leaving France? You told me when you left but not why,' Fern said quietly. 'Did you not want to leave?'

'No. I begged and pleaded with my mum to let me stay behind,' Belinda answered. 'Even when we got back to England, I kept on and on at her to let me return. Threw all the tantrums a teenager is so good at.' She sighed. 'It was weeks before Mum finally gave in and told me that Dad had been having an affair.' Saying the words out loud to Fern brought the long-ago scene from that dreadful afternoon thirty-five years ago flooding back into her mind. Belinda gnawed on her bottom lip and closed her eyes before she began to talk about the scene that had finished her childhood and fractured her family...

For the last time, the school bus had dropped her at the top of the lane and she'd swung her bag happily as she strolled homewards. She'd finished with school. The last Baccalauréat exam, the dreaded chemistry, had been taken, she could now forget all about chemical reactions because they would have no relevance in her life ever again. She'd felt free and wonderful, with the summer stretching ahead of her. She was a country girl at heart, had never known anywhere else really. She loved the changing seasons here in Brittany (sometimes all four in a day!), the magical light that had drawn famous artists down the years to paint, the sense of history that pervaded the crop circles and the ancient woods. Of course, she'd loved visiting nearby towns, Pontivy, Carhaix, Quimper for shopping, but the thought of living in such close proximity to other people had made her shudder; she was always glad to get back home. Even if it meant eating her mum's home-made pizza rather than being able to go to a McDonald's like her friends who lived in a nearby town.

The thought of a summer of working weekends in the village café, riding Lucky, her pony, helping her dad with the animals and haymaking and then, in the afternoons and evenings, hanging out with her friend, Amelie, made her smile. And this was the summer, too, that Dad was going to prepare her for taking the driving test. He'd bought the car he'd promised to give her, a fun 2CV painted sunshine yellow, months ago, and had sat at her side as she'd driven it around the smallholding, getting used to steering it and changing the gears smoothly. 'A natural driver,' he'd called her. 'Take after me you do.' By the end of summer, she'd be as free as a bird, driving here, there and everywhere.

Strolling up the lane, she'd thought about Dominique, the local heart-throb. Maybe she'd be casually driving through the village and see him. His eyes would light up as he saw her and he'd jump into the car and she'd drive them to the coast for a picnic. She remembered thinking, yeah, like that was going to happen.

As much as she might daydream and imagine herself and Dominique cast as Sandy and Danny in her favourite film, *Grease*, Belinda had a streak of realism in her – she knew it was never going to happen. She wasn't his type – unlike Sandrine, whose parents ran the local bar. So, this summer, the last one before college in Rennes in the autumn to study Accounts and Business Management, she was going to give up having a crush on someone unobtainable (because that's all it was, right? A crush) and enjoy being free of all the responsibilities everyone assured her would start once she was out in the big bad world.

Her mum's car had been parked in front of the granite-built mas and unusually Belinda didn't have to struggle to open the blue wrought-iron gates at the entrance to the smallholding as they were propped open. Belinda saw her parents standing by the car, her mum making angry gesticulations at her father, her father raising his arms in a useless protest. Butch, the sheepdog, was barking frantically at them both. Something terrible must have happened. She'd never known her parents to behave like this. Belinda remembered quickening her steps until she was running towards them.

By the time she'd reached her parents and yelled, 'What's happened?' her dad had started running his hands through his hair, a sure sign that he was upset. Her mum was trying to push a suitcase into an already full car. Neither of them had noticed Belinda's arrival.

'Mum? Dad? What's going on?' Belinda remembered staring in astonishment at the car, the inside stuffed with boxes, several small suitcases and a jumble of coats and boots all flung in on top.

'Get in the car, Belinda,' her mum had said, finally registering that she was there. 'We're leaving.'

'Jean, we need to talk. All of us. You can't leave like this. Belinda might not want to come with you.'

'She's coming, whether she wants to or not. One thing she's not doing is staying here with you and your... your... Get in the car, Belinda.'

'Not until one of you tells me what the hell is going on.'

'Don't swear,' her mother had answered automatically. 'I'm leaving your father and you're coming with me.'

'What if I don't want to – which I don't.' Bewildered Belinda looked from her mum to her dad. The last thing she needed was to have to choose between them but if she had to she knew which it would be. She loved her mum but there was no way she wanted to leave either her dad or the smallholding.

'You don't have a choice, you're under age.' Her mother had pushed another bag of things into the back of the already stuffed car and slammed the boot shut.

Belinda hadn't moved. 'Why are you leaving Dad?' she demanded.

Her mother's shoulders sagged. 'Because he lied to me and I won't stay around to be the laughing stock of the village. I've packed up most of your stuff – clothes and things. Dad will pack the rest up and send it on. Please just get in the car and we can leave.'

Belinda could see her mum was close to tears. She'd never seen her in such a state before. Her dad never, ever lied, always said he couldn't abide people who told lies, so what was that all about? She'd sighed and walked over to her dad, gave him a hug and said quietly, 'I'll go with her for now, but I'll come back tomorrow and talk to you.' When he shook his head, she insisted, 'Yes I will.'

'Belinda! Now!'

'Okay. I'm coming. See you sometime tomorrow, Dad.'

She'd pretended not to see the knowing look that passed between her parents as she got in the car and pulled her seat belt on.

'So where are we staying? Please not Agatha's!'

'We're catching the evening ferry and going to live in England,' her mother had answered as if it was the most natural thing in the world to be doing. She'd started the car and turned the wheel slowly until the car was facing down the drive.

A jolt had gone through Belinda's body at her mother's words and she'd felt physically ill. 'What? I don't want to live in England,' she'd shouted and struggled to undo her seat belt as her mother revved the car and started to drive down the lane. 'Stop the car and let me out. I want to stay here. You'll ruin my life if you take me to England.' Belinda forced down the bile that was forming in her throat at the thought of losing touch and not seeing her dad regularly.

'No I won't. I'm giving you a new one. You'll soon get used to living in England. And the fact we're never coming back.' As the words sank into Belinda's brain, her mother had wound down the car window and yelled at her husband, 'I hate you. I'll never forgive you and I'll make sure Belinda doesn't either.' She'd revved the car even harder, spinning gravel from out under the wheels as she sped down the lane.

Belinda took a deep breath.

'The next day when we arrived in Devon and the knowledge that the only life I'd ever known and wanted was over sank into my numb brain, I was finally physically sick.' As she finished telling Fern the sorry tale, Belinda's voice cracked. 'She never did forgive him, she refused to tell me the whole truth about what had happened or to let me contact him. This is the first time I've been back to Brittany since we left.'

Fern stared at her. 'Belinda, I'm so sorry. I don't know what to say. My marriage didn't have the most civilised of break-ups, but I did try to make sure the children had a relationship with their dad.'

'My mother was so bitter, it coloured the rest of her life. It wasn't until she was ill and dying that she seemed to regret things. Even extracted a deathbed promise from me to return and lay a few ghosts.'

Fern looked at her questioningly, but Belinda shook her head.

'What about your dad?' she asked instead.

'I did write to him secretly a couple of times, wanting to know how he was and asking about Lucky and Butch. But then one of my letters was returned, marked "Gone Away". I began to believe the vitriolic things mum was constantly saying about him to me were true, so I gave up. I figured it was up to him.' Belinda shrugged. 'Now I don't know whether he's alive or dead. Down the years I did think about trying to contact him without telling mum but life was busy. Besides I knew that if she did find out what I'd done the fallout would be massive. And then she lands me with a deathbed promise – ironic or what?' Belinda sighed. 'I did think though it was something I might investigate while I was here. You know, visit the old home, ask questions, but somehow there hasn't been time.'

'Maybe when you come back after Easter? I'll come with you, if you want me to,' Fern said quietly.

'Thank you. I might take you up on that offer. It was a long time ago, maybe it would be best to let sleeping dogs lie, but it's something that had a huge impact on my life. Don't know about everyone's life having baggage by a certain age, mine seems to have gained a few ghosts loitering under the surface too. Every now and again, it hits me just how different my life has been against what I expected at seventeen. Anyway, enough about me,' Belinda said determinedly and picked up her empty wine glass. 'I think another glass of red please, while you tell me about your day.'

Fern cleared the plates and placed their main course on the table as she told Belinda about her day. 'I've got another booking for the weekend after Easter – two couples for two nights. That will stop me missing you.' She picked up a serving spoon. 'I hope you like fish pie with white wine sauce?' She ladled a generous amount onto Belinda's plate when she nodded. 'Help yourself to broccoli and carrots.' She paused. 'I went to Huelgoat today and had coffee with Anouk, my ma-in-law. We saw Fabian, my stepson – Anouk's grandson – who told me the lovely news that Carole, his wife, is expecting their second child. Which is lovely and I'm truly thrilled for them.'

'I sense a but coming,' Belinda said.

'Fabian had another go at me about the auberge being half his and wanting to live here.' Fern sighed. 'It does seem unfair when you look at it from his point of view.' She pushed a piece of broccoli around her plate before glancing at Belinda. 'Can I run something past you? And please will you give me your honest opinion?'

Belinda nodded. 'Of course.'

'I'm thinking of suggesting that Anouk moves in with me. And Fabian takes over her house. I'm not even sure that she'll agree. I know she'd prefer to spend the rest of her days in her own home, so the chances are she's going to say no.'

'Do you get on with her?'

'Yes. Anouk is lovely. She is getting increasingly frail though, and I know at some point in the future, if she does come and live with me, I'd end up as her carer. Which is something I'm happy to do.'

'Would you still run the auberge?'

'Yes, but more like a B&B – no evening meals. I have to keep some income coming in and there would still be five bedrooms available for guests.'

'Would Fabian be happy about moving into Anouk's house and not this one?'

'He's already suggested we house-share. He'll inherit his grandmother's house in due course,' Fern said quietly. 'As well as this one.'

'It's a colossal decision to make, which will impact hugely on your life, as well as Anouk's,' Belinda said as she studied her friend. 'I know you'd be doing this for Anouk, someone you're very fond of, but it's one hell of a commitment to take on someone you're not technically related to. She could live for another ten years. What happens to your own life in that time? You put it on hold?'

17

Waiting for the first woman to turn up for her interview about the receptionist's job, Belinda began to tick things off her action plan. The shop cleaned and spruced up, tick. All current painting jobs done, tick. Picnic tables pressure-washed and placed in position, tick. Boules pitch down by the entertainment area, tick. Manager's house clean and tidy, tick. Office ready for action, tick. Not that there would be a lot of action, Easter would be like a dry-run experiment for the season when, hopefully, everything would be in tip-top condition. Information board, tick. She glanced across at it in position already by the door.

The Tourist Office had sent a large bundle of brochures and she'd been amazed at the number of attractions there were these days in Brittany, especially local ones that she'd never dreamed existed back in the day, which, of course, some of them hadn't. Château de Trévarez, known locally as The Pink Chateau, had always been there, but the Valley of the Saints was definitely new, with its hundreds of granite statues standing on a hillside. There was Lac de Guerlédan for a day of water activities and the newly discovered Roman remains in Carhaix – so much to take Chloe and the twins to see when – if – they still came for their holiday at the end of May.

Belinda looked up as the office door opened and Marie walked shyly in. Belinda saw her glance down, embarrassed at the scruffy clothes she wore for the cleaning jobs.

'Desolé. I wanted to smarten myself up for the rendezvous, but time, it was impossible. I 'ave better clothes at home,' she hastened to assure Belinda.

'No worries, Marie. I understand,' Belinda said. 'I'm not exactly dressed for the office today either. I was about to suggest you sat down, but I've realised we only have the one chair between us in here. Must sort out at least another two, I think. Now, I already know you're reliable and a hard worker, so tell me why we should employ you as a receptionist?'

'Because I'd be good at it, given the chance. I like 'elping people and I know about the area. I speak a little English. And I know how to use a computer. I am 'appy to do whatever is needed.'

Belinda asked a couple more questions and watched Marie as she spoke and tried to work out how old she was. Early twenties at a guess. About the same age as Chloe.

'It would be part-time initially until about mid-June and then full-time,' Belinda explained. 'At the height of the summer season, it would be necessary to work several evenings a week, including Saturdays. Would that be a problem?'

Marie shook her head. 'Non.'

'Okay. I have one other person to see. Once I've seen her, I'll let you know later this afternoon.' Belinda smiled at Marie as she showed her out. She had a good feeling about Marie. Alain was right. She'd almost told her the job was hers, but morally she was duty-bound to at least see the other candidate.

Belinda glanced at her watch. The woman the employment

agency were sending was late. Not a good start. In fact, not a start at all. An hour later when she'd neither shown up nor phoned to apologise for being late, Belinda went in search of a delighted Marie to tell her the job was hers.

Alain and Hervé were standing on the office steps when Belinda retraced her steps, intending to phone the agency and tell them about the missing job candidate.

'Bonjour, Hervé,' she said politely and went to carry on in, but Alain stopped her.

'Hervé has given me all the information about the vide-grenier – okay to book it for Sunday, May the third?'

Belinda nodded. 'Of course.' She smiled at Hervé. 'I hope it's a success, I'll be sure to ask Alain how it went. Maybe he'll want to make it a regular feature.'

'You won't be here for it?' Hervé asked.

'I doubt it. I'm going back to Devon for Easter and possibly staying on for a few weeks.' Belinda turned to Alain. 'I've just told Marie she's got the job. You'll have to sort out her starting date and the initial hours you'll need her over Easter. I won't have time before I leave. Goodbye, Hervé, nice to see you again. Bon chance for the vide-grenier,' and Belinda carried on into the office to tick yet another item off her list.

* * *

As Fern worked her way through her normal daily chores, Belinda's question, what would happen to her own life if she did take on the responsibility for Anouk rattled around in her brain. She knew Belinda had been right to throw that question at her, but she couldn't answer it readily. Her life would change, she knew that. Life as she currently lived it would cease to exist in many ways, but would that be such a bad thing? Having

Anouk living with her could turn out to be the best thing all round.

Living alone for the past year and a half hadn't exactly been a fun-filled existence. She'd spent a lot of time alone, especially in the winter months when she didn't have guests to look after. She'd taken Lady for long walks in the countryside in all weathers, read a lot of books and watched a lot of rubbish TV shows. Anouk might be old and fragile in many ways, but she was still good company and hopefully would be for years yet. Having Anouk living at the auberge would put purpose back in her life. Someone to care for on a daily basis.

Fern picked up her mobile and pressed Anouk's number. 'Hi, may I come and see you this afternoon? There is something I need to ask you. I'll bring some coffee eclairs,' she promised, knowing that they were Anouk's favourite cake.

'Always delighted to see you, and with coffee eclairs, double delight,' Anouk said.

* * *

Anouk was sitting out under the loggia in the sunshine when Fern arrived, cups, saucers and plates already on the wrought-iron table. 'Coffee in the machine is ready to go,' she told Fern. 'So, my dear, what is it you want to ask me?' Anouk said when Fern had fetched and poured the coffee and put the eclairs on plates.

Fern took a deep breath. Driving over she'd formulated a plan. 'Have you anything planned for this Easter weekend? Meeting up with friends? Or seeing Fabian and family?'

'Not many friends left these days.' Anouk shook her head. 'Carole has persuaded Fabian to visit her family for the 'oliday up in Normandy. Which leaves me entirely free to get up to mischief with you. What are you planning?' Anouk gave her a beaming smile.

Fern laughed. 'I don't know about mischief, but I was wondering whether you'd like to come and spend the weekend with me? We could go for a drive down to the coast if you like. Have lunch out. You could go to church in the village Sunday morning if you wanted.'

Anouk looked at her. 'Yes, I would like to do that. First, though, 'ave you been thinking about Fabian and his suggestions? Is this some sort of trial to see if we could live together before you suggest I move in with you?'

Fern laughed and shook her head. 'Nothing gets past you, does it? Yes, I have been thinking about Fabian's suggestions, but, honestly, asking you to stay for the weekend was not a ploy to see if we could live together. It was more to see if you would even consider the idea of moving in with me. I promise you I shall not be upset if you say no, but I really, truly hope you will say yes.'

'Why would you want to take on the responsibility of an old woman who isn't related to you? What happens if I get dementia and – oh, what's the word you English use? Do... do...'

'I think you mean doolally,' Fern said, laughing.

'Doolally, that's it. What if I get that in a few months' time?'

'Just because the man that linked us together via marriage is no longer with us, doesn't mean that I don't still regard you as my mother-in-law, a part of my family,' Fern answered quietly. 'And I promise you, I'll never stop caring about and for you.' She took a drink of coffee. 'As for you going doolally – I don't see that happening for a long time, if ever.'

Anouk nodded thoughtfully. 'D'accord. I too 'ave been thinking about Fabian wanting to move one of us out of our homes. The reasons you want to stay in the auberge are as valid as Fabian's are for wanting you to move out. We will spend the weekend together and talk it through properly. Mais.' She looked at Fern with a glint in her eye. 'We 'ave no need to mention this to Fabian. He is away and we will decide without the pressure. It is for the best. D'accord?'

'D'accord,' Fern agreed.

18

When Belinda arrived back at the auberge that evening, she listened as a happy Fern told her about the conversation with Anouk and her weekend plans. 'I'll pick her up Saturday morning and by the time she leaves sometime on Tuesday she promises to have made a decision.'

Fern looked at Belinda. 'I did think about what you said about putting my life on hold, but I think having Anouk here will do the opposite in reality. Life since Laurent died has been lonely and inconsequential. Having someone relying on me will make me do things again. I wish you could meet her before you leave.'

'From what you've told me about Anouk, I think if she does come here, it sounds as though it will benefit you both,' Belinda replied. 'Hopefully I'll be back to help finalise things for the opening of the campsite. I can meet her then.'

'At least you'll be able to see your daughter and the twins,' Fern said.

'That's what I'm looking forward to the most,' Belinda answered. 'What about your girls? Are you likely to see them over the holiday?'

Fern shook her head. 'No, sadly. They both have their own busy lives. I expect they'll be over later in the summer though.'

After supper, Belinda apologised to Fern and went upstairs to finish sorting her things out. Once she'd packed and prepared everything for the morning, she stood in front of the bedroom window, looking out over the dark countryside. An almost full moon was illuminating the fields and owls were tooting in the copse at the far side of the field.

Belinda sighed. She'd felt so at home here in Brittany for the past few weeks, she'd be sad to leave tomorrow. The time here had woken something inside her that had been buried for far too long.

The next morning at work, she made sure everything on her to-do list was as up to date as she could make it, and the booking page on the website was properly loaded and working. She hoped that Maria was as computer-literate as she said and would soon get the hang of things. If not, Belinda could only hope that Alain would be more helpful to Maria than he had been with her. Afterwards, she wandered around outside for a while, taking some photos on her phone to show everyone back home. So much had changed in such a short time and the place was really starting to look good. She even managed to snap an unsuspecting Alain as he chainsawed some branches into logs. Putting her phone away, she headed over to him and waited until he saw her and silenced the chainsaw.

'I'll be off in about ten minutes,' Belinda said. 'I'll leave my keys in the office desk drawer. Hopefully I'll see you at the end of the month.'

'Okay. 'Ave a safe journey. See you when you get back,' and Alain opened up the chainsaw again, making further conversation impossible.

Once BB was settled in his travelling cushion in the back of the car, Belinda started the engine and drove away. Driving slowly down the potholed lane, she remembered that first day when she'd driven equally slowly in the opposite direction, not wanting to be there, her mind full of unhappy memories. This time, though, it was a feeling of not wanting to leave that kept her speed down in an effort not to reach the end and turn onto the road and make for the ferry at Roscoff. She was surprised to realise that she'd made a number of happy memories during the last few weeks. New memories that were slowly replacing old sad ones.

19

The first morning back in her flat at the top of the Riverside hotel, Belinda struggled to remember where she was when the alarm went off and woke her. She lay there for a few minutes listening to the early-morning sounds of people and traffic down on the quayside. Sounds that felt alien to her after the silence of the Brittany countryside for the past few weeks.

After showering, Belinda moved across to the wardrobe. Jeans and a sweatshirt, her normal workday attire for the campsite, wouldn't do here. Businesslike and professional was the look she needed. Reluctantly, she pulled out one of her navy work suits that she teamed with a white shirt. She caught her light brown hair up in a neat ballerina-type bun at the back of her head, instead of simply brushing it and leaving it loose. There, back in proper work mode, so why didn't she feel excited at the prospect of spending her days once again working in a job that had always given her a sense of purpose, of being needed? Smothering a sigh, Belinda picked up her work bag and laptop.

'Come on then, BB, back in the old routine.' The little dog gave a quick bark and followed her out of the door.

Downstairs in the hotel's dining room, she helped herself to a mug of coffee from the machine on the buffet table and stood looking around, making sure everything was up to standard before heading for reception.

Donna, the senior receptionist, was on duty and welcomed Belinda back with a smile. 'Nigel will be pleased to see you.'

'I'm heading over to Torquay this morning to see him and Molly,' Belinda said. 'Everything ticking along here? Anything I need to know about?'

Donna shook her head. 'All good. We're full for the Easter weekend. Housekeeper is on top of everything for that.' She hesitated. 'There is one thing, but that's up to Nigel to tell you.'

Belinda raised her eyebrows and looked at her, but Donna shook her head.

'Sorry, I shouldn't have said anything.'

'Okay. I'll see you later,' Belinda said, feeling unsettled and wondering what Nigel needed to tell her.

'Give my love to Molly,' Donna said.

'Will do.'

Half an hour later and Belinda was driving along the Torquay ring road approaching the turning to take for the coastal road where the hotel was situated. Traffic was heavy and Belinda found herself thinking wistfully of the quieter Brittany roads. Once in the hotel grounds, she quickly parked and, taking the pot of tulips she'd bought at the garden centre en route, made her way through the hotel to Nigel and Molly's cottage hidden away in the grounds. The door was on the latch and she pushed it open.

'Nigel, it's me Belinda,' she called.

'Come through – we're in the conservatory,' he answered.

An efficient looking nurse was writing something on her tablet as she stood alongside Molly lying on a daybed.

'Sorry to interrupt. Shall I go and have a look around the hotel and come back in fifteen minutes?' Belinda asked, hoping she didn't sound as shocked as she felt at seeing Molly, a woman who was always on the go, lying down, a pale imitation of her normal self.

'No, you're fine,' Nigel answered. 'Nurse here has finished her morning routine, making Molly comfortable.'

'Come here right now,' Molly ordered, at least sounding something like her old self. 'I want to hear all about France and how things are going over there. Nigel just tells me it's all in hand, which is, of course, good, but I want the nitty-gritty.' She saw the pretty pot of tulips. 'For me, thank you.' She looked at Belinda. 'You're looking well, positively glowing with health. Less stressed than usual.'

'How are you feeling?' Belinda asked. 'I hope it was nothing too serious? Nigel didn't say what was wrong.'

Molly smiled. 'Let's call it women's problems and leave it at that, shall we?'

'I wasn't expecting you to have had your operation already. When did you get out of hospital? Should you even be home?' Belinda said.

'I was allowed to leave on one condition, that Nigel hired a private nurse. Now I've got six weeks of taking it easy to look forward to.' Molly pulled a face. 'Hence Nigel wanting you back. At least I'll be able to tackle the pile of books on my TBR. Mixed blessings, eh?'

The nurse declined Nigel's offer of coffee and left. A few minutes later, Nigel had brought the coffee through into the conservatory, along with a plate of chocolate brownies. The three of them sat companionably chatting about the hotels.

'I'll need to sit down with you after Easter and make a plan for the season,' Nigel said. 'Molly insists she'll be fine before the real summer rush begins, but I'm not having her do too much, too soon. There are a few things we need to discuss.'

'Okay,' Belinda agreed. 'In the meantime, I'll carry on as usual. How's everything out at Moorside? I was planning on driving across the moor tomorrow.' She registered the guilty look that passed between Nigel and Molly and waited.

'Ah, there's something we have to tell you about Moorside,' Nigel said. 'We've sold it.'

'Really?' Belinda said, trying to hide her surprise. Being on Dartmoor, Moorside had always been different from the other two hotels in attracting a divergent, usually older, guest, but its annual turnover had always been more than acceptable to the groups' accountants.

'It's always been that bit too far away to manage easily, so when the brewery unexpectedly made us an offer, we haggled a bit and then accepted,' Nigel explained.

'Fair enough,' was all Belinda could think of saying as she wondered where the sale of one of the hotels would leave her job. It would certainly give her more time to devote to the remaining two.

'Tell us about the campsite,' Molly said. 'Is it starting to look good?'

Belinda reached for her tote and took out her notebook. 'I took some photos before I left.' She handed the tablet to Molly. 'Have a scroll through. Alain and the workers have done a grand job getting the place up to scratch. Shame we've had to delay the opening really, but at least it will give Alain and the others time to really get the place sorted for a grand reopening for the late May Bank Holiday.' She turned to Nigel. 'We need to decide about the shop and café. Are you happy to lease them both out? The village shop seems keen to expand, but the café is maybe different. I think there is huge potential there that we'd miss out on if we allow someone else to develop it.'

'Do you know how Alain feels about that?'

'Honestly? I think Alain would be happy for the site to become set in a time warp, say the 1970s where there was no internet, definitely no social media and everyone was happy with their lot. As for pods and glamping,' Belinda laughed, 'he'd never heard of them. I think he would say that a café serving, pizzas, frites, sandwiches, wine, beer, coffee and ice creams is all that is needed for a campsite.'

Molly nodded. 'That pretty well sums up the cafés I remember from my childhood.'

'And we all know people's expectations are so much higher these days,' Belinda added. 'Anyway, it's your campsite now and you two get to decide how you want it.'

'Let's get Easter out of the way and then have a meeting to discuss things,' Nigel said. 'Alain is a good bloke and I know he has his own reasons for wanting the campsite to succeed. He told me more about them when he was here recently.'

'He was here?' Belinda couldn't keep the surprise out of her voice. 'What was he doing here?'

There was a slight pause before Nigel answered. 'There were some things he wanted to discuss face to face about his parents, since they are old friends of ours. Have you met them yet?'

Belinda shook her head. 'No.'

'Lovely couple.'

Belinda waited for him to expand on that, but he changed the conversation by asking Belinda how Chloe was and talk became veered away from hotel and campsite business. Belinda made a mental note to ask Nigel at their next meeting what he'd meant about Alain having his own reasons regarding the campsite succeeding and – importantly – how the sale of Moorside affected her job.

Belinda turned down an invitation to stay for lunch and left soon afterwards. Driving home, she found herself thinking about Alain, wondering in what way his reasons differed from Nigel's in wanting the campsite to succeed. And why hadn't Alain mentioned his visit to Nigel to her? What was the big secret?

20

Saturday morning of the Easter weekend Fern drove to Huelgoat and collected Anouk as promised. The sun was shining, the cherry trees in the main square were in blossom as she drove through and people were strolling by the lake. It was a beautiful day that filled Fern with hope for the future. Everything would come right.

Anouk was ready and waiting for her and while Fern collected her suitcase from the bedroom and locked the front door, she walked with the aid of her stick and settled herself in the car.

'It's a long time since I had a weekend away,' she said as Fern started the engine. 'I'm really looking forward to it.'

'Shall we stop for a coffee on the way, or even lunch?' Fern said.

'Knowing you, my dear, I'm sure you 'ave prepared something – and your coffee is better than most cafés. We go and sit on your terrace,' Anouk said. 'Tomorrow, maybe after church, we go out.'

Fern, as usual, took a scenic route home, taking her time so that Anouk could enjoy the scenery. Ten minutes before they reached the auberge, Fern said, 'I've some guests tonight – just a couple, bed and breakfast, no evening meal, so I doubt we'll see much of them. The room I've given you for the weekend is on the ground floor and opens onto a small private terrace. If you'd prefer one upstairs, you can choose another one. After the guests leave, you can have a look around and choose which room you'd like. If you decide to come permanently, of course.'

Anouk nodded and smiled but didn't say anything.

Fern parked the car in its usual place to the side of the house and helped Anouk out. 'Come and sit on the terrace while I make the coffee and get your suitcase out of the car. I'll show you your room later. Look out for Lady – she has a dreadful habit of weaving in and out of legs. We don't need her knocking you over.'

Anouk waved her free hand in the air. 'Now don't fuss, Fern. That, I think, will be our number one rule. I've got my stick.'

'Sorry, I promise no fussing.'

Fern pressed the button on the coffee machine and went back outside to collect Anouk's suitcase. As she was reaching in for it, she heard rather than saw a car drive in and park. Damn. She knew her guests had gone out for the day and she really didn't want any more guests for this weekend. The next few days were to be all about Anouk and her. She lifted the suitcase out, slammed the car door and turned to see who it was.

The man getting out of the 4 x 4 looked vaguely familiar and Fern struggled to remember where she knew him from him.

'Bonjour, Madame LeRoy. We meet again.' An American accent and Fern recognised him then as the man she'd met in Tronjoly park.

'Scott. What are you doing here?'

'Hoping you've got a room for a night or two. The Tourist Office said you might have. If not, maybe you can point me in the direction of one.' He regarded her hopefully.

Fern looked at him steadily. Some instinct told her that Scott turning up here asking for a room was no coincidence.

'Would you like a coffee while I think about it?' she said. 'My mother-in-law is here and we were just about to have one.'

'I'd appreciate a coffee for sure, so long as I'm not intruding,' Scott said, taking the suitcase from her. 'Let me carry that.'

'Thank you.' Fern led the way into the auberge. 'Just leave the suitcase in the kitchen and come on out to the terrace.'

'Anouk, we have company for coffee,' she said, wondering what Anouk would make of Scott. She was about to make the introductions when Scott moved across to Anouk as she politely started to stand up.

'Madame LeRoy – it's a pleasure to meet you. I'm Scott Kergoëts. Please don't get up for me.'

'American?' Anouk asked, settling back down. 'With a Breton surname?'

'Guilty as charged.'

'Maybe you'd like to talk amongst yourselves for a couple of moments while I fetch the coffee,' Fern said, leaving them to it.

She stood by the kitchen window watching the two of them for a moment. Should she give him a room? Or send him to the auberge in the next village? She'd decide after coffee. And after asking him a couple of searching questions.

When she carried the coffee and the plate of biscuits out, she smothered a smile. Anouk was holding her own interrogation of Scott.

'Your Breton ancestors came from Gourin then?'

'They sure did, ma'am. All I heard growing up was how beautiful the old country was and how desperate things had been, forcing them to emigrate.'

Anouk nodded. 'My father had two uncles who emigrated, looking for that better life.'

'Did they find it?' Scott asked gently.

'For a while. Then the letters stopped coming during the Depression. It was sometime before he 'eard they'd both died during that terrible time in America.' Anouk sighed as she accepted a coffee from Fern.

'So you're here researching your family history then?' Fern asked, handing Scott a coffee. 'Help yourself to biscuits.'

'There was an album at home all the time I was growing up, full of faded photos and other mementos of the area. I've wanted to visit forever, but it's taken until now to happen.'

'D'you still have relatives over here?' Fern asked. 'If you do, surely you could stay with them?'

'Sadly no.'

'I went to school with a Marie-France Kergoëts,' Anouk said thoughtfully. 'I think she died last year. Married someone from Josselyn. Moved back this way when she was widowed. Maybe she was a relative?'

'That's interesting,' Scott answered. 'I'll have to do some research. As far as I know, my last relative living in the Gourin area died a few years ago.'

Fern, watching Scott talk so easily to Anouk, couldn't help but be drawn to the man. He was just so open and honest. She'd tell him he could have a room, she decided, as soon as she could get a word in edgewise between Anouk and him. And then Anouk paved the way.

'Where are you staying?' she asked.

'Ah, well, at the moment nowhere. But I'd heard about this rather good auberge run by a certain lady and I was hoping she might have a space?' he answered, looking at Fern.

Before Fern could say anything, Anouk answered him.

'Yes she does, don't you, Fern?' Anouk leaned conspiratorially towards Scott. 'Fern's not doing evening meals for the other guests, so you'll 'ave to join us for supper in the kitchen.'

'That sounds wonderful,' he said quietly back, looking at Fern questioningly.

Before she could react, Anouk went to stand up, and Scott was instantly on his feet to help and handed her stick to her.

'Thank you. Please excuse me for five minutes,' and Anouk turned to walk slowly into the house.

It was Scott who broke the silence that fell between them. 'Do you have a room I can rent like Anouk says? Or would you rather send me away?'

'How did you find me? You're not going to turn out to be a stalker, are you?' Fern said.

Scott grinned at her. 'No way. You'd told me your name and the direction you lived in. And in the last Tourist Office I found, when I mentioned your name, the lady behind the desk knew you. Bingo – here I am.' He looked at Fern for several seconds before he added, 'I promise I'm not a stalker. I simply liked you when we met and wanted to see you again. Maybe make amends after I upset you with my offer of dinner. I'll understand if you'd rather I didn't stay here, but I hope you'll allow me to buy you dinner one evening. Anouk too, she reminds me of my grand-mother. Feisty, utterly incorrigible and so French.'

In spite of herself, Fern laughed. 'That's one way of describing her. Scott, just so you know, you're welcome to a room here.'

'And supper in the kitchen with you two?'

'If you would like to join us, you're more than welcome. Now, fetch your suitcase and I'll show you to your room. I need to get lunch. Would you like to join us? I'm sure Anouk would like to interrogate you some more.'

Scott laughed. 'Thanks. I'd love to have lunch with you both.'

Fern was in the kitchen making a green salad when Anouk

returned. 'Can I 'elp you, and before you say non, remember I still managed to feed myself at home.'

'I was going to make a mozzarella salad – cheese and tomatoes are in the fridge, basil on the windowsill.'

'He is nice your Monsieur Scott,' Anouk said as she deftly sliced tomatoes a few minutes later. 'He reminds me of someone.'

'He is not mine,' Fern protested. 'I've only met him once before. But I agree he does seem nice.'

'Where did you meet?'

'I took Lady for a walk a few weeks ago in Tronjoly park and we got chatting.'

'Ah Tronjoly. That figures,' Anouk said.

'Why?'

'That would be his ancestral home. The Kergoëts owned it for a couple of centuries, but eventually it passed out of the family before falling into disrepair. The council own it now.'

Fern took the country-style baguette she'd put to warm in the oven and cut it into chunks to go with the asparagus and pea soup she had put to gently heat on the stove. She carried the plate of cold meats and the cheeseboard with Cantal, brie and a Roquefort out onto the table at the end of the terrace. More than enough food for three people, she thought, especially with the soup, bread and salads. And the special cake she'd made to go with coffee. Plates, cutlery and wine glasses were next before she opened the wine, a bottle each of white and red. She pulled the corks absently, thinking about Scott. That day in the park, he'd told her he was retired but hadn't mentioned a wife or a family. No doubt Anouk would have obtained that information from him by the end of lunch. Not that it was any of their business of course but Fern couldn't help wondering.

Fern turned as Scott came from the kitchen carrying the

basket of bread and the mozzarella salad. 'Gosh, what a spread. Anouk said the soup is ready to serve.'

'Thanks. Help yourself to a glass of wine,' and Fern went back to the kitchen.

A few minutes later, the three of them were tucking into their lunch. As she finished her soup, Anouk said, 'Where is it you live in America, Scott?'

'New York. There's a vibrant Breton community there, you'll be surprised to hear. They're all eager for news about the old country from me.'

'Anyone in particular? Like a wife? Children?' Anouk asked the question while Fern was dithering about voicing it. She collected the empty soup plates and placed them on the small serving table to the left of her chair.

'I've been a widower for longer than I care to remember,' Scott answered quietly. 'And, no, I don't have any children. We lost our little boy in an accident when he was four. My wife couldn't bear the thought of ever losing another child, so...' he shrugged. 'I have cousins, a few godchildren and a couple of aunts and uncles.'

Anouk reached out a hand and squeezed his arm. 'Desolé. So sad for you and your poor wife.'

'I really don't know how anyone gets over something like that,' Fern said. In the silence that followed, she gave Scott a sympathetic smile before excusing herself and taking the soup bowls into the kitchen. She set the oven temperature at 100 degrees and switched it on ready to heat through the Kouign-amann cake she'd made.

Glancing out of the kitchen window, she saw Anouk laugh at something Scott had said. It was the first time really since Laurent's death that Fern had seen Anouk so animated, her eyes were bright and her whole persona seemed to be charged with new energy. Anouk, Fern realised, had hidden her loneliness from everyone over the past months. Looking at her now, Fern smiled to herself. She was definitely doing the right thing inviting Anouk to move in with her.

Fern was relieved to find the conversation had changed when she went back outside. Scott had clearly asked a question or two of his own and Anouk was telling him about her life. Conversation flowed easily throughout lunch between the three of them and there was a lot of laughter.

When Fern placed the warm Kouign-amann on the table to accompany coffee, Scott looked at her. 'Is that what I suspect? Heart attack on a plate?'

'You can call it that. I call it a traditional Breton cake made with local butter, lots of it. I only make one on special occasions, like Easter. I will cut small slices, but if you're worried about it not being good for you and prefer not to have a slice, that's fine.'

'You joshing me? My grandmother used to make it once in a blue moon and I was always begging her to make it more often.' Scott picked up a plate and held it out. 'Thank you.'

'I hope it matches up to your memories of your grandmother's cake,' Fern said, as she cut small slices for everyone. This cake was not one to indulge in large portions.

Scott ate his slice before looking up at the sky. 'Sorry, Granny, but I've just eaten the best Kouign-amann I have ever had. And it was made by a wonderful English cook.'

Fern laughed, feeling ridiculously pleased at his words.

Shortly afterwards when Fern started to clear the table, Anouk stood up ready to help.

'I think I'll go for my afternoon nap after this,' she said, taking her stick in one hand and an empty plate in the other.

Scott gently took the plate from her. 'Why don't you go now and I'll help Fern?'

'Maybe I will,' and Anouk let Scott take the plate out of her hand before walking into the house.

Fern watched her go anxiously before turning to Scott. 'You really don't have to help clear things. It won't take me ten minutes.'

Scott ignored her words and started to clear up. 'Take the two of us five minutes then. Do you have plans for the rest of the afternoon?'

'Walking Lady and, later, cooking dinner,' Fern answered, following him into the kitchen with empty plates.

'May I join you and Lady?' Scott asked.

'Of course,' Fern answered. 'Give me ten minutes to change and to tell Anouk and I'll give you a walking tour of the immediate area.'

21

Anouk was asleep when Fern went to tell her she was walking Lady with Scott, so she quickly scribbled a note and left it on the bedside table where Anouk would see it when she awoke.

Clipping Lady's lead on, Fern joined Scott, who was waiting outside for her, and they started to walk in the direction of the church and the village. Only the first day of the weekend and already it was turning out to be so different to how she'd imagined it would be when she'd invited Anouk. Scott turning up had been a surprise, changing the whole ethos of the day and probably the whole weekend.

'Have you been doing the touristy thing of going here, there and everywhere since the day we met in Gourin? Or have you been concentrating on family history?' Fern asked, glancing across at him as he strolled at her side.

'A bit of both,' Scott said. 'Gourin is where the family is from, so I've tended to stay around that area, but I've been further afield too. North coast, west coast and south coast. Brittany has so much coastline, it should be an island!'

Fern laughed. 'All three coasts are so different too. Do you want to look inside the church? I can wait outside with Lady if you do,' Fern said as they drew level with the entrance to the church.

'Not this afternoon,' Scott replied. 'I'll wander up another time.'

They both paused to look at the Easter arrangement of fluffy yellow chicks, eggs, artisan chocolates and daffodils in the window of the village shop. 'I love Easter time,' Fern said. 'To me, it signals that winter is nearly over and spring is finally on its way back.'

When they reached the crossroads, they turned left onto the road leading to the campsite.

'Shall we turn back now?' Fern said a few moments later as they approached the top of the lane leading to the campsite. 'I don't like to leave Anouk on her own too long.'

'Does she often spend time with you?' Scott asked.

'This is the first weekend. It's meant to be a test to see how we'd get on if she moved in permanently.'

'Ah, that explains something,' Scott said. 'She invited me to have coffee with her one morning but said she had to decide where that would be first. She's very independent, she'll find it hard living in someone else's home, even yours, I suspect. Is there a need for her to move in with you?' Scott asked.

'It's complicated,' and Fern gave him a quick run-down as to why the idea was under consideration. 'And, if I'm honest, I know I would benefit from having Anouk in the house too. It would make me feel needed again.'

'How old is Anouk?'

'It's her ninetieth birthday this year,' Fern said. 'Do you mind holding Lady for a minute or two while I go into the village shop?'

'Sure thing,' and Scott held out his hand for the lead.

In the shop, Fern collected the Easter egg she'd ordered for

Anouk and hesitated over buying one for Scott before selecting one for him too. Carrying the bag, she rejoined Scott and took back Lady.

'Thank you.'

'D'you want to start walking home and I'll catch up with you?' Scott asked. 'I've just realised I need a new tube of toothpaste.'

'Okay,' and Fern smiled at him as he turned away to go into the shop.

To her surprise, she was home and indoors and he still hadn't appeared. The shop hadn't been that busy. There was no sign of Anouk either. She was about to go and check on her when she heard Scott return and go straight to his room – presumably to put his toothpaste in the bathroom. Minutes later, he walked into the kitchen carrying a bottle of champagne.

'My contribution to Easter Sunday,' he said, holding it out.

'Oh goodness, thank you, my favourite brand,' Fern said, looking at the orange label. 'I'll put it in the fridge now.'

'If I may, I'm going to spend the afternoon sitting in your wonderful garden and read,' Scott said. 'Unless I can do anything to help you?'

'No thanks. You'll find loungers and cushions in the small shed. See you later.' If he'd been a proper guest, she'd have rushed to get them out, but somehow Scott didn't feel like a paying guest even though he was.

To even think of him as a new friend was a dangerous thought though. She'd known him for far too short a time to treat him as anything but a paying guest. Besides, he'd be moving on soon. Returning to America.

22

Belinda was up early Easter Sunday morning checking everything in the hotel was ready for the busy day ahead. She'd booked a family table for lunch in the restaurant and was looking forward to a couple of hours with Chloe and the twins before spending the rest of the day on duty. Chloe's husband, Max, manager of the local marina, was working and couldn't join them, which was a shame. When they all arrived at 12.30, she took them upstairs to give them their Easter eggs and the small gifts she'd brought them from France.

'No chocolate until after lunch,' Chloe said, confiscating the eggs from Charlie and Aimee. 'But you can each open your other present carefully.'

Watching them open the books, crayons and colouring posters Belinda had bought them, Chloe looked at Belinda. 'You and Dad spoil them, Mum.'

'That's what grandparents do,' Belinda replied. 'How is your dad?'

'Good, I think. Totally enamoured with Gina.' Chloe glanced carefully at Belinda. 'There's talk of a summer wedding. He wants Charlie and Aimee to act as pageboy and bridesmaid.'

'Aimee will adore that, not so sure about Charlie,' Belinda said.

'Do you mind?'

Belinda hesitated. She'd expected Peter to marry Gina before now and had steeled herself not to mind when it was announced. Hearing it was finally going to happen this year, she waited for the jolt of pain to make itself felt, but nothing. She was happy for them both, she realised, and didn't mind in the slightest that Peter was remarrying, she'd moved on.

'Do I mind that your dad is marrying again? No, I don't and I wish them every happiness. Do I mind that I won't be there to see the twins? Yes, that I do mind. I shall insist they dress up for me in all their finery after the event.'

Chloe gave her a hug. 'I hope you meet someone new too, then the twins can do the same for you.'

'The chances of that happening before they're teenagers is unlikely.' Belinda laughed. 'Anyway, back to the pressies. There's nothing big, just Easter eggs and things I managed to buy on the ferry. I didn't have time to go shopping before I left.' She picked up two bags she'd left on the table and held them behind her back. 'I've got you and Max something too, but if you don't want them?'

'Oh, you know I do,' Chloe said, accepting the bags Belinda held out. 'Thank you.'

'I know you'll like your pressies, but Max's is a bit boring, I'm afraid, his favourite aftershave. Men are notoriously difficult to buy for, aren't they?'

'Oh it's good to have you back, Mum,' Chloe said as she carefully unwrapped the first of her presents, a cream silk scarf printed with French scenes. 'This is beautiful. Thank you again,' and she tied the scarf around her neck straight away. The second present, a traditional nautical Breton top with red stripes, was also greeted with delight.

'I bought myself one of those too,' Belinda said. 'One with blue stripes. I practically lived in similar ones a long time ago and they're still incredibly popular.'

'Thanks, Mum. So how long are you here for?'

Belinda shrugged. 'I'm not sure if I'm going back to the campsite at all, from the way Nigel was talking. Says he needs me while Molly recuperates. Did you know he's sold Moorside? I'm just hoping he and Molly don't decide to get out of the hotel business completely and my job disappears.' She didn't add, *my home would be gone too if that happens.*

'If they do, you'll find another job, Mum,' Chloe said. 'Another top hotel group would snap you up. What about our camping holiday though? I was looking forward to it. And to you showing me places you knew growing up,' she added. 'Like where you went to school. You lived over there for a long time, but you've never really talked about it to me.' She glanced at Belinda. 'How was it really being back over there, Mum? Is the campsite close to where you lived? Did you meet anyone from those days?'

Belinda hesitated and then Chloe's words 'you've never really talked about it' echoed in her head.

'You can still go on your holiday, even if I'm not working over there. The campsite should be fully functional by the end of May and Alain is sure to be happier, not having me bossing him around. As for talking about that time of my life,' Belinda shrugged, 'you know how upset Granny always got if anyone brought up the subject of Brittany. Leaving it in the past was her way of coping. I guess I've followed her lead. But, yes, it did feel strange in the beginning, although after a few days, it was like I'd never been away. And I've made a new friend, Fern. The lady who owns the auberge where I stayed.'

Thankfully Chloe didn't press her on talking about the past but picked up on Alain. 'What's this Alain like?'

'Initially we rubbed each other up the wrong way, mainly because he's got definite ideas about how he wants the site to be which are different to the way Nigel sees it. Nigel being the owner though, as far as I'm concerned, gets the final say.' Belinda laughed. 'Alain called me bossy and uptight at one stage. And I thought he was a Frenchman with a bad attitude. But we got over it.' Belinda took her phone out. 'These don't do it justice and once all the work is complete it will look even better. It's very child-friendly in the old-fashioned way – places to build dens, play games and generally just have fun. And that's down to Alain.' She handed her phone over to Chloe, who scrolled through.

'It does look nice. Oh, who's the hero with the chainsaw?'

'That's Alain,' Belinda said. 'Mr Attitude himself.'

* * *

Fern smiled to herself Sunday morning as she took half a dozen hot cross buns out of the freezer to heat through. As far as she was concerned, Easter wasn't Easter without a spicy bun and she'd enjoyed one for breakfast on the traditional morning they were eaten, Good Friday. She hoped that both Scott and Anouk would enjoy the warm spicy buns slathered with creamy local Breton butter. Standing in the kitchen preparing breakfast for everyone, Fern realised the whole Easter weekend had somehow started to resemble a mini Christmas celebration, with the emphasis on extra-special meals.

Last night, dinner had been a fresh seafood platter with salad, followed by individual lemon soufflés. Lunch today would be roast lamb with roast potatoes and parsnips, tender asparagus, petite carrots and, because she was English, gravy and mint sauce. There was a fresh fruit salad to follow the ubiquitous cheeseboard that she knew Anouk would expect. And, of course, that expensive bottle of champagne that Scott had provided would be opened and enjoyed.

Last evening over supper, Scott had offered to accompany Anouk to church when she said she'd like to go to morning service. After breakfast, when they'd both sampled the buns and enjoyed them, they set off together, Anouk leaning on Scott's arm rather than using her stick.

Once her routine chores were done, Fern started to prepare lunch. Memories of the previous evening floated into her mind as she peeled vegetables. Memories of happy laughter between friends. Sitting out on the terrace as dusk fell and the solar lights dotted around the garden came on, she'd felt truly happy for the first time in months. Anouk too was smiling and laughing more than she had done since Laurent's passing. Perhaps they were both coming to terms with their loss and exiting that dreadful depressing time of their lives.

Scott's presence this weekend, although unexpected, had been a real gift. It was surprising how quickly he'd turned from stranger to friend. Even Anouk, normally restrained with strangers, had come under his spell, talking for hours about local families, looking for links between the two of them. As for Fern herself, she felt at ease with him, as if she'd known him forever. Lady too was more than content to curl up at his feet.

When the two of them returned from church, Fern made coffee, put the Easter eggs she'd bought for the two of them on a tray and carried it out to the terrace.

Before she could pour Scott a coffee, he disappeared to his room. 'Two minutes. I've forgotten something.' He returned carrying an Easter egg for each of them. 'Happy Easter, everyone,' he said. 'And may I just say I think this Easter is going to turn out to be one of the best of my life, thanks to you two ladies.' He took his phone out of his pocket. 'A special time that I would like a memento of.' He hesitated. 'Please may I take a photo?'

Before Fern could respond, Anouk had given an enthusiastic, 'Yes. Fern, get your phone as well, then I can take one of you and Scott so that we too can have a reminder when you leave.'

Within minutes, several photos had been taken. Scott had even managed to take a group selfie on both phones.

Fern stood up. 'I must check lunch. Talk amongst yourselves for five minutes.'

Once she'd checked the roasties, and taken the lamb out to rest, Fern stood by the kitchen window looking out over the terrace. As she watched, Anouk threw back her head and laughed at something Scott had said. They seemed to be on the same wavelength for lots of things, no cultural or generation gap between them. Just a genuine friendship. Anouk had been pleased last night when Fabian had rung to wish her a Happy Easter and had had a naughty tone to her voice when she'd thanked him and said it was promising to be the best Easter for several years.

Indeed, this weekend was turning out to be different to the one Fern had planned for her and Anouk, but she wouldn't change a thing. It was a long time since she'd had so much fun. And that was down to Scott, with his American go get 'em attitude, although it was clearly toned down these days. A polite version, Fern thought. He still oozed enthusiasm for life though and that all-American college-boy vibe that certain men carried off so well – Scott amongst them.

Fern smothered a sigh. It was good to have a new friend, even knowing that it could never be more than a long-distance friendship when he returned to America. She'd enjoy his company while he was here, and take comfort from the fact that technology united everyone these days at the press of a smartphone button wherever in the world they happened to be.

And tomorrow another fun-filled day beckoned. Scott was taking them both down to the historic and picturesque coastal town of Pont-Aven, famous for the presence of the artist Paul Gauguin back in the nineteenth century. Fern was looking forward to showing Scott around the town she'd always loved visiting with Laurent.

23

Early evening on Easter Monday, Belinda wearily stepped out of
the lift that stopped on the floor below her flat, unlocked the door
marked private and climbed the hidden flight of stairs that led to
her flat. She'd forgotten what it was like to be so busy that she
couldn't even stop for a break. Being short-staffed for the last day
of the holiday hadn't been in the plan and she'd had to help out
on reception and in the restaurant. She couldn't kick her shoes off
quickly enough and change from her work clothes into her PJs –
or leisure suit, as the advert had called them when she'd ordered
them online. Once that was done, she fed BB, poured a glass of
wine and stepped out onto her little secret terrace outside the
sitting room.

The terrace was one of her favourite things about the flat. Big
enough for a small circular table and two chairs and a lilac tree
that was budding up to blossom in the terracotta pot she'd placed
in one corner, she had a wonderful view of the inner harbour and
river, but she herself was so high up and set back from the front
of the hotel as to be unseen by the ant-like people she could
watch below walking on the quayside. With a sigh of relief, she

sank onto a chair, took a sip of wine and glanced at her watch. Jane had sent a text earlier saying she was back after spending Easter with her family and would see her about eight o'clock.

Time to make a phone call, take a shower and generally relax before Jane arrived. She'd asked the kitchen to prepare a supper tray for two people – slices of quiche, a salad, and chocolate mousses – which Jane would collect on her way through the hotel and bring up. A bottle of chardonnay was already cold in the fridge.

Belinda picked up her mobile, but her finger hovered over pressing Alain's number. Would he regard it as an intrusion if she phoned him? After all, this wasn't an emergency. But they were working colleagues and she wanted to know how the Easter weekend had gone over in Camping dans La Fôret – whether there had even been any campers turn up. She'd worked hard to help get the place set up and she wanted to know about the first visitors. She didn't need an excuse to phone him. Defiantly, she pressed the button and listened as the call rang out.

'Bonjour, Belinda, you are missing me a little, mais non?' Alain's voice held a teasing note.

'No, of course not,' Belinda protested. 'I was simply wondering how the weekend went. Did anyone turn up and stay after you'd explained about the lack of facilities?'

'Half a dozen caravans and three camper vans. Two of the caravans are staying on for another week. No tents.'

'How was Marie?'

'Good. And Easter, it was good for you and the hotels?'

'Usual mayhem, with the added problem of staff shortages thrown into the mix. I've only just finished today. At least it will quieten down tomorrow.'

'Your daughter and the grandchildren? 'Ave you spent time with them?'

'Yes.' Belinda hesitated. She wanted to ask him more about the campsite: whether the weather had been good, whether things had gone smoothly or whether they had overlooked anything important, whether Bernie had been useful. But Alain was already winding up the conversation.

'I 'ave to go. Everything, it goes like clockwork here, so no need for you to worry. Take care. Bye Bye.'

Belinda smiled at his heavily accented 'Bye Bye' as she echoed it. She'd phone one morning later in the week, maybe Alain would have more time then to chat and answer her questions.

Right, time to jump in the shower and get dressed.

* * *

The fairy lights Belinda had looped around the door frame outside on the terrace were twinkling and Belinda was putting glasses and cutlery out when Jane buzzed the door. She quickly ran down the stairs to let her in and to take the tray from her. Five minutes later, they were settled on the terrace and they both tucked into their supper.

'Phew,' Jane let out a deep breath, 'I really envy you this little hideaway. I love my family dearly, but after three days of 24/7 with them, this is just what I need,' Jane said. 'Wine, food, just you and me. Perfect.' She waved her fork in the air. 'I bet you missed this view when you were in France.'

'To be honest, I was too busy to have much time for views. My bedroom at the auberge I stayed in looked out over countryside and that was pretty lovely too.'

'So how is the campsite?'

'Pretty run-down and basic, but we're slowly getting to grips with it. It's going to be a rather special place, I think.'

'We?' Jane looked at her, eyebrows raised.

'Alain who will be in charge when I return here permanently.'

'What's he like? Married?'

Belinda, knowing what her friend really wanted to ask was 'is he hot?', which would be followed by 'do you fancy him?', deliberately kept her answer work-related. 'Divorced. He's a hard worker and has decided views on things. Got that typical male French attitude, you know the type.'

'Are you telling me he's all moody Serge Gainsbourg and Gauloises cigarettes?'

'I've never seen him smoke, but yes,' Belinda nodded thoughtfully. 'Now you mention it, that sums him up perfectly.' Seeing the speculative glint in her friend's eyes and not wanting to discuss Alain any more, she changed the subject back to Jane. 'So how was the weekend really?'

'It was mainly good. The grandkids were full on as usual and you know how my beloved mother-in-law tuts when she thinks the kids are out of control. Well, let's just say she did a lot of tutting this weekend and I ended up as peacekeeper. My daughter owes me big time.' Jane took a sip of her drink. 'And don't think I didn't notice what you did then. We haven't finished talking about Alain or the campsite. I need to know more, especially as Brett and I are still planning on being one of your first visitors. I loved the camping holidays my parents organised when I was a child.'

'I need to talk to you about that,' Belinda said. 'I'm not sure if Nigel is sending me back, so if you do go over, I might not be there. And, to be honest, I'm not sure it's Brett's scene, or yours come to that, these days,' Belinda said. 'It's being dragged into the twenty-first century, but in May it will still be pretty basic. The cabins do have their own bathrooms, so you'll at least be spared the shower block. Maybe wait until one of the new glamping pods is installed? Although, as they're not even on order yet, that could be late summer.'

Jane shook her head. 'No, I want a nostalgic, old-fashioned camping experience. I want to see it before the place is totally transformed so that when I go back for a posh glamping holiday next time, I can make comparisons. Have to admit though, it won't be the same if you're not there.'

Belinda swirled the wine around in her glass at Jane's words. Would she even be going back to help to Alain? And afterwards, when the site was up and running, would Nigel want her to do a yearly visit to keep an eye on things for him? Although he had said he and Molly were looking forward to visiting when the site was ready, so maybe they would do the necessary checks themselves. If they sold the hotels though, would they keep the campsite? All questions she resolved to ask Nigel and Molly in the near future.

Draining her glass of wine, she picked up the bottle and proffered it to Jane. 'Top-up?'

Jane nodded and held out her glass.

'Well, if the site is too basic for you in May, I'm sure Fern would find you a room at the auberge I stayed in,' Belinda said as she topped up both glasses.

Jane left at ten and Belinda went down in the lift with her to give BB a last walk along the embankment. There was still a chill in the evening air, spring might have arrived, but night-time temperatures were still on the cold side. Belinda shivered as she stood looking out over the gently flowing river. Surely the Brittany evenings had been warmer than this before she left?

Alain had seemed upbeat and pleased with the way things had gone over there when she'd spoken to him earlier. Although she would have liked more detail. Had the weather been kind, had the shop been busy, had the campers been friendly, had... Oh, the list was endless. She was surprised at how involved she'd become with the place in the short time she'd been there.

With a start, she realised she was missing Brittany. The weeks there had passed quickly with all the work, whilst here, yes she'd been busy over the holiday weekend, but with Nigel looking after things at the Torquay hotel, it had been less frantic than previous years.

Standing there, her conversation yesterday with Chloe flitted into her mind. It was true she had never talked to Chloe about Brittany; hadn't deemed it necessary. What good would it do? It was in the past and didn't affect Chloe's life in any way. Why did she need to know about past unhappiness? On the other hand, it was part of their family history. Part of what had made Belinda who she was.

Maybe she'd been wrong to stay silent like her mum, but it had been the easy way out. If people didn't know, they couldn't judge. But that deathbed promise her mother had extracted from her – did that mean she'd lived her life feeling guilty over things? Or simply that she wanted Belinda to know the truth?

Belinda gave a small groan. How was she going to find the truth all these years later? She glanced up at the hotel building as she turned to walk back and remembered the box in the cupboard. Perhaps that would hold clues? She quickened her pace. Tonight was the night she'd finally go through the box and examine its contents properly.

Once upstairs, Belinda quickly cleared the debris of the evening away and poured herself the last of the wine before opening the cupboard and dragging the box out. Settling down on the floor alongside it, she lifted the lid off and began to take things out.

An hour later, she was stiff, barely able to move and surrounded by small piles of stuff. A pile to throw away consisting mainly of old utility bills, out-of-date passports (hers and her mum's), old batteries and several old-fashioned Valentine cards.

There was another pile of envelopes containing black-and-white photos. Belinda had spent some time looking through these and had pulled out one of her mami to frame and place on her bedside table. There was a small (very small) pile of home-made cards from her to her mum – birthday, mothering Sunday, Christmas, stretching over about five years. She was touched that her mum had kept those, but she didn't need to keep them, they were destined for the bin. Her school reports and her Baccalauréat certificate were at the very bottom of the box under a large brown envelope with a lot of official papers.

Belinda put the last envelope to one side while she struggled to her feet and began to tidy up a bit. She'd sit on the settee to go through the final envelope once she'd put all the things to keep back in the box.

She was too tired to do more than a cursory look through of the contents of the envelope before she went to bed. It was full of family birth, marriage and death certificates. A real find if she'd been researching family history. And that was it. The box was empty. It hadn't been hoarding incriminating papers, or the diary that Belinda had secretly been hoping she'd find. A diary that would hold the key to her mother's life all those years ago.

She glanced at her watch, nearly midnight. Better go to bed and get some sleep or she'd be fit for nothing at work tomorrow.

But sleep wouldn't come and she tossed and turned for hours until at nearly four o'clock she found herself sitting bolt upright.

Two vitally important things were missing from amongst everything in the box. Two things that would begin to, if not explain everything, at least give her a starting point. But for that she needed to return to Brittany.

24

Tuesday morning and life was almost back to normal in the auberge. The guests had checked out and Fern had left Anouk and Scott chatting over breakfast on the terrace while she made a start on her after-guests routine of changing linen, cleaning bathrooms and vacuuming everywhere.

The weekend had been so good. Saturday and Sunday had been full of fun, laughter and food, so much food! And yesterday Scott had driven them down to Pont-Aven as he'd promised and they'd had a leisurely walk along the river there and then lunch in the hotel overlooking the estuary. The sun had shone, the tide had been in and, all in all, it had been a wonderful day.

Fern pushed the thought of how much she was going to miss Scott when he left out of her mind. Hopefully organising Anouk to move in with her would keep her busy. Not that Anouk had told her yet what she had decided. Fern was driving her home after lunch and would press her for a decision then. She hoped Anouk's decision would be the one she was praying for.

Anouk was quiet as Fern helped her into the car after she'd said goodbye to Scott, who'd unexpectedly given Anouk a hug before walking her out to the car. Fern had packed up some food into a basket for Anouk to take home with her, not a lot but enough for a day or two, and placed it in the car. Scott had said he'd walk Lady and then spend time in the garden and read until she returned. Driving away, it was a strange feeling to see Scott standing in front of the auberge waving goodbye.

Anouk waved back. 'Such a nice man,' she said. 'A kind man too.'

'Yes, he is,' Fern answered, concentrating on her driving and wondering how to broach the subject of moving. In the end, she decided to ask the question outright, but Anouk spoke first.

'He likes you, you know.'

'I like him too,' Fern said warily. 'We had a lovely weekend, didn't we?'

'I mean he likes you seriously,' Anouk insisted. 'And I think you like 'im too?'

'Yes, of course I like him. And I hope he stays in touch when he leaves. But our lives are lived in different countries. He's an American and he will be returning to New York soon and I live here in Brittany.'

'You're both single. There's nothing stopping you getting together in either country. You'd like New York.'

Fern sighed. 'I like it here. I don't want to up sticks and move a thousand miles away. Moving here from England was traumatic enough,' she said, deciding to change the conversation. 'Now, what have you decided about moving in with me?'

Anouk was silent for several seconds. 'I think we'd get on very well together, but I worry about saying yes. What 'appens if things change? You're still a young woman. If you and Scott become a couple, or if not 'im, you meet someone else, who doesn't want an old woman hanging around.'

For once Fern was glad to see a herd of cows blocking the

country lane ahead. She stopped the car and turned off the engine. This was an important moment in both their lives. She had to get it right.

'Anouk, whether I meet someone else or not is immaterial. I promise you that you will always be a part of my life, living with me for as long as you want to. I could never have a relationship with anyone who didn't accept that. It will be a case of love me, love Anouk. Understand?'

Anouk nodded. 'I don't want to be a burden.'

'You will never be a burden to me,' Fern said. 'I know there will be occasional days when, for some reason or other, we might irritate each other, but we'll make a pact that when that happens we will talk about it. Not brood.'

Anouk reached out and patted her arm. 'You're the daughter I never had.'

Fern smiled at her and patted her arm back, pretending not to notice the tears glistening in Anouk's eyes.

'So we'll start putting things into motion this week then? Tell Fabian and Carole, decide what you'd like to bring to make your room feel like your home. I'll come and help you pack up things and we can start to take clothes and other bits and pieces over and then move you slowly to the auberge. How does that sound?' Fern said, starting the engine again as the last of the cows disappeared into a field and the farmer waved his hand in acknowledgement.

'Not too slowly, I hope,' Anouk said. 'At my age, I can't afford to wait too long. I think next week would be a good date to aim for. Will Scott still be staying?'

'No idea,' Fern said. 'I don't know how long he plans to stay. There is one thing though,' and she glanced across to Anouk, 'just don't expect every weekend to be like this last one. Scott made Easter extra special. The season starts soon and Saturday becomes changeover day – the busiest day of my week.'

'I can 'elp,' Anouk said. 'It will keep me out of mischief.'

The rest of the journey to Huelgoat passed quickly as the two of them made plans. Fern in particular was looking forward to being able to keep a proper eye on a woman she was very fond of.

* * *

When Fern got back to the auberge a couple of hours later, Scott was reading in the garden, Lady sprawled at his feet. He got up instantly as she appeared.

'Anouk settle back home all right?'

Fern nodded. 'Yes, and she's decided to move in with me ASAP. I can't tell you how relieved I am about that. Independent she may be, but living alone isn't good for her. It's a long time since I've seen her as animated as she was this weekend. Although, I think that was down to your presence. She really likes you.' She smiled at him. 'I know it's early, but I fancy a nice cold wine. Will you join me?'

'Thank you. I'll fetch it. Sit down, you look exhausted,' and Scott disappeared indoors.

Fern did as she was told and sat down. She closed her eyes and took a deep breath. She was exhausted. These days, when she drove, even though she used the quiet country roads, she could feel the tension building in her shoulders, across her back, try as she might to relax.

'Here you go,' Scott said.

Fern opened her eyes and took the glass he was holding out to her. 'Thank you. Cheers,' and they clinked glasses.

'Cheers.' Scott hesitated before continuing, 'I have to ask this.

Are you happy for me to stay here now that your guests and Anouk have left? I wouldn't want you to feel uncomfortable being in the house on your own with me. I'll find somewhere else tomorrow if you want me to.' His gaze caught and held Fern's. 'Although I hope you don't.'

'Anouk thinks you're a nice man, as well as a kind one,' Fern said slowly, unable to look away. 'I agree with her. I'm not worried about being in the house alone with you. Please stay.'

'Thank you.' Scott smiled at her as Fern blinked and took a sip of her drink.

'How long do you think you'll be staying? I know Anouk is hoping you'll still be here when she moves in.'

He smiled. 'I can't possibly disappoint Anouk – I'll be here.'

'About supper tonight,' Fern said. 'There's so much food left over from the weekend – lamb, cheese, salad, even some Kouign-amann cake that needs finishing. Would you mind if we had what I call a fridge bits-and-pieces supper?' She looked at him anxiously. He was technically a paying guest, although she had no intention of charging him for the evening meals they shared.

'Sounds good to me, I adore cold lamb,' Scott said. 'And it means you can stay there and relax while I put everything on the table. Okay?'

'Oh, but I can't let you do that,' Fern protested.

'Yes you can because I'm not taking no for an answer. Now, drink your wine and let me take care of... dinner.'

Fern watched him go and sat back, closing her eyes again. Had he been about to say 'take care of you' not dinner? She'd forgotten how good it was to have someone who cared about you and took the trouble to show and help. Scott was a lovely man and she knew Anouk was right when she'd said he seriously liked her. But liking someone 'seriously' when in a few weeks there would be an ocean between them would only lead to heartbreak, and Fern had suffered enough of that. What was the point of getting close to a man who would soon disappear out of her life?

25

The week after the Easter holiday was quiet in the hotel, with everyone back to work and the children at school, Belinda used her time to make sure everything was up to date. She rang Nigel and told him she wanted to talk to him about the campsite renovations. To her disappointment, he said she'd have to wait until the following week.

'Molly has a temperature, she thinks I'm fussing but I want to keep her quiet. If you come over, I know she'll want to see you, so can we leave it please?'

'Of course,' Belinda agreed. 'Do you want me to take over Torquay's books again while you're looking after Molly?'

'No thanks. I keep on top of them while Molly sleeps.'

'Okay. Give my love to Molly and tell her I'll see her soon.' Belinda ended the call, wondering what she was going to do to fill her days before she could talk to Nigel. With one hotel sold and Nigel looking after another, she was beginning to feel more than a little redundant. And unsettled, if she were honest. Was this what her job was going to be like in the future?

When Chloe rang to invite her to dinner, she accepted immediately. 'I'd love to come over. Can I bring anything?'

'No, just yourself. Do you want to come early and bathe the twins?'

'I'll be there at six,' Belinda promised. She'd missed helping with the twins' bath and bedtime routine, and then snuggling up together while she read them a story or two. Family time was just what she needed today. It would help smooth away her current frustrations about not being able to deal with certain issues both here and in Brittany.

There was a palpable air of excitement radiating off Chloe when Belinda arrived at their cottage close to the marina.

'Has something happened? You have that look you used to get as a little girl when you couldn't contain your excitement over something.'

Chloe shot a look at the twins. 'We'll talk later, after these two are in bed. Max has had some exciting news.'

It was almost eight o'clock before the twins were settled and asleep and Chloe began placing dinner on the table. Max opened a bottle of Prosecco and carefully poured three glasses. A knot in Belinda's stomach made its presence known. She had a feeling that she wasn't going to like what she was about to learn.

'Come on, you two. Put me out of my suspense. What are we celebrating?' She forced herself to sound bright and cheerful as she looked at them.

'I've been promoted at work,' Max said. 'The company have just taken on a new marina and have big expansion plans they want me to oversee.'

'It's in the Vendée,' Chloe interrupted him. 'We're going to live in France, can you believe? And we want you to come with us.'

'Congratulations, Max. You've worked so hard, you deserve the promotion.' A stunned Belinda raised her glass to him, trying to ignore the knot in her stomach that was growing by the second. 'I'm really pleased for you. Even I know how important that area of France is in the boating world.'

'You will come with us, won't you?' Chloe asked. 'It will be a new beginning for you and us, together. I can't bear the thought of us living in different countries.'

'Darling, I'm not sure I can,' Belinda said. 'It's a wonderful opportunity for Max and it will be a great experience for you as a family.' She took a deep breath. 'I'll think about it, I promise. I'll be a very frequent visitor even if I don't move over with you.' Was moving to France with Chloe really an option for her? She couldn't wish for a better son-in-law but would Max truly welcome his mother-in-law tagging along on his family's big adventure? And, importantly, did she deep down want to go and live in the Vendée?

'Mum,' Chloe pleaded, her eyes glistening with tears. It was Max who interrupted her this time.

'Darling, give your mum some space. It's a lot to take in and your mum does have her own life. She's promised to think about it.'

Belinda looked at Max gratefully. 'Tell me more about your actual promotion.'

Listening to Max explaining about what he would be doing, Belinda tried hard to concentrate. Difficult when all she could think of was 'this time next year they'll have left'. Apparently, Max would be going over on his own for a few weeks, coming back at weekends to help Chloe pack the house up. Their actual move to France would happen in the autumn. Max brought up the website on his laptop and showed her pictures of the marina and the big yachts that were based there already. One photo showed the large hotel that was part of the complex. If she went perhaps she'd be able to get a job there. Mentally she dismissed the thought as soon as it arrived. With Max overseeing things at the marina she wouldn't want the question of nepotism being raised.

As she left, Chloe gave her a tight hug. 'Please come with us, Mum.'

Belinda hugged her back but didn't answer her daughter.

On the way home, her thoughts went round and round in circles. Why was she surprised at this turn of events? Max was ambitious and determined to give his family a good life. She should have anticipated the possibility of Max and Chloe moving away. She'd missed the twins so much the last few weeks while she'd been in France – how was she going to cope with longer separations? Missing milestones in their lives. Not birthdays and Christmas because she'd definitely join them for those important dates. No, it was things like their first day at nursery, visits from the tooth fairy, learning to ride a bike, teaching them to bake biscuits. Everyday things she would still be part of if she went with them. She wanted to be a part of their young lives like Mami had been in hers and her own mum had been with Chloe.

Belinda brushed the tears away as she climbed the stairs to her flat. Talk about being at a major crossroads in her life with NO idea which way to turn. Embrace yet another new beginning like Chloe wanted and go with them? Or stay put and... and what?

26

Tuesday afternoon and Anouk's move to the auberge was under-way. After a week of toing and froing, her possessions were installed in the large downstairs bedroom at the back overlooking the countryside that she'd chosen, rather than an upstairs room. Fern had done her best to make it more than just a bedroom. She wanted Anouk to feel it was her own space with some of her own things around her. The cane chair, the three-drawer modern chest, the bedside tables and the small dressing table had all been removed. Fern knew she was indebted to Scott for his help in carrying them out into the garage for storage. Not an ideal place, but it would do for now until she could find somewhere else.

Anouk had been of the opinion that Fabian could jolly well help as he was benefiting from the arrangement. When she'd told him that she was moving to the auberge and that he could move into the Huelgoat house, she'd insisted that he would be her removal man. Accordingly, he'd hired a small van, coerced a friend into helping him and loaded the few things Anouk had decided she wanted and driven them over to the auberge.

A chintz-covered armchair by the window replaced the cane one, a bedside table and lamp was placed on one side of the bed, a small bookcase on the other. An antique dressing table with several drawers went against a side wall and a cream deep-pile rug was placed on the floor. Once the pieces of furniture were in place, Fabian brought in a couple of boxes containing Anouk's personal bits and pieces and the two suitcases with her clothes.

'Shall I give you a hand hanging everything in the wardrobe?' Fern asked.

Anouk shook her head. 'Non merci. I'll do some this evening before bed and finish it tomorrow.'

Together they unpacked the box of books and photographs, placing the books on the small bookcase and standing the photos on various surfaces. The silver framed formal black-and-white photo of Anouk and Jean-Marc on their long ago wedding day went on the bedside table along with the well-worn black leather bible. Taking a framed colour photo of herself and Laurent out of the box, Fern smiled remembering the day it had been taken.

'I'd forgotten we gave you a copy of this,' she said. 'Our last holiday.' They'd taken the train from Antibes along the coast to Monaco and spent a day indulging themselves with impossible daydreams: which super yacht moored in the harbour they'd buy; which prestigious apartment block contained 'their' home; which luxury car parked outside the Casino belonged to them. The photo, taken outside the Monaco Yacht Club by a passing stranger who'd stopped and asked if they'd like him to take a photo of them, had been an unexpected bonus. 'We were so happy that day,' Fern murmured, standing the photo on the small table before turning to face Anouk. Thankfully they'd had no suspicion of how any future happiness would shortly be so brutally shattered.

'If there's anything you've forgotten, we can fetch it next week.

I hope you're happy with the room once you've settled in,' Fern said, glancing around the room. Somehow, now that the room contained Anouk's things, including mementoes of Laurent, she felt reassured that inviting her mother-in-law to live at the auberge had been the right thing to do. Not only for the two of them but she knew Laurent would have approved of the arrangement too.

'It's going to be good having you here. I'm going to go and give Fabian and his friend a cup of tea and a slice of cake before they leave. Would you like one too?'

'Please,' Anouk answered. 'I'll come with you,' and the two of them made their way to the kitchen together.

'Where's Scott today?' Anouk asked.

'Taken himself off to Roscoff for an hour or two of sea air. He didn't want to get in the way. Promised he'd be back in time for your welcome dinner though,' Fern said.

Fabian was placing a large flower arrangement on the kitchen table, alongside a box of chocolates and a bottle of champagne when they walked in.

'Carole sent these for you both. She is so grateful to the two of you. As I am of course, Mami,' and he gave Anouk a hug before turning to Fern and hugging her too. 'I have to return the van this evening. If there is nothing else for me to carry, I will go.'

Anouk beckoned him to her, and gave him a long hug. 'I hope you and Carole are as happy in the house as your grand-père and I were.'

Fabian returned the hug. 'I 'ope so too. I already have the 'appy memories of the two of you living there.'

As Fabian left, Anouk looked at Fern. 'He's a good lad. More like Laurent than he realises sometimes.'

27

In Devon, Belinda was beginning to feel as though her life had been put on hold. Routine hotel work was not enough to keep her mind wandering back and forth over her problems. It was another three days before Nigel phoned and said Molly was much better and they would both love to see her. And she was to stay for lunch this time, Nigel insisted. At least she'd had time to think things through and make a sort of plan to put to them.

They both greeted Belinda warmly when she arrived and she sat chatting to Molly while Nigel made coffee.

'Good to see you looking better, Molly,' Belinda said. 'You had me worried for a while.'

'Happy to say I'm feeling a lot more like my old self,' Molly answered. 'How's Chloe and the family? I expect the twins are growing.'

'Yes they are,' Belinda said. She opened her phone and showed Molly the photos she'd taken over Easter.

'Oh, doesn't Aimee take after you and your mum,' Molly exclaimed. 'So pretty. You are lucky to have little ones in your life.'

'Would you like me to bring them to see you when you're

better?' Belinda offered, knowing how much Molly loved children.

'Would you?'

Belinda nodded. 'Of course.' She hesitated. 'Max has been given a promotion at work. A marina in the Vendée. They're going over there to live in a few months.' She hoped Molly didn't hear the catch in her voice. 'They've asked me to go with them, but...' She shrugged.

'In my experience, things always work out for the best,' Molly said and patted her arm. 'This will too. Ah, here's Nigel with the coffee.'

Belinda was grateful that Molly didn't pursue the subject in Nigel's hearing.

Nigel put the coffee on the table next to a pile of files, including one Belinda couldn't help notice labelled Camping dans La Fôret. He turned to give Belinda a cup of coffee.

'Everything all right the other side of the river?'

Belinda gave him a brief nod as she took her drink. 'Yes, the madness of Easter has died back. Everything is ticking over. In fact, now that you've sold Moorside and you're spending more time here, I haven't really got a lot to do.' She took a deep breath. 'I think I'd earn my keep more back in Brittany at the moment.' She felt bad about not telling them that returning to Brittany had been at the foremost of her mind for days, ever since she'd looked through the box of her mum's belongings. Now it wasn't just about getting the campsite fully functional, although that was important too of course.

Nigel regarded her thoughtfully before picking up the campsite file. 'I think I overreacted asking you to come back and stay. I didn't think Molly was going to be such a model patient. I was actually going to suggest today over lunch that you returned to Brittany. We'll take a look through the file and decide which jobs can go on hold and which should be marked urgent.'

Molly stood up. 'I'm going to leave you two to sort out the details. I'll be in the conservatory if you need me, with my book.'

'Alain tells me the campers that have turned up were happy to stay despite the lack of facilities,' Belinda said, trying not to show her relief that Nigel was all for her returning to Brittany early.

'He told us that too when he rang yesterday but said there were a couple of things that needed sorting.'

Belinda bit back on a retort about Alain not talking to her, saying instead, 'Off the top of my head, that would be the old café-cum-restaurant, the cabins still haven't been refurbished completely, the drive potholes need filling in, the communal washing-up area and the loos need updating. And then there is the question of deciding where to put the glamping pods and sourcing them.'

'We've decided not to go for pods this year,' Nigel said. 'Maybe next year, but Alain has suggested a couple of tree houses would be more in keeping.'

Belinda stared at him. 'I thought the whole idea was to go upmarket. Appeal to modern-day families.'

Nigel shrugged. 'They're only on hold, not cancelled. As for the other things, let's work through them, decide what needs to be done and reset the budget.'

For the next hour, the two of them went back and forth over things until they were both happy with the plan going forward.

'That's sorted,' Nigel said. 'Are you happy to go back and work with Alain again?'

'Of course,' Belinda answered. 'I want to finish the job.'

'From what he tells me, you've both sorted out your initial antagonism towards each other. He reckons you're okay.' Alain looked at her. 'You think the same about him?'

Did she think he was okay? Yes, she supposed she did really. He couldn't help his annoying French attitude that hid his good traits, from her especially.

Belinda sighed. 'Let's say we muddle along together now. There is one thing we haven't discussed – Bernie living in one of the cabins. Does he stay or do you want him to leave?'

'He stays. Alain says he's not a problem, just somebody who hasn't had the best deal in life. He's going to help around the site.'

'Have you two finished yet?' Molly called out. 'It's almost lunchtime and I'm hungry.'

'Two minutes,' Nigel answered. 'Just need to sort out a ferry ticket for Belinda.'

Two hours later, after an enjoyable lunch, Belinda left to drive home, her mind buzzing with plans for the campsite. The feeling, though, that her input hadn't been strictly necessary because certain things seemed to have been already decided between Nigel and Alain niggled away at her. She wished Alain had seen fit to discuss the tree house plan with her rather than have her find out from Nigel. Bespoke tree houses would certainly offer campers something different and would fit in with the ethical side of the campsite that Alain seemed to be pushing. But was her determination to make it a profitable business for Nigel going to cause more problems between her and Alain?

The fact that she was able to return to Brittany so soon filled her with mixed emotions too. Nigel and Molly thought she was going back just to help finish the campsite improvements for them. They had no idea of her secret agenda to dig around in the past and try to uncover the bitter truth behind her parents' break-up all those years ago.

That evening, as Belinda took BB along the river for his last walk before bedtime, she phoned Chloe to tell her she was returning to France the next day.

'That quickly? I thought Nigel needed you here?' Chloe said.

'The campsite needs me more if it's to be ready for the summer season,' Belinda explained. 'Now that Nigel's sold one hotel and manages the other one himself, that doesn't leave me a lot to do at Riverside for the time being, so it makes more sense for me to be over there.'

'I suppose so,' Chloe agreed. 'I was just hoping to see more of you over the next couple of weeks. Have you thought any more about the Vendée?'

Belinda hesitated. How could she explain to her daughter that since the night she'd opened the box and made her discovery, she'd pushed everything else outside of work to the back of her mind. 'Still weighing it all up, darling. There's months before you go yet.'

'I'm going to be so busy, it will fly by,' Chloe said. 'Especially with Max away so much. I was hoping you'd be around to help with... with things,' Belinda heard her daughter sigh down the phone.

'I'll be back by the second week in June,' Belinda said. 'And don't forget you're coming for a holiday in May.'

'Is that still on then?'

'Don't see why not, especially now that I'll be out there. Why not come in the middle of the month, you're not tied to school holidays yet. Even if Max can't make it, you and the twins can come.'

'Okay, but please, Mum, do think seriously about coming to France with us.'

'I will,' Belinda assured her.

'Right. Got to go, one of the twins has woken up. Love you,' and Chloe was gone.

Belinda put the phone in her pocket and continued walking for a few moments before turning and making for the apartment.

Lots of things to do before she caught the three o'clock ferry tomorrow afternoon. To think this time tomorrow evening she'd be back in Brittany – and she actually wanted to be there this time. There were certain things she needed to face up to, whatever the consequences turned out to be.

28

The sun was shining as the ferry pulled out of Plymouth and stayed with them all the way across the Channel. The sea was a little choppy, but Belinda remained out on deck with a coffee and a sandwich to read her book, looking up to people-watch occasionally.

Six hours later, standing with other passengers on the front deck, Belinda watched the lights of the French coast, and then Roscoff ferry port itself, get closer. This time, there were no feelings of dread, of not wanting to set foot on French soil, churning away inside her despite being at another crossroad in her life. Instead, there was the strange feeling of coming home to a place she recognised and an overwhelming sense of being in charge of things; in charge of her emotions. She'd deal with the package of official papers in her suitcase she'd decided to bring with her, lay a few ghosts and then get on with her life.

There was no need to set the satnav this time as she collected her car, with BB sleeping happily in the back, before joining the stream of traffic driving down the boat ramp and making its way up to the main road. The traffic quickly thinned out and within the hour Belinda was driving up the campsite lane. A newly resurfaced lane with not a single pothole, she was pleased to note.

She parked in front of the office and let BB out of the car. The office was closed and locked. Belinda glanced across at the staff house. No lights inside, but an outside one by the door was on.

The house had a lived-in feel to it this time when she unlocked the door, walked in and switched on the lights. Mugs and plates drying by the sink. A car magazine on the coffee table in the sitting room. The wood-burner stove was warm and the firebed was glowing, taking the evening chill off the air. Milk, ham, cheese, butter, a bottle of white wine and several small bottles of beer were in the fridge when she went to put in the food she'd brought with her. Briefly she wondered if Alain was going to sleep here tonight now that she was back, or return to his parents' house. She knew that Nigel had emailed him to tell him she was returning early.

Taking her suitcase upstairs, Belinda was surprised to find that Alain had opted to use one of the smaller bedrooms rather than the one she'd prepared before leaving. She unpacked her suitcase and put things away in drawers and the wardrobe. The envelope she placed on the bedside table. Taking a towel and her toiletries bag, she made her way to the one and only bathroom, intending to leave her things there, ready. A toothbrush and toothpaste were on the shelf by the sink, a large bath towel on the towel rail. She retraced her steps to the bedroom. Probably best to keep her personal stuff in her bedroom.

A door slammed downstairs.

'Belinda?'

Alain was waiting for her in the small hallway as she went downstairs. 'Welcome back,' he said. 'Good trip?'

'Thank you. And yes, it was.'

'You 'ave eaten?' he asked. 'I think to have a sandwich and a beer before bed. Peut-être you join me?'

Surprised at the offer, Belinda nodded. 'I'd love a sandwich and a glass of wine,' she said and followed him into the kitchen. She poured herself a glass of wine and opened a beer for Alain while he buttered some bread and made some ham sandwiches. Minutes later, they were sitting companionably on the settee in front of the fire, which Alain brought back to life with a few small logs.

There was something different about Alain tonight, Belinda decided, trying to work out what it was. Sitting there with BB sprawled across his feet waiting for stray crumbs and the odd crust that Belinda realised Alain was feeding him, the man looked positively at home. Definitely more relaxed. Definitely friendlier. Definitely happier.

'Nigel and I had a good discussion yesterday about the camp, about what needs doing for the season,' she said. 'We've got a busy few weeks ahead of us. I've come back with revised plans and a new budget. We'll go through it together tomorrow. Nigel said the glamping pods were cancelled until next year and that you had suggested building a couple of tree houses?' She looked at him questioningly.

'Much more in keeping with a family-orientated site, don't you think?' Alain said.

'They won't bring in as much money as pods.'

'It's not all about the money though, is it?' Alain asked quietly. 'I know the site 'as to be profitable, but it needs a balance too. We're in the 'eart of the countryside 'ere, people should be able to enjoy the things nature offers. Rather than a plastic bubble filled with luxuries.'

Belinda watched him as he drained his bottle of beer and replaced it on the table. Why was he so set on everything being as nature intended? This was the twenty-first century. They needed some technology to be available for campers.

'It's all coming together. Everything that needed painting and smartening up has been done. All the white goods 'ave arrived for the cabins, new furniture is on order and the grounds are looking spring-like. Bernie, he 'as been working hard with me on them,' Alain said.

'Do we have anybody staying on site at the moment?' Belinda asked.

'Six camper vans and one caravan.'

'I'll wander round tomorrow and take some photos for the website,' Belinda said. 'We need to keep it up to date. Now it's live we'll soon start to get some bookings and money in.' She finished her sandwich and stood up. 'That was good, thank you. It's been a long day, so I'll say goodnight, see you in the morning.'

'I'll shut the fire down and lock up. The bathroom's all yours.'

'Thanks.'

Belinda was in and out of the bathroom in five minutes flat and back in her bedroom with the door closed. She hadn't shared a house or bathroom with a stranger since college and then, being long before the days of unisex accommodation, it was an all-female house share. Maybe they should sort out some sort of rota for the two of them if he continued to stay in the house?

She gave a quiet laugh. She could just imagine Alain's reaction to that.

* * *

Belinda, awake early the next morning, could hear Alain singing in the shower so stayed where she was until she heard the water being turned off and Alain making his way back to his room. When she got downstairs half an hour later, the coffee machine was on, but there was no sign of Alain. She made herself a coffee and drank it standing up looking out of the kitchen window at the limited view of the forecourt area in front of the office. Alain's car was parked next to hers, the office light was on and the door open.

She picked up her tote and the file with all the new paperwork, locked the cottage door behind her and went over to the office.

Alain looked up briefly as she walked in before returning his attention to the computer screen. 'Bonjour.'

'Bonjour,' and Belinda put the file on the desk. 'I'm planning on having a walkabout, seeing what's happened while I've been away, taking those photographs I mentioned for the website. Do you want to come with me, or shall I leave you the file and you can go through the paperwork and new budget Nigel has given us, ready for a discussion when I get back?'

'I'll go through the file,' Alain said. 'Ready for the argument when you get back.'

Belinda shook her head at him, irritated by his attitude but then realised when she saw his lips twitch that he was teasing her. 'No arguments. Discussion.' She took her camera out of her bag. 'Right. I'll see you in a bit.'

With BB excited to be back and enjoying the freedom of being off the lead, Belinda wandered down the path, leading to the tent area, knowing it was empty. Still barely past eight o'clock, she didn't want to disturb the people in the camper vans or caravan.

The shower block and the toilet block were positively gleaming with their new paintwork and tiles. The pathways were clear all round the camp, the shrubs cut back, wooden signs painted, windows of the cabins freshly washed and their wooden decking freshly varnished. Belinda took photo after photo. The transformation of the site was amazing.

She'd only been away for less than a fortnight, but so much had been achieved. The entertainment area had been pressure-washed and the picnic tables cleaned and put in place. The outside of the restaurant had been washed down, but peering through a window, Belinda could see the inside was still a shambles. Getting that ready for the season would be top of her agenda now, especially as Nigel had decided to employ staff to run it rather than lease it out.

Wandering on down through the site, Belinda stood and looked out over the river and remembered Fern saying something about an annual fishing competition. Fern. She needed to let her know she was back and arrange to meet up. See if she could give her any advice on how she should approach finding the missing link to her past.

As she turned to walk back past the cabins, BB bounded ahead happily and barked joyfully at Bernie sitting drinking a coffee at the table in his patch of garden. He raised his cup and pointed at it, looking at Belinda nodding and smiling. Belinda smiled back but shook her head, gently refusing what she took to be an offer of coffee. 'Merci, Bernie, but non.'

If only he spoke French he could probably tell her something about the fishing festival. Maybe he liked to fish. Belinda remembered Fern saying she thought he understood simple French, he just didn't like speaking it.

She gestured in the direction of the river. 'Pêchez-vous?'

Bernie nodded vigorously.

'Avez-vous pêche au festival de la pêche ici?' Belinda said slowly and clearly.

Bernie's face broke into a big smile at her words. He held out his arm and hand towards her, indicating he wanted her to wait and dashed into the cabin. Seconds later he was back and handed her a photograph of himself proudly holding a big fish and a plaque that said 1st Prize.

'Félicitations,' Belinda said, smiling as she handed the photo back. She tapped her watch. 'Le travail. À bientôt.'

Leaving Bernie, Belinda made her way back to the office, hoping that Alain would be there and free to discuss the things in the file. Half an hour later, she was regretting that hope. They'd gone through everything, including the siting of the tree houses to replace the pods, except the plans for a newly refurbished restaurant. It was then the discussion turned into an argument.

'There isn't time to refurbish the restaurant for this season, so it makes sense to keep it as a basic café and employ a couple of people to work there for us. I've had an idea too about sourcing food, which I need to research more. Then, at the end of summer, we can organise a complete renovation,' Belinda said. 'After that, we can advertise its availability for functions in the spring.'

'Functions? Why? And what sort?' Alain almost snapped at her.

'The restaurant refurbished, with decent tables and chairs, a bar and a sound system would be a wonderful place for weddings, parties, even some of those bonding weekends that companies are so fond of these days. Revive the old fishing festival maybe. It's a way of keeping the site open and paying for itself all year round. It would all bring in good money.'

'You're turning it into the kind of campsite I don't want to run.' Alain glared at her.

'Well, as this campsite is Nigel's, he gets to make the final decisions, so if you're not happy, maybe you'd better find yourself another one,' Belinda said quietly.

Alain looked at her, opened his mouth as though to say something, before changing his mind and walking out.

The happier Alain of last evening had definitely disappeared.

When Marie turned up for work after lunch, Belinda saved everything on the website she'd been working on and returned to the cottage to work. Thankfully there was no sign of Alain. It was late afternoon before she remembered to phone Fern and tell her she was back.

'You're here,' a delighted Fern said. 'When did you get back? How was it?'

'Last night. There were one or two unexpected changes, but on the whole it was okay. We need a catch-up. Fancy coming here tonight for a glass of wine. Or do you have guests?'

'No guests, but Anouk and Scott are here. I could come after dinner. They're quite happy to spend time together. You wouldn't believe how competitive they get over a game of scrabble,' Fern said, trying to organise her thoughts.

'Excuse me? I'm away for two weeks and you not only move your ex ma-in-law in but a new man as well. This Scott, he's the American you met a few weeks ago, isn't he? And now he's living with you?'

'Yes that Scott, but he's not living with me. Well, he is, but he's a paying guest. I'll explain when I see you. He'll be leaving soon anyway. Would you like to come here for supper?' Fern asked.

'Another night would be lovely. I can meet Anouk and check out your Scott then. Tonight, I need to talk to you alone and ask your advice.'

'Right. I'll do an early dinner and see you about eight, okay?'

'Perfect. Bring Lady too. And, Fern? Thanks.'

29

Belinda opened the door of the cottage as she heard Fern drive up and went out with BB to greet her and to let the two dogs have a play before they went indoors.

'This place is starting to look smart again. Love the coloured lights at the foot of the trees,' Fern said as she looked at the cutback shrubs and the newly planted flower beds by the office and the cottage. 'Can I smell a barbecue? I can definitely hear someone strumming a guitar.' She handed Belinda a plastic box.

'What's this?'

'Cantucci biscuits I made this afternoon. Delicious dunked in wine. Should be white wine, but I personally prefer red – which you have?'

'I do,' Belinda said, leading Fern inside and tipping the biscuits onto a plate. 'It's in the sitting room. I opened it earlier to let it breathe.'

'Is Alain here tonight?'

'He left a message with Marie for me. He's gone over to check up on his parents. Said he'd be back about ten, so we've got the place to ourselves until then. Come on, let's make ourselves comfortable,' and she ushered Fern into the sitting room.

'So how come you're back so quickly?' Fern asked as Belinda poured wine into two glasses.

'Nigel has sold one of the hotels, he's managing another, and the third isn't really busy at this time of year, so it made sense for me to come back and help Alain with the final things to get this place up to scratch for the summer. And...' Belinda paused. 'There is something I've decided I need to do, so I'm quite pleased it worked out like this.' She handed a glass to Fern. 'Cheers.'

'Cheers.'

'But first, tell me all about your Scott.'

'I told you he's not my Scott.' Fern swirled her wine around in the glass reflectively. 'Anouk adores him. He's really nice. But...'

'But?'

'He's American and that's where his life is, so there is little point in being anything other than friends.'

'He might be happy to relocate to Europe,' Belinda said. 'Didn't you say his family are originally from here? Maybe he feels at home here, a pull of the old country.'

Fern shrugged. 'I don't think so. Anyway, we've not known each other long and I'm not sure whether I'm completely over Laurent, so...' She took a swig of her drink. 'What was it you wanted to talk about?'

'Two things. Let's get the first one out of the way.' Belinda took a deep breath and looked at her friend. 'I finally went through some papers of my mum's. Some of them are in that envelope on the coffee table.' She pointed out the envelope to Fern. 'Have a look through them, will you, and tell me what's in there.'

Puzzled, Fern looked at her before she reached out for the envelope and emptied its contents onto the table. 'Birth certificates. Marriage certificates. Death certificates. A decrees nisi. Two old Passports. Normal family official papers.'

'Agreed,' Belinda said. 'You remember my mum left my dad because he had an affair?' As she spoke, she sorted the marriage certificates into one pile, the birth certificates into a second and the decree nisi into another.

Fern nodded. 'Yes.'

Belinda handed her a pile of papers. 'These are marriage certificates for my great-grandparents through to me. Birth certificates, again from my great-grandparents through to me. Look there's my father's name – Enzo Belrose. And this single decree nisi is mine.'

'Where are you going with this?' Fern asked.

'I didn't realise a couple of papers were missing at first. There's no marriage certificate or decree nisi for my parents,' Belinda said quietly. 'I don't think my parents were ever married.'

'Maybe your mum kept them in a different place and you didn't find them. Or could your mum have destroyed them in a fit of anger after your father's affair?' Fern asked.

'I went through the house methodically, I would have found them. I did think about her wanting to be rid of them, but I don't think she did destroy them.' Belinda put everything back in the envelope. 'Ever since I realised they were missing, I've been thinking about my mum. She never talked to me about her wedding day. Even when I asked her a direct question – what was her dress like, for instance, or where did they go on honeymoon – she'd brush me off. Called me an old romantic.

'I remember asking to see their wedding photographs. I mean everyone has photos of their wedding, don't they? Even if they don't have an album as such. Mum laughed and told me they were too broke when they got married to afford a photographer and that's why she didn't have any photos. When I asked if that didn't make her sad, she just shrugged and said, who needed photos when she had the person.'

Belinda took a biscuit and carefully dunked it in her wine. 'Mmm, these are so good. The best nibbles ever.'

'They're a bit addictive,' Fern said, taking one. 'I don't make them very often – they tend to lead me to the wine bottle when I have them in the biscuit tin. Too much temptation.'

'I've been thinking too about Mum's reactions when I was planning my marriage to Peter,' Belinda said. 'I bought every bridezilla magazine I could lay my hands on and Mum fell on them every time. She'd go through them muttering, "Who'd wear a dress like that? How much?" and other things like that. When I wanted her advice on wedding etiquette and how to do things, can you guess what she said?'

Fern shook her head.

'"You don't want a wedding like mine, darling. We were just two crazy hippies who didn't make a big deal out of it. Your wedding day though is going to be wonderful." And it was. Shame the marriage failed to live up to expectations.' Belinda sighed. 'The more I talk about it, the more I think they never married. Which raises the obvious question, why not? I remember them as loving parents to me and loving towards each other, until that dreadful day when Mum dragged me away because Dad had had an affair.'

'Do you have any relatives who might know the truth?'

'No. Damn, I should have asked Molly while I was over there. She and Mum were quite close. I do remember them having a party on the thirtieth of June every year and claiming it was for their anniversary. Mind, it could have been the anniversary of the day they met or got together, for all I know.' Belinda helped herself to another biscuit and dunked it. 'You're right, these are addictive.' She glanced at Fern. 'You remember that waitress, Sandrine? I was wondering whether I'd go and talk to her. She, or probably her parents, would have heard all the gossip after we left. Not sure that I want to bring it all out into the open again.' She groaned to herself. 'But I really really want to know the truth about my parents.'

'We're talking about the late 1960s here, aren't we?' Fern said thoughtfully. 'What was the name of the village your grandmother lived in?'

'Saint-Herbot,' Belinda answered. 'Why?'

'I was wondering whether Anouk would have heard anything all those years ago. You said you lived on a smallholding nearby and Huelgoat isn't a million miles away from Saint-Herbot.' Fern did some mental calculations. 'Anouk has lived in Huelgoat since she married sixty-five years ago. And villages in those days thrived on gossip even more than today. She may have heard something but not necessarily known the people involved.'

'It's worth asking her, I suppose,' Belinda said.

'Come for supper soon and you can ask her yourself,' Fern said. 'I'll introduce you to Scott too.'

'Thanks. I can always go and see Sandrine afterwards if Anouk doesn't know anything,' which Belinda thought was more than likely to be the case. Everyone knew that old people's memories weren't always the most reliable.

The cottage door slammed, startling them both, as well as the two dogs, who jumped up, barking simultaneously.

'Evening, Belinda, Fern,' Alain said, appearing in the doorway. 'I won't disturb you, just going to make a spot of supper. Anyone like anything?'

'No thanks,' Fern said, standing up. 'I must go.' She turned to

Belinda. 'I'll see you soon and I'll also have a quiet word with Anouk.'

'Thanks. I'll see you out.'

Standing watching Fern drive away, Belinda realised that she'd never got around to asking her what she should do about Chloe moving to the Vendée. Let her go? Or go with her? It would keep until the next time she saw Fern. Sighing inwardly, she went back indoors.

Alain was sitting on the settee, a plate of sandwiches in front of him, a car magazine on his lap. He glanced up as Belinda returned. 'I 'ope I didn't drive Fern away?'

'No of course not. She needed to get back for Anouk,' Belinda answered and gave him a sharp glance. 'You've got over your bad temper from this morning then?'

'Oui, it is all sorted now,' Alain said. 'You 'ave un problème? You look préoccupée.'

'I wanted to ask Fern's advice about something, but we were so busy talking about... about something else, that I didn't get time.'

'Want to ask me?'

Honestly, she never knew where she was with this man. One minute he was being obnoxious and the next, well, the next he was being friendly.

Belinda, went to shake her head and say no, but found herself saying instead, 'It's my daughter and her husband.'

Alain waited.

'Max has been promoted at work. They're moving to the Vendée and want me to go with them.'

'Do you want to go?'

'I don't know,' Belinda said helplessly. 'I can't see the wood for the trees.'

'Excuse? I do not know that English saying.' Alain looked at her.

'It means I can't see my way to making a decision. There are too many "ifs".' She sighed. 'Anyway, I think I'll have a shower and then go to bed. See you in the morning.'

30

Over the next few days living in the house together, Belinda and Alain slipped into a comfortable routine without noticing it happen. Alain was always up first to shower and leave the bathroom free for Belinda. By the time she went downstairs, coffee was ready and fresh croissants from the village bakery were on the table. Some mornings, Alain was still around and joined her for breakfast before they left for the short walk across to the office together.

It seemed only fair to Belinda that the afternoons when she was home first she organised supper for them both. Nothing fancy, she knew her limitations. The shop was opening for a couple of hours every day now and Belinda picked up various cold meats, salad stuff and fresh bread on the evenings she did supper for the two of them.

After supper, they settled in for a couple of companionable hours together in the sitting room. Whether by accident or design on both their parts, the ongoing work on the campsite was rarely mentioned. The evenings were getting warmer and they were able to open the French doors onto the little terrace. Sometimes they watched TV, but mostly they read. Belinda a book and Alain one of his endless car magazines. Conversation was limited but friendly and the silences were becoming those that happen between people who were becoming comfortable with each other.

Alain went out every evening at about ten o'clock to check all was well on the campsite and Belinda usually said goodnight then and went to bed before he returned.

One particularly lovely evening, she stood up with him.

'Mind if I join you tonight? It's such a lovely evening, I fancy a walk.'

'Bring a jacket, it's always a bit cooler down by the river at this time of day,' Alain said.

A couple sitting outside their camper van with a glass of wine called out 'Bon nuit' as they walked past. The other two nearby vans had their lights on and curtains drawn, the muted tones of TV programmes could be heard. Bernie was sitting outside of his cabin, Ging curled up on his lap. Belinda stood and smiled at him as Alain had a brief conversation with him, before they moved on down towards the river.

Belinda gave a happy sigh. 'I love this part of the site. The noise of the upstream river weir, the ducks, watching the herons. I can't wait to show it all to Chloe and the twins when they arrive. I'm so pleased she's coming for a holiday.'

Alain, staring out over the river, nodded. 'My son used to love it here.'

Belinda turned to look at him. 'He doesn't come here any more?'

'No. He's thirty this year and lives in Canada now, so he's got all the wide-open spaces he needs. I rarely see him these days.'

'That must be hard,' Belinda said quietly.

'I am used to it. He lived with his mother after the divorce and seeing 'im has always been difficult. Especially when I lived in Africa. His mother refused to let 'im travel there.'

'What were you doing in Africa?'

'I oversaw several charitable projects building schools for the local children,' Alain said briefly, keeping his gaze on the river.

'Sounds like a rewarding thing to have done.' So, not a mercenary then. Working for a charity was more in tune with the kind of man Alain was turning out to be, Belinda realised.

Alain nodded at her words.

'Did you come home because of your parents? To help them?'

'Oui. They're at an age when they need me around. Although if you'd heard my maman telling me off the other day for not wearing a coat, you'd think I was still six years old.' He paused. 'And there was this place of course.'

'Were you upset when you discovered Nigel now owned it?'

'Non. It stops my parents worrying about money and they're 'appy for me to have a job while things sort themselves out.'

Belinda waited for him to explain what things needed sorting out, but he stayed staring out over the river.

'Were you living with them before the cottage was ready? Or have you got your own place in the village?'

'I was back in my old childhood room with them. Still covered with motorbike posters.' Alain grinned at her. 'A virtual time warp.'

'Did they mind you moving out again so soon?' Belinda asked. Then, as something Alain had said the day she did her first site inspection flashed into her mind, she turned to look at him. 'Hang on, why are you still living in the cottage now I'm back? Why haven't you returned to your parents' place to keep an eye on them? You told me you had no intention of living on site until the season started properly.'

Alain returned her glare with one of his own. 'And leave you living on site by yourself? Don't be ridiculous. And don't accuse me of being a chauvinist again. It's the way I was brought up – you don't leave any woman in a vulnerable situation.'

'We're in the middle of the countryside, not the inner city,' Belinda said. 'There are campers around. I have a phone to call the gendarmes if I have to. And I have BB. I don't need looking after. You should be looking after your parents.'

'Like it or not, I'm staying put in the cottage until you leave for good. Now let's get back,' and Alain waited for her to start walking before he fell into step alongside her.

Back at the cottage, Belinda said a polite bon nuit and went straight to her room to get ready for bed. She supposed she should be grateful that Alain was such a gentleman. The campsite was in an isolated position and under the cover of darkness it could be eerily spooky with the owls calling to each other and the nocturnal animals rustling through the bushes as they hunted for food. But she'd have coped. Although, if she was honest, she did sleep better knowing that there was someone else in the house with her. Any emergency and help would be instant.

Perhaps she was overreacting? It had been a long time since anyone had thought to protect her from real or imagined trouble. Despite their differences, she liked Alain and after their conversation this evening, knew he had hidden depths that he kept well concealed. She was beginning to value his friendship and didn't want them to fall out. Tomorrow at breakfast she'd apologise and lay the blame on becoming fiercely independent since her divorce.

31

There was an unusual atmosphere in the kitchen during breakfast at the auberge Thursday morning that worried Fern. The four guests in the dining room were happy and friendly as she served them, talking about where they were going for the day, Quimper. One of the party was vegan and asked if she could recommend anywhere for lunch. 'Try my favourite place for lunch in Quimper, The Sherlock Holmes Restaurant. Lots of choices for both vegans and meat eaters,' Fern said. 'You'll all find something tasty to eat. You need to get there early, it's very popular.'

In the kitchen, though, something was different. Scott and Anouk normally set the world to rights over their coffee and croissants, but this morning, they were both strangely quiet. Fern struggled to get a word out of either of them. In the end, after the guests had gone upstairs to get ready for their day out, Fern poured herself a cup of coffee and sat down at the table with them.

'Right, you two. Why the long faces?'

Anouk stood up. 'I'll let Scott tell you. I'm going to write a letter in my room.'

Fern watched her go as a feeling of sadness threatened to engulf her. She knew what Scott was going to tell her before he even opened his mouth to speak.

'You have to return to America, don't you?'

He nodded. 'I was planning on staying for another month, but my god-daughter has emailed me to say her mother, my cousin, isn't well and wants to see me.'

'When are you leaving?' Fern asked, her voice low, surprised at how empty she felt at the thought of saying goodbye to Scott.

'I've had a look at flights and the first direct flight I can get from Paris to New York is Tuesday, which means I have to leave on Monday from Brest.'

Fern smiled at him. 'We knew you'd be going back sometime, it's just a bit sooner than we... I expected.' She put her cup down on the table and Scott caught hold of her hand and squeezed it gently.

'I will be back I promise,' he said, looking at her, 'but Kylie's illness complicates things. I'm not sure how long I will need to stay in New York. It could be a couple of weeks or it could be months.'

'Well, I'm not going anywhere, I'll be here when you do return. What about your hire car? Where will you drop it? Brest or Carhaix? I can always drive you to the airport if it's Carhaix.'

'Appreciate the offer, but I can leave it at Brest.' Scott looked at her. 'I'm not very good with airport goodbyes. Arrivals I love. Departures, not so much.' He hesitated. 'What I would like you to do though is to have dinner with me Saturday night. Just the two of us. Is that possible?'

'Yes. I'd like that. Thank you. And tonight when my friend,

Belinda, comes here to meet you and to talk to Anouk, the three of us will put on happy faces.'

* * *

Thursday on the campsite was surprisingly busy considering it was a weekday at the end of April. The last few days had been wonderfully sunny and spring-like and it seemed as if the world and his family had taken it upon themselves to get out into the countryside. But it wasn't until Alain pointed out that Friday was the first of May that Belinda realised the real reason.

'Of course. How stupid of me to forget the Labour Day holiday. And everybody is "faire le pont" – making a long weekend of it.' She glanced at Alain. 'It's the vide-grenier this Sunday too, isn't it?'

Alain nodded. 'Oui. Hervé and Yann's Gang will be here Saturday afternoon to start setting things up.'

Both Belinda and Alain took great care to make sure visitors realised that the site was barely operational yet and most people took it all in their stride. There were one or two disgruntled guests, who decided to drive on a bit further when they realised the lack of facilities. Which made Alain grumble under his breath. Belinda didn't exactly say 'I told you so', but she did say again there were certain twenty-first-century technologies that were necessary.

It was late afternoon before things slowed down and Belinda took the opportunity to make some coffee while Alain showed a family of four to one of the cabins.

'I think we definitely need Marie working weekends from now on,' Belinda said, when he returned.

Alain nodded in agreement. 'And probably for most of the

week while Chloe is here. You'll need to spend some time with her.'

'True, so long as that's okay with you.'

'Of course it is. They stay in the cottage with us?'

Belinda shook her head. 'I thought I'd put them in a cabin.' She glanced at her watch. 'I think I'm going to slip off in a moment and leave you to it for any late arrivals. I really fancy a long hot soak in the bath before I head out for the evening.'

'You're not home tonight?'

For a moment there Belinda thought she heard a disappointed note in Alain's voice.

'I'm having dinner with Fern to meet Anouk, her ma-in-law, and Scott, her American friend.' She looked at Alain. 'I'm hoping that Anouk will be able to help me solve a mystery from my past.'

'Your French past?'

Belinda nodded. 'Yes. There's nothing I can do to change it, whatever happened, happened. But I do need to know the truth.'

'Good luck. I hope Anouk can help,' Alain said. 'You'd better go and have that soak you wanted.'

* * *

A quarter of an hour later, the bathroom was steamy and smelt of strawberries from the bubble bath Belinda had poured into the water before she'd stepped in and lowered herself into the hot water. Bliss.

Laying there, she thought about the evening ahead. Would Anouk remember that far back and would anything she remembered be relevant to the questions Belinda wanted answered? Perhaps it would be better to see Anouk on her own, not with other people around, eating and drinking.

Her mobile, which she'd placed within reach on the bath

stool, began to ring, breaking into her thoughts. Belinda sat up, reached out for the towel she'd put on the nearby rail, quickly dried her hands and picked up the phone.

'What's up?' she answered Fern's quiet hello. 'You sound down.'

'I haven't mentioned anything to Anouk yet about the two of you talking, but you are still coming tonight, aren't you?'

'Yes of course. Why?'

'Scott's leaving on Monday. This evening is in danger of turning into a bit of a tearful farewell dinner for him. I need you here for some light relief.'

'In that case, do you have room for another guest? Alain is at a loose end,' Belinda said impulsively.

'Bring him. There's lots of food and it will be good to have another man at the table. See you soon.'

As the call finished, Belinda decided if Fern still hadn't mentioned the reason for tonight's dinner to Anouk when she got there, then she wouldn't bring the subject up. Tonight didn't look like the night to ask questions.

Belinda was drying herself when she heard Alain moving around in his room and quickly pulled on her towelling robe before opening the bathroom door.

'Alain,' she called. 'Your lonely evening has been averted. Fern is in desperate need of another man at the dinner table, would like you to join us for dinner?'

* * *

Leaving the cottage, Belinda automatically had her car keys in her hand and pressed the unlock button.

'We go in mine,' Alain said.

Belinda looked at him, surprised, as he held the passenger car door open for her. She shrugged. What did it matter which car they went in? She pressed her key fob again and the lights flashed and the door locks clicked back down.

'If Anouk tells you something upsetting tonight, peut-être you drink more than is good. This way, I make sure you get home safely.' Once Belinda was sitting in the passenger seat, Alain slammed the door closed and walked around to get into the driving seat.

'I had a car like this once,' Belinda said quietly. 'The year we left France, Dad was teaching me to drive.' She didn't tell him that it had been another four years before she finally learnt to drive.

'You like to drive?'

'I do now, yes. Especially here in Brittany where the roads are quieter.'

The rest of the short journey to the auberge passed in silence.

Anouk and Scott were out in the garden when Fern let them in. Alain handed her the bottle of wine they'd stopped to buy in the village shop.

'Thank you. You really didn't have to. Come on through and meet Anouk and Scott.'

Introductions were made quickly and Scott poured everyone their wine of choice before disappearing to help Fern with something in the kitchen.

Anouk looked at Alain. 'How are your parents? Fern tells me you're running their old campsite now. I remember some good times there years ago, before they owned it of course. I'm talking about back in the sixties.'

Belinda glanced at her. The late sixties were when her father had brought her and her mum to France to live. Maybe Anouk would be able to tell her something about her parents after all. As Scott returned, Belinda excused herself and went to talk to Fern in the kitchen.

'The smells coming from this kitchen are, as always, delicious,' Belinda said. 'How are you really about Scott leaving?'

Fern, concentrating on pouring a sauce into a jug, pulled a face. 'I'm fine. It's not as if we're in the throes of a mad passionate relationship. We haven't passed more than the friendship stage really.' She turned to face Belinda. 'I've always known he would have to return to his life in New York. I've always known too that long-distance relationships rarely survive.' Fern hesitated. 'Which is why I've struggled to keep things on a friendship basis, even though I really like him.'

'My mum had a favourite song from her teenage years, she was always humming it or singing the words out loud. It used to irritate me like hell,' Belinda said. 'But now I understand her need to keep saying it. Que sera sera. What will be will be.'

Fern nodded. 'I remember that song too. And you're right... it is an irritating phrase.'

Belinda gave Fern a quick hug. 'I know it doesn't change anything, but it's true. You have to hang on to that thought. If Scott wants a proper relationship with you, he will find a way. If not, you will be happy that you met him even for a short time and carry on with your life here.' She moved away from Fern and picked up a stray cube of cheese from the work surface. 'Listen to me, don't I sound all grown-up and philosophical about things? When I'm truly not. If I was, I'd know what to do about Chloe's recent bombshell.'

'Which is?'

'Max has a new job at a marina in the Vendée. Brilliant promotion for him, from what they say, and Chloe is desperate for me to go with them. Give up my job and my flat. I'm not sure.' It was her turn to grimace at Fern. 'Que sera sera.' Belinda picked up a dish of olives and cashews. 'Enough. Shall I take these through and we can get the show on the road?'

'Good idea. You and Alain look very comfortable together by the way. I'm guessing you no longer want to shoot him?'

'I wouldn't say that,' Belinda smiled. 'He has his moments. But he's definitely growing on me,' she added quietly.

* * *

Conversation between the five of them flowed from subject to subject. As they all made appreciative noises and tucked into the maigret de canard with caramelised onions and sauté potatoes that Fern placed in front of them, Belinda remembered something she wanted to ask Fern that had been floating around in her mind for days now. Something that she should really run past Alain before putting it out there, but she decided she'd risk upsetting him.

'We're looking to employ a couple of people to run the café for us this season,' she said. 'And I know you don't want a full-time job like that, but would you be interested in providing the cakes, desserts and possibly a couple of main meals like lasagna.' Without looking at him, Belinda sensed that Alain was staring at her.

'What about the village bakery?' Fern asked. 'Won't that be stepping on their toes?'

'They're already providing croissettes, bread and a few cakes to the shop and, of course, we'll sell some of their stuff too in the café, but it would be nice to have a bit of variety.' She looked at Fern hopefully. 'You're such a brilliant cook. And it would keep you out of mischief for the next few weeks.'

'It's a big commitment, but I'll definitely think about it,' Fern said.

After that, the conversation turned to other things and it

wasn't until Belinda and Alain started to say their thank yous prior to leaving that Anouk spoke directly to Belinda.

'Fern tells me that you'd like to talk to me about your French family?' She raised her eyebrows as she looked at Belinda, who managed a surprised shaky nod. 'Scott is taking Fern out for dinner Saturday night, so why don't you come and spend the evening with me? We can talk then and I can tell you what I know about the Belrose scandal.'

'Thank you. I'll see you then.' A stunned Belinda followed Alain out to the car. Anouk did know about the past. Saturday evening she would finally, hopefully, learn the truth about what had really torn her family apart. Why had the locals back then dubbed it the Belrose scandal? Why did those three words strike fear into her heart?

32

Fern took extra time and care getting ready for her dinner date with Scott. It wasn't that she wanted to impress him, simply that she wanted him to remember her looking as good as possible on what could turn out to be their last date. A last date that in reality was their first one. Yes, they'd spent a lot of time in each other's company since Easter. Walking Lady, gardening, preparing meals together. None of which constituted a date, like going out for dinner did. Her hand trembled as she started to apply her favourite lipstick. Fern wanted him to remember her tonight as someone he would like to date again when he was a thousand miles away across the Atlantic Ocean. Someone he would return to when he'd dealt with the problems that had called him back.

She took one last look in the mirror and decided that she looked good. Not sure where Scott planned on taking her, she'd opted for her favourite red dress with a scooped neckline, long sleeves and a flared skirt. Because the evenings could still be chilly, she teamed it with a cream jacket with pale silk raised embroidery.

Anouk was in the conservatory when she got downstairs.

'You're looking very glamorous tonight. Scott is going to have a 'ard time getting on that plane,' she said with a twinkle in her eye.

'But we both know that get on it he will,' Fern said quietly.

Anouk nodded. 'You do like him, don't you?'

Fern nodded. 'I do.' There, she'd finally admitted it out loud.

'So you must enjoy this evening, make 'appy memories to tide you over until he returns. Because he will, I know.' Anouk smiled.

'Belinda will be here soon to keep you company,' Fern said. 'I hope she's ready for anything you might have to tell her. I've left a small supper tray out in the kitchen and a bottle of wine. Ah, I can hear Scott coming. I'll see you later.'

As the two of them were getting into Scott's car, Belinda drove in.

'Anouk's waiting for you in the conservatory,' Fern called out.

'Have a good evening you two,' Belinda answered. 'Scott, it's been a pleasure to meet you. Hope to see you again sometime.'

'Oh you will definitely see me again,' Scott assured her as he closed his car door.

Fern glanced across at him. He sounded so sure, so confident that he would return, she would have to trust he would.

Scott turned to look at her before he started the car. 'Am I allowed to tell you that you look beautiful tonight? Because you do.'

Fern smiled. 'Thank you. You're looking very smart too. Where are we going?'

'I found a small family-run restaurant in Carhaix that sounds as if it could be good. Lots of positive reviews on TripAdvisor anyway. To be honest, I just want to spend the evening with you. I don't really care what the food is like, probably won't be up to your standard anyway,' he said, grinning at her. 'In which case, I apologise in advance.'

When Scott turned onto the N164, Fern caught her breath. *It will be all right*, she muttered to herself. *It's the quickest way to Carhaix. It's not the same stretch. You're not driving. Just take deep breaths.* She closed her eyes but sensed Scott glancing across at her.

'Are you okay?' he asked.

'I'm not very good on this road. I'll be fine when we get to town,' Fern replied, deciding to be honest.

'Why this road? Oh,' Scott said as he realised the problem. 'I'm sorry. It didn't occur to me. This is the road I've been using since I've been here.'

'It's not your fault, Scott. But maybe I can show you a different route when we go home.' So much for wanting Scott to have special memories of her and the evening. He'd forever remember her now as the woman who almost had a panic attack in his car.

The rest of the journey passed in silence as Fern concentrated on her breathing and Scott on his driving. Parking in the main street, Scott took her hand as they made their way down a narrow lane towards the restaurant he'd chosen.

'Good choice,' Fern whispered as he pushed open the door and they were greeted by the maître d'. The table they were shown to was in a secluded corner, with candles in sconces on the walls alongside and a bowl of floating candles surrounded by red rose heads had been placed in the centre of the white tablecloth.

Scott ordered Kir royale aperitifs for them both while they looked at the menu. Once they'd given their orders and the large menus had been whisked away, Scott picked up his Kir and held it out for her to clink glasses. 'Here's to us,' he said. 'And to the future I hope we'll have.'

Fern gave him a tremulous smile. 'To our future.'

They chattered away like old friends over the course of the evening, when in fact they were new friends finding out about each other and liking what they learnt.

After their main course was finished, steak for Scott and lamb for Fern, Scott took a small package out of his pocket and, placing it on the table, pushed it towards Fern.

'I bought you something. I hope you like it and when you wear it, you'll think of me while I'm away.'

Fern's fingers trembled as she opened the small box she found inside the package. When she saw the contents, she looked at Scott and laughed. 'I love it. Thank you,' and she took the silver pendant of a Scottish Highland terrier out of the box and fastened it around her neck. 'Now I've got two Scotties.'

Scott reached across the table and picked her hand up. 'I will come back as soon as I can – you will wait, won't you?'

Fern felt her heart skip a beat as Scott looked deep into her eyes, almost willing her to answer. Did she like this man enough to do as he asked and wait for him to return? Deep down she already knew the answer.

'Yes of course I will.' As Fern smiled at him, she saw Scott give a deep sigh of relief.

'Good. Now, have you thought any more about Belinda's job offer?'

'Making cakes and desserts for the campsite? I have to admit it's the kind of thing I'd have jumped at years ago. I was surprised when Belinda suggested it though.'

'I think you should take her up on the offer. It would keep you busy.'

'I'll definitely think about it,' Fern said. 'I do like that sort of cooking. In fact, I made a tiramisu this afternoon, just to take my mind off things.'

'In that case I suggest I ask for the bill and we go home and sample it. Did I tell you I put a bottle of champagne in the fridge earlier?'

'No you didn't,' Fern said, laughing. 'Is that why you barely touched your aperitif and why I was the only one to have wine with our meal? You were saving yourself for later.'

'That and the fact I never drink and drive. Come on. You can show me the way to go home.'

Fern laughed.

'What's so funny?'

'That reminded me of the old song my dad used to sing when he came home from the pub after too many beers.'

'I wonder if it's the same one I know? You can sing it for me in the car,' Scott said.

Once in the car, after Fern had given him the scenic-route directions and they were driving homewards, Scott glanced at her and started to hum the tune. Within minutes they were both laughing as Scott sang an American parody of the song, while Fern tried to stick to the words she knew.

Half an hour later, after creeping into the house so as not to disturb Anouk, they were sitting on the auberge terrace, glasses of champagne on the table, two spoons and a dish of tiramisu between them. As she shared the dessert with Scott, Fern knew that the sense of connection between the two of them had deepened. It was a connection that she was beginning to want more from. Having agreed to wait for him she could only hope that Scott would fulfil his promise to return when he had sorted things in America.

33

Anouk was in the conservatory as Fern had said she would be. Belinda, about to call out 'Hello', stopped. The old lady was sat there, her eyes closed and her breathing slow, facing out over the garden. Belinda hesitated for a moment. As much as she longed to hear the truth about her parents, she didn't want to upset Anouk by asking her to drag up memories from the past. She would have been newly married in the late fifties, talking about those times would surely remind her of her husband and her life then. Belinda could only pray that Anouk's personal memories would be good ones because now she knew Anouk could tell her things about her parents, there was no way she couldn't ask the questions that she desperately needed the answers to.

'Anouk, I'm here,' Belinda said softly, walking into the conservatory. 'How are you this evening?'

'Bonsoir,' Anouk said, opening her eyes and smiling at Belinda. 'Come and sit down. Fern has left us some nibbles and some wine in the kitchen. Do you want to fetch it or save it for later?'

'Later,' Belinda said. 'I might need a drink after you've told me the truth about what you called the Belrose scandal.'

'I will tell you what I know but you must remember times were different back then.'

Anouk regarded her shrewdly. 'Do you really know rien – nothing – about your parents' break-up?'

Belinda shook her head. 'Nothing. Mum would never talk to me about it and I never got the chance to ask Dad. Mum died three years ago, but it was only recently that I finally went through the last of her papers. When she was dying, she said sorry and told me to visit and lay the ghosts to rest. I had no idea what ghosts she was talking about.' Belinda rubbed her face distractedly. 'It was the final box of papers that really made me realise there were things I did not know about. There were certain things missing that should have been there. Like a marriage certificate and divorce papers.'

Anouk nodded and sighed. 'I went to your father's wedding, you know.'

'You did? So they were married, even though I didn't find a marriage certificate.' Belinda's voice died away as Anouk shook her head.

'Not his wedding to your mother – Jean, wasn't it?'

Belinda nodded miserably.

'This was his first marriage. Helena Colbert was a local girl, in fact she's a distant relation of mine through my father's family. Younger than me, but we'd see each other at family get-togethers. Enzo and Helena grew up together and from an early age it was understood by everyone that they would end up marrying each other.' Anouk sighed. 'They were both so young, still teenagers. It was a beautiful day, Helena looked like a picture-book bride and Enzo couldn't take his eyes off her. Three months later, Helena was pregnant.'

Belinda caught her breath. Did that mean she had a sibling, or even siblings, somewhere?

'The two of them were apparently giddy with excitement at the thought of being a family. Sadly, the child was stillborn.' Anouk paused for a few seconds. 'And the bubble that 'ad encased their love and their lives burst. Helena went to pieces and then one day she just disappeared. No one heard anything about her for years. Her parents were devastated. Blamed Enzo, of course. They died still not knowing where Helena was.'

'That must have been very difficult for them,' Belinda said, trying to get her head around everything Anouk was telling her.

Anouk nodded. 'Enzo too was beside 'imself. His parents were good to him though and understood when he said he 'ad to get away. It was nearly six years before he came back, with a woman we all assumed was his new wife and you.'

'Had anyone heard from Helena in the meantime?' Belinda asked.

'No. Her parents were dead, there were no brothers or sisters.'

'Right, so Mum and Dad just settled down in the village near my grandmother and lived happily. I mean I had a lovely childhood, they rarely argued, I assumed my parents were happy together. I also assumed, of course, they were married. My parents were known as Mr and Mrs Belrose. Dad's named on my birth certificate. So what happened thirty-five years ago that made my mother run away?'

'Helena came back,' Anouk said simply. 'And all hell broke loose because...' Anouk took a deep breath. 'She told everyone Enzo was still married to her and she wanted him back. And that was the gist of the scandal: Enzo was living as a married man with a woman who wasn't his wife. The devout churchgoers around here couldn't accept that easily.' Anouk looked at Belinda. 'What was regarded as a scandal then wouldn't cause such a furore now.

Marriages break up and people move on these days with no stigma attached.'

Belinda stood up. 'I think I'm ready for that drink now.' She went into the kitchen and fetched the tray Fern had prepared and carried it out to the conservatory. She poured them both a glass of wine and handed one to Anouk and pushed the plate of sandwiches Fern had left for them towards her.

'So, Mum thought she'd be the laughing stock of the village – or worse,' Belinda said, finally able to fill in the blanks. 'And she ran away taking me with her, leaving Dad with Helena. I thought that Dad had had an affair.' Belinda smothered a sigh. For years she'd blamed her dad's affair for being the sole reason behind her mum leaving him and ruining their lives. Learning about Helena made it impossible not to feel a degree of sympathy for both her parents. But being secretly married to someone else was far worse than having an affair. Her dad might have been caught up in the middle but he was still guilty of letting her mum and herself down. Wasn't he?

Belinda helped herself to a sandwich before glancing at Anouk. 'That's half the story I had no idea about. Now, can you tell me what happened after we left?'

Anouk looked at her, sympathy clearly etched on her face. 'Helena moved in with your father, telling people as his wife she had every right to live there. Apparently the fact that Enzo told her he didn't want her there counted for nothing. She just stayed put. So Enzo himself moved out.' Anouk took a sip of her wine. 'Did you never try to contact Enzo without telling your mother?'

'Of course. I secretly planned to keep in touch with him by letter until I was old enough to come back and join him. I wrote a couple of letters but told him to reply to a friend's address so that mum wouldn't know. The last letter I wrote to him was a long one telling him how much I missed and loved him. That letter came back to our normal address, not the one I'd been secretly using. It had been opened and resealed, and marked Gone Away. Return to Sender. Mum saw the French stamp and was livid with me that day,' Belinda said reflectively. 'I was miserable and unhappy that Dad was rejecting my... Oh, it was her, wasn't it, Helena? Not Dad who returned the letter.'

Belinda could feel tears threatening and bit back on the names she wanted to call Helena but wouldn't in Anouk's presence.

Anouk gave her a sad smile. 'I think you could assume that.'

Belinda sat for several moments thinking about things and realised there was another question she needed to ask.

'He's still alive, you know.' Anouk's quiet voice broke into her thoughts.

'What?' Belinda stared at her.

'I rang a couple of people when Fern told me of your connection to Enzo to try and get some up-to-date information for you. While Helena has lived in the cottage permanently for a number of years, Enzo has been living down on the Morbihan coast. Recently though he moved back into the cottage.' Anouk hesitated. 'He's not well and Helena has taken on the task of nursing him.'

'Do you know what's wrong with him?' Belinda's voice trembled as she asked the question.

'No, but there's talk of moving him to a hospice in the not too distant future.'

Belinda took a drink of wine. This was all too much to take in – the burning question though was, should she go and see him? And importantly did she want to? He'd not been in contact with her for over thirty years so he probably wouldn't care one way or the other. But maybe seeing him in the flesh again would help her come to terms with the way he'd abandoned her.

Anouk stood up and reached for her stick. 'Belinda my dear, I do 'ope you'll forgive me if I go to bed now. The news this evening will have come as a shock to you and I know I've given you a lot to think about. But it's important to remember two things. The past has gone and you can't change anything about it. It's the future you need to pay attention to and nurture with a kind heart.'

Belinda stood up and moved across to the old lady to give her a gentle hug. 'Thank you for talking to me and reaching out to people to find out about my father. I sincerely hope I haven't tired you out. Can I get you anything before you retire?'

'No thank you. Fern always makes sure I have water in my bedroom and I have a book. Goodnight and see you again soon, I hope.'

'I'll take the supper tray through to the kitchen and close the front door behind me when I leave,' Belinda said.

Closing the auberge door behind her and reeling from the things Anouk had told her, Belinda pressed the key fob to open the car doors and sank down into the driver's seat. It was five minutes before she'd pulled herself together sufficiently to drive the short distance to the campsite.

As Belinda parked her car, Alain was coming out of the cottage with BB.

'Late-night patrol? May I come?'

'Of course. How did it go this evening? Did Anouk know anything?' Alain asked when Belinda rejoined him, having grabbed a jacket as well as changing her shoes.

'Yes. She'd taken the trouble to make some phone calls too. She knew the whole story bang up to date.'

As they walked, Belinda told Alain everything Anouk had told her, including the fact that her dad was still alive, if very ill.

'The thing I can't get my head around though is, did he ever tell Mum about Helena and the fact he was married? And did she convince herself she didn't want to get married because there was no chance of it happening. Or did the two of them decide together that they didn't need a marriage certificate? Mum always said they were a couple of hippies.' Belinda stopped. 'Actually, I don't think she did know. I still remember the way she flipped the day she dragged me away. Totally out of character for her.' Belinda shook her head. 'So much I don't understand and probably never will now.'

She stopped walking suddenly and turned to face Alain.

'How old are you exactly?'

'Fifty-five.'

'Two years older than me, so you would have been nineteen when the so-called "Belrose" scandal erupted,' Belinda said thoughtfully. 'Did you hear about it at the time?'

Alain shook his head. 'At the time, non. I am away in Rennes studying. Besides, I'm a young man and more interested in le football and les girls.' He paused and looked at her. 'Mais, my parents knew about it when I asked them today. I think they knew your mama.'

Belinda started walking again, her thoughts in turmoil.

'Do you want to go and see your father?' Alain asked quietly.

Belinda didn't answer him straight away and he didn't push her.

'I don't know,' she said eventually. 'I'm not sure I can forgive him for the hurt he caused Mum and me. Mum might have wanted me to lay the ghosts as she put it, but I'm not sure whether she knew he was still alive. One thing I forgot to tell you. He's back living in our old cottage with Helena. She's actually looking after him. Now, her, I definitely don't want to see.' Belinda could feel tears starting to break through and rubbed her eyes hard. 'I cried an ocean of tears years ago. How can I possibly have any left to cry over him?'

Alain gently and unexpectedly put his arms around her and held her tight. 'If you decide to go and see your father, I take you. Don't go alone.'

'I lost my father years ago. This man, Enzo Belrose, is a virtual stranger.' Belinda lost the fight with keeping the tears at bay and they soaked into Alain's jumper, but she didn't want to move. 'Sorry I'm making you all wet.'

'It doesn't matter.'

Standing there secure in Alain's arms, Belinda had a flashback to her father holding her tight when she'd been crying after her grandmother had died. She was shocked to realise the feeling of security she felt now with Alain's arms around her resembled the same sense of belonging she'd felt when her father hugged her.

'He lost you and your mama,' Alain said. 'I doubt he expected Helena to ever turn up again, let alone lay claim to 'im after all those years. Peut-être that was foolish of 'im, mais I think he's been a victim in all this as much as you and your mama.' Alain held her tightly as he said softly, 'Even if you can't forgive 'im, he might want to see you one last time.'

34

After their late-night patrol, Alain had accompanied Belinda back to the house and made her a hot chocolate.

'Things, they always look better in the morning,' he'd said, handing her the drink. 'Take this and go to bed and try to sleep. I told Hervé that I'd make sure the vide-grenier signs were all in place tonight for the morning. Twenty minutes and I return.'

Obediently, Belinda did as she was told and five minutes later she was sitting up in bed nursing the mug and sipping the rich drink. Sadly, despite the fact she felt emotionally exhausted, sleep didn't come when she turned off the light and snuggled down under the duvet. Everything Anouk had told her was going round and round in her head, throwing up new questions. Did it matter that her parents had never married? No. Had her dad loved her? Yes, she was sure he did. But why hadn't he kept in touch with her? Why hadn't he divorced Helena? Surely the five-year separation rule came into force here? Why had her mum turned on her dad and run away? Why? Why? Why? The questions kept coming. It was 3 a.m. when Belinda admitted to herself that if she wanted answers to at least some of her questions, as selfish as it probably was, she needed to visit her father before it was too late.

* * *

The smell of coffee woke her Sunday morning from the fitful sleep she'd finally sunk into and Belinda dragged herself out of bed at eight o'clock, feeling drained. A quick glance in the bathroom mirror confirmed she looked as bad as she felt. A hot shower went someway to making her feel better and a careful application of foundation and eye make-up managed to camouflage the worst of the lack of sleep damage to her face.

Alain was in the kitchen when she went downstairs and poured her a cup of coffee. 'Croissant?' he said, pointing to the plate on the table.

Belinda pulled a chair out and sat at the table before helping herself to one. 'Thanks.' She took a mouthful of coffee. 'Thank you for last night too,' she said. 'You make a mean hot chocolate.' She smothered a yawn. 'Sorry, I didn't get a lot of sleep. What time can we expect the hordes to arrive?'

'Hervé should be here any time soon and people wanting to set up in about twenty minutes.' Alain looked at her. 'You okay? You prefer to stay 'ere? 'Ave a day off?'

Belinda shook her head. 'Thanks, but I prefer to be doing something.'

A car door slammed outside and a minute later Hervé knocked on the door. 'Bonjour à vous. Ready for a fun day?'

'Oui. Allons-y. Belinda will follow us later,' and to Belinda's relief, Alain ushered Hervé away before he came into the kitchen. She needed the caffeine to kick in before she was up to meeting and greeting people properly.

It was half an hour later, after two cups of coffee, before she felt ready to face the busy day ahead. Checking she had some money in her pocket and clipping BB's lead on before locking the cottage door behind her, she ventured outside to find the campsite bustling with activity.

Alain had nailed signs to trees pointing to the parking area and also roped off the area where people could set up their tables. Belinda knew that Hervé was expecting about fifty stallholders to set up their individual tables and already most of these were in place, ahead of the official opening at ten o'clock.

As she wandered around, Belinda walked past tables selling children's toys, clothes and games, books, bric-a-brac, plants, kitchen utensils, furniture, pictures. Everything, in fact, including the kitchen sink, was for sale. Belinda stopped by one particular seller who had simply set out her things on two large cloths on the ground. In amongst the plates, the coffee grinders, the pictures, the candles and the miscellaneous cutlery the woman had laid on the second cloth, was a battered and chipped painted plaster cast of a horse's head. Belinda bent down and picked it up as her mind went straight back to her childhood.

For her tenth birthday, she'd received a modelling kit with several different horse moulds, a large bag of Plaster of Paris and paints. Her favourite mould had been a horse head just like this one that her dad had helped her to make. Once it was ready, she'd painted it to look as much like Lucky as she could. She'd mixed colours until she'd obtained just the right shiny chestnut colour for the head and carefully added the long white baize down the face once it was dry. She'd been so proud of herself. The finished head had sat on the shelf in her room until...

'C'est five euros.' The stallholder's voice brought Belinda out of her reverie.

She smiled at the woman before pulling a five-euro note out of her pocket and handing it to her. She didn't really want the chipped ornament but couldn't find it in her to say so. It had brought back a precious happy memory. 'Merci.' Belinda turned and moved away. She'd put it on the table in her room and take it back to the UK when she left.

The car park was filling up and more people were milling around, laughing and joking as they met up with friends and family, all scanning the tables and stalls for that elusive item that could be worth a fortune, or at the very least be a bargain they couldn't refuse.

Because the café wasn't open, she and Alain had agreed to Yann setting up his catering van, selling coffee, cold drinks and, later in the day, there would be glasses of wine and beer for sale. She could see Alain was over there, talking to Yann and Hervé, and she wandered over to join them.

'Something tells me that you were horse-mad when you were younger,' Alain said, looking at the head.

'I was. I even made plaster models like this one,' Belinda confessed. 'Trip down memory lane. A happy one,' she assured him when she caught his anxious glance.

'Peut-être you ride these days?' Hervé asked. 'I 'ave two horses.'

'I haven't ridden for years,' Belinda said, shaking her head. 'But thank you.' She turned to Alain. 'I thought I'd go and see if Marie would like a break from the office and have a look round. I'll see you later.'

Wandering back to the office Belinda delighted in seeing the campsite brought to life with people milling around, searching for bargains on the stalls and generally enjoying themselves. There was even a game of boule being played on the pitch at the edge of the entertainment area. Maybe Alain was right – access to traditional things was vital and that a feeling of community was still important in these days of hi-tech.

35

Fern and Anouk went back into the kitchen after waving Scott goodbye on Monday morning. Wordlessly, Fern made another pot of coffee and the two of them were lost in their own thoughts for a few moments as they drank.

Anouk was the first to break the silence. 'If it's all right with you, I thought I'd spend the morning tidying up the pots on the terrace. The tulips have gone over now and need sorting.'

'We can do it together,' Fern said. 'I haven't got anything pressing to do.'

Anouk gave her a stern look. 'I'm more than capable of sorting out a few bulbs on my own. If I was still in Huelgoat, I'd be doing my own pots by myself. Besides, this morning you're taking Lady for a walk to the campsite. Belinda will be pleased to see you, I think, after our talk Saturday evening.'

'Were you able to tell her much about what happened in the past? Was she upset?'

Anouk nodded. 'Yes to both questions. I think this morning she will appreciate a fellow countrywoman to talk to. As for you, a walk in the countryside is good for the soul. While you're there, you can discuss terms and conditions with Belinda for the baking you're going to be doing this summer.'

'I haven't decided yet whether I—'

Anouk's stern look silenced her in mid-sentence. 'It will be good for you to have something definite to concentrate on.'

Fern laughed. 'Okay. I'll go and talk to Belinda. I shall have a moan to her about this bully I unwittingly invited to live with me.'

'You think I'm bullying you?' Anouk said, her eyes twinkling. 'You wait until I've really settled in.'

Fern took her time walking Lady to Camping dans La Fôret, listening to the birds singing in the hedgerows and enjoying the sight of primroses nestled in the verges. She'd always found this time of year joyous as the countryside burgeoned back from the drabness of winter's bare branches and started to wear its summer clothes. This year, it seemed to her that the early colours were that little bit brighter.

Belinda was in the office with Alain, both of them intent on some papers spread out over the desk as Fern opened the door and walked in.

'Hi, you two. Am I interrupting a busy morning? Anouk virtually threw me out of the house this morning for a walk,' Fern said, looking at her friend and noting the puffy eyes and tiredness etched on her face. 'Can I drag you away for a walk down to the river?' She saw Belinda hesitate and look at Alain.

'Sounds like a plan to me,' Alain said. 'You can grab a croissant from the shop too, since you didn't 'ave any breakfast. This can wait until later,' he added, looking at Belinda and gesturing at the plan.

'You sure? Thanks,' Belinda said. 'Come on BB,' and she clipped his lead onto his collar.

Fern waited outside the shop with the two dogs while Belinda bought a couple of almond slices and together they ambled down through the campsite towards the river.

'Are you okay?' Fern asked quietly. 'You don't look too good, if I'm honest.'

'Didn't sleep very well last night,' Belinda admitted. 'Did Anouk tell you what she told me?'

'Just the barest outline of your dad being married before he met your mum.'

'Did she also mention my father is still alive and living back in our old family home with his wife – the one he was legally married to while supposedly married to my mum,' Belinda said bitterly before sighing and biting her bottom lip. Fern realised she was struggling to find her next words. 'The fact that he is dying is another "something" that has added to my angst.' She was silent for a few seconds. 'Do I go and see him or not?' Belinda turned to Fern. 'Alain has offered to take me but...' She wiped tears off her cheeks. 'What do you think?'

'Will you regret it if you don't go and see him?' Fern asked.

'There's already a long list of regrets in my head concerning him. Adding one more to the pile won't make a difference.'

'Possibly not, but the fact that this particular chance will never be there again once he's dead is inescapable,' Fern said.

'But I can't even be sure that he'll want to see me,' Belinda muttered.

They walked along in silence for a few moments until they reached the gate in the hedge. Belinda pushed it open and they went through and stood on the river path for a minute until they both turned and sat on the nearby wooden bench.

Fern glanced at the paper bag in Belinda's hand. 'Might be a good idea if we ate those almond slices before you mangle them completely.'

Belinda glanced down at the bag. 'I'm not very hungry,' she said, holding the bag out to Fern.

'You need to keep your sugar levels up, especially as you didn't eat breakfast according to Alain,' Fern insisted, opening the bag and waiting until Belinda had given in and scooped out a few pieces of broken cake.

'The thing is, I'm so angry with him for not being honest with Mum and me that I'm scared I'll lose it when I see him. The other things is, I'm not sure I'm brave enough to go the cottage when "she" is there – the last person on this earth that I want to meet.'

'I can understand that might be difficult.' Fern nodded thoughtfully. 'Oh, Belinda, I honestly don't know what to suggest as it's a decision you'll have to live with for the rest of your life and it's one only you can make.'

'It's so hard to know what to do for the best.' Belinda sighed. 'And Chloe is coming for a visit soon. I have to tell her about her unknown grandfather.'

'Why don't you give yourself a twenty-four hour respite before you decide how to handle things?' Fern said. 'I know you won't be able to stop thinking about it totally and it will still be churning away in your subconscious.' She hesitated. 'But, you never know, the decision may simply make itself apparent. I know I've agonised over problems in the past, but the moment I stopped giving them my full attention, consigned them to my subconscious, the solution came to me. I'm sorry if that sounds all a bit airy-fairy, but sometimes it can happen like that.'

'It does a bit,' Belinda said, giving her a watery smile. 'Certainly worth a try though.'

'Just remember, whatever you decide has to be the right decision for you. Nobody else. I'm always ready to listen, but I can't make the decision, okay?'

Belinda nodded. 'Thanks.'

'Now, in an effort to take your mind off things for five minutes, do you want to tell me more about the kind of cakes and food you're thinking of for the café?'

Belinda turned to Fern delighted. 'You're going to do it? Brilliant news.'

'Hang on. I haven't agreed yet, despite Anouk telling me I need to do it.' Fern smiled.

'Come on. I've got the keys to the café in my pocket. I'll show you round. You won't need to cook up here because your kitchen in the auberge is fully up to standard, but I want to tell you about the kind of set-up we hope to create.'

Belinda glanced at her friend. 'And I'm hoping too that you'll do more than provide some of the food.'

Fern looked at her, eyebrows raised.

'I'll explain more in a moment,' Belinda said.

36

After Fern had left to walk back to the auberge, Belinda returned to the office.

'Good you're back,' Alain said, pushing some papers into a briefcase that Belinda had never seen him use before. 'I'm sorry, but I've got to go out for an urgent meeting. Will you be all right for a couple of hours?'

'Yes.'

'Nigel phoned. Said he's going to call you after lunch.'

Puzzled, Belinda looked at him. 'I had my phone with me. Why didn't he phone me? I'd better call him back.'

'Non. Wait for him to phone you,' Alain said, giving her a look she couldn't interpret. 'Think he's a bit busy for a couple of hours. Right, I'm off. Wish me luck.'

'Why do you need luck?'

'I'll explain when I get 'ome,' and Alain was gone.

Belinda gave a little laugh. His words about getting home made it sound as though they were living together. Which they were, of course, but not quite in the way it had sounded.

The rest of the day trundled on routinely. When Marie

arrived to take over reception for a couple of hours, Belinda took her laptop and returned to the cottage. It was a lovely sunny afternoon and she opened the sitting room French doors and went out onto the small terrace. She was sitting out there working yet again on the website when Nigel phoned.

'Hi, Nigel, how's things? Molly?'

'Molly is much better, thank you. And things, well things here have changed.'

She heard the troubled note in Nigel's voice and instinctively responded. 'Nigel, please tell me you're not ill now, are you?'

'No, it's nothing like that, but...' He sighed. 'This is a difficult conversation to have on the phone, but the truth is, I've accepted an offer for the rest of the business, lock, stock and barrel as they say.'

Belinda sat in stunned silence. The thing she'd been worried about had happened. Nigel was actually selling the other two hotels.

'You still there?' Nigel asked. 'I'm sorry to break it to you over the phone, but it's happened so quickly, I'm still spinning myself.'

'You never mentioned the possibility of this when I was over,' Belinda said, dazed, trying to gather her thoughts and work out what Nigel's news meant for her.

'It hadn't kicked off then. It was when word got out about Moorside being sold that I started to get enquiries for the other two. Molly and I talked about it and decided that it was too good an offer to refuse and now would be a good time for us to retire to our place in Cannes and enjoy some sunshine.'

'Can't see you retired somehow,' Belinda said. 'I give you six months and you'll be running a club somewhere on the coast.'

'Don't think Molly will let me,' Nigel said. 'With this health scare of hers, she's determined we're going to take things quieter, enjoy life. Now, Belinda,' and Nigel's voice changed.

Belinda tensed, dreading what was coming next.

'The new owners are happy to keep you on as manager for Riverside and for you to live in your apartment until New Year. But in January they intend to review the situation.'

Belinda suspected there would be a hidden agenda in there. Use her expertise and pick her brains and then, come January in all probability, they'd 'restructure' the business and she'd lose her job and her home. Maybe it would be better to leave before she was pushed.

'Can I have time to think about it before agreeing to stay on? Perhaps it's time for me to have a change too,' Belinda said. 'When is the sale due to be completed?'

'End of June. Whatever you decide, I promise Molly and I will see you all right. We've already earmarked a healthy bonus for you from the sale proceeds. A reward for all you've done over the past few years.'

'That's so good of you, Nigel, thank you. Have you sold the campsite as well?'

'Still under negotiation, but yes, the idea is to sell that too.'

Briefly, Belinda wondered how Alain would feel about that. She knew how she felt as Nigel ended the call. Sick at the unexpectedness of it and shattered as yet another problem reared its head in her life. It seemed as if her whole world had started to implode since she'd arrived back in Brittany.

Belinda was still sitting outside when Alain got home, playing an aimless game of solitaire on the laptop while trying to get her head around the three major problems life had hoisted on her. First, there was the problem of her father. Should she go and see him while she was over here in France? Or would it be too painful for both of them? Second, should she stay, keep her home and work for the new company until the end of the year – or leave?

And last, but not least, was Chloe's imminent move to Vendée. Go with them? Or not?

She could hear Alain moving around in the kitchen and the oven being slammed before he appeared on the terrace.

'Hi,' she said. 'How did your meeting go?'

'Good. Fancy a slice of pizza in about five minutes?'

'Just a small slice. I'm not that hungry,' Belinda said.

Alain looked at her. 'Where do you want to eat, out 'ere or in the kitchen?'

'Here please. I'll come and get plates and glasses,' Belinda said.

Five minutes later, Alain placed the pizza on the table and pushed it towards her. 'Eat.'

Belinda picked up the smallest slice she could see and dutifully started to eat. Three mouthfuls in and she realised she was in fact starving and she devoured two more slices while Alain watched her in amusement.

'Nigel phoned,' Belinda said between mouthfuls. 'Did he tell you he's sold the other two hotels and probably this place?'

Alain nodded.

'Apparently the new owners will keep me on in Riverside until the end of the year, if I want to stay. What about here? Are you going to stay and work for the new owners if this place sells?'

'Definitely.'

Belinda looked at him. 'Aren't you worried about them? Don't expect them to be as easy-going as Nigel has been over everything here,' Belinda said darkly. 'And what about Bernie. You'll have to warn him. Where will he end up if he has to move?'

'I make sure Bernie will be okay and the village will rally around to 'elp. Don't worry. Everything will work out,' Alain said. 'More pizza?'

Belinda stared at him, puzzled. How could he be so laid-back about this latest turn of events? What if the new owners insisted on major changes like, heaven forbid, Alain's dreaded pods being installed. No, she figured, Alain hadn't yet thought it through properly. It was nothing to do with her, she didn't even live here, but she felt sick at the thought of the possible changes that the new owners would want to make to the campsite. There were sure to be unforeseen effects spreading out like ripples on the river.

37

The next morning, Belinda phoned Chloe and told her about the hotels being sold as well as, probably, the campsite. 'If I don't agree to stay on until the end of the year, my job and home will disappear in a few weeks.'

'Oh, Mum. What are you going to do?'

'Right this moment, I have no idea.' Belinda sighed wearily. 'I hadn't planned on changing my job or losing my home this year.'

'If you decide not to stay with the new owners you can come and live here until we move or you could find a new place.' The hesitation was clear in Chloe's voice as she added, 'It would mean you'd be free to come to the Vendée with us without worrying.'

'I might need to take you up on the offer of moving in with you for a few weeks, so thanks for that,' Belinda said. 'But as far as the Vendée is concerned, I'm still not sure about moving there permanently, although I might come for a couple of weeks and help you settle in.' Belinda paused. 'Chloe? You are still coming to stay with the twins at the campsite, aren't you?'

'Of course. Looking forward to it. Why, is there a problem?'

'No, not a problem for you as such. It's just that something important has happened recently here in Brittany.'

'You're not ill, are you?' Chloe said.

'No, I'm not ill. It's just something I need to talk to you about when I see you.'

'Can't you tell me now?'

Belinda hesitated. 'I'd rather wait and tell you face to face. Explain things properly.'

'Okay, if you're sure,' Chloe said. 'I'll try not to worry about what it is.'

Belinda immediately began feeling guilty for worrying Chloe. 'It's absolutely nothing for you to worry about. It's... it's just some family history that has surfaced.'

Finishing the call with Chloe, Belinda phoned Jane. As usual, Jane was bright and breezy when she answered the phone.

'Hi. How you doing over there with the Serge Gainsbourg lookalike? Can't wait to meet him.'

'You need to visit fairly soon if that's going to happen,' Belinda said flatly, and gave her the news about Nigel selling up and retiring. Jane was suitably horrified for her friend when Belinda gave her the details.

'What are you going to do?'

'The answer to that question is floating in the air somewhere and I have yet to catch it,' Belinda said. 'I've got a few weeks to sort something out. Anyway, right now I'd better go and do some work. Ring me when you've worked some dates out.'

Working around the campsite for the rest of the day, Belinda struggled to concentrate on the various jobs she'd earmarked to do. By the time she'd finished work for the day though, she'd made one of three important decisions. She'd tell Nigel she'd decided she didn't want to work with the new owners and would therefore resign. Apart from the fact that working for somebody other than Nigel and Molly in what for her would always be their hotels didn't appeal, Belinda was starting to think that all her current problems were a sign. A sign that it was time she moved on with her life. The next two decisions would follow on from that one. She'd go home at the end of the month, pack the flat up and move in temporarily with Chloe. If she hadn't found a new job and a place to live when they moved, she'd go with them for a few weeks and, after that, who knew? The Vendée might be the place for her too, although if she was going to live in France, she realised she'd prefer to live in Brittany. She just had to trust that she'd make the right decision when the time came.

She was relieved too that Chloe knew she needed to talk to her when she came. As well as talking, she'd give her a guided tour of the places she'd known when growing up. It wasn't fair to keep Chloe in ignorance about her grandparents; their history was part of hers and she had a right to know.

Belinda sighed. Life was being a bit of a bitch right now, but at least she was making plans to sort things out. Besides, no one could ever predict what the future might hold, could they?

* * *

The next few days passed in a blur of work. Belinda and Alain left Marie in charge of the office and concentrated on getting the café and its kitchen ready for the inspectors' visit. After her initial visit to the café and Belinda's surprise job offer, Fern had agreed to become the part-time manager of the café as well as supplying cakes and some meals. Most days she joined them for a couple of hours, helping to get the café ready. Alain had put the word out in the village that they were looking for catering staff and Fern joined them when they interviewed the five or six people who applied for jobs.

One afternoon, Fern arrived to tell them about a delivery for the next day and also to give them a broccoli quiche for supper. 'It a different recipe – a bit spicier than I usually make it. Need to know what you think.'

Belinda picked up a crusty baguette and prepared a salad to go with the quiche when she got back to the cottage that afternoon. Placing the meal on the table, she called out 'À table' to Alain, who'd gone upstairs to take a shower, just as her mobile rang. Fern. They'd only said goodbye half an hour ago.

'Hi, Fern. Everything all right?'

'I thought I'd let you know, Anouk heard from a friend this afternoon that your father has been moved into the hospice this morning. So, if you do decide to go and say farewell, you wouldn't have to go to the cottage. You might still come face to face with Helena at the hospice though.'

Belinda closed her eyes and sighed. The message was clear. Her dad was edging closer to the end. If she was going to see him alive one last time, then she would have to visit soon. She thanked Fern and ended the call as Alain came downstairs and she went into the kitchen for the wine to accompany the meal. She poured two glasses and handed one to Alain.

'My father has been moved into the hospice.' She took a deep breath. 'Did you mean what you said about taking me? If you did, I think I'd like to go the day after tomorrow if possible.'

'I'll take you,' Alain said gently. 'But you must eat something as well as drink, otherwise you'll be too weak to go anywhere,' and he pushed the quiche towards her.

38

The morning of the visit to the hospice, Belinda showered and, feeling foolish, hesitated over what to wear for meeting her dad after such a long time. What did it matter in the scheme of things what she wore? But somehow it did matter. Dad had always liked to see her dressed stylishly. Belinda smiled to herself. He'd have been horrified if he'd ever seen her during her goth phase. The problem was her current wardrobe was purely practical: a couple of pairs of jeans, sweatshirts, T-shirts and two or three white long-sleeved cotton shirts. She felt ridiculously pleased when, having decided on a sweatshirt and jeans, underneath the sweatshirts in the drawer, she found the Breton striped top she'd bought on her visit home and hadn't yet worn. Perfect with her best jeans and her wedge sandals.

There was no sign of Alain when she went downstairs, but the coffee machine was on and there was a note propped against it. 'Bernie will have BB for the day. Can you walk BB down to him? As soon as Marie arrives, we'll go. P.S. You need more than coffee. Have a croissant.'

Belinda forced herself to eat half a croissant and washed it down with her coffee. The way her tummy was churning she prayed it would stay put during the journey. Clipping BB's lead on, she walked down to Bernie's cabin. Still early, there were a few campers sitting out enjoying the early-morning sunshine quiet and eating breakfast outside. Bernie was sitting outside his cabin with a mug of coffee on a small table next to him, waiting for her. Ging was curled up again in the bicycle basket.

'Demat, Bernie,' Belinda said.

Bernie smiled. 'Demat, Belinda,' and he held out his hand for BB's lead.

'Trugarez,' Belinda said, remembering the word for thank you in Breton. She bent down and stroked BB, who was already curled up at Bernie's feet. 'You be good. Au revoir,' she said, trusting it was such a universal word that Bernie couldn't fail to know it and waved before turning to walk back to the cottage to collect her bag, car keys and jacket.

There was a large Mitsubishi 4 x 4 car parked outside the office when she went to find Alain. Hopefully Marie would be able to deal with whoever had arrived and not delay Alain and her leaving. Belinda stood by her car waiting and wondering whether she should go and seek Alain out. Before she could climb the steps to the office though, he appeared.

'Ready?'

Belinda nodded. 'Yes. Who does that belong to?'

'Me,' Alain said, pressing the key fob. 'Come on, in you get.' He opened the passenger door for her.

Belinda couldn't contain her surprise. 'Yours? You've traded the 2CV in?'

Alain shook his head. 'Non. The 2CV is for local trips and is fun. This, this is for serious journeys.' Once she was in, he closed the door and walked round and got in the driver's seat. 'I've set the satnav for the quickest route. Should take under an hour.'

Belinda, thankful she didn't have to concentrate on driving, sat lost in thoughts and memories that chased themselves around and around in her head as the miles flashed past. The car radio was switched to a classic station playing gentle piano music, the sort that could send you to sleep if you weren't careful, Belinda thought. Alain, concentrating on his driving, glanced across at her once or twice but didn't attempt to make conversation, something for which Belinda was grateful.

'I've forgotten to buy him something. I should have brought a gift,' Belinda said, suddenly in a panic at the thought of the forthcoming meeting. 'Flowers or something.'

'I think seeing you will be a gift enough,' Alain said.

Belinda sank back down into her seat. 'I hope you're right.'

When Alain pulled up into a visitor's parking space to one side of the hospice, Belinda didn't want to get out of the car. Her legs seemed to be frozen into position and wouldn't move.

'Alain, I don't think I can do this,' she said.

'Yes you can,' Alain said gently. 'Take deep breaths and think positive thoughts. You want me to go first and see if Enzo is well enough for visitors? I tell them who you are? I make sure that you don't bump into Helena.'

'Please.'

Alain got out of the car and walked round to Belinda's side. 'Come on, out you get. There's a bench by the main entrance, you can sit there and wait. The fresh air will be good for you.'

Belinda sat on the bench waiting for Alain to return, trying not to shake with nerves. She'd had over twenty-four hours to psych herself up for this visit and suddenly it wasn't enough. She needed more time – except there would never be enough time. She stared at the modern L-shaped single-storey building. Her father was in there dying. Wouldn't it be better to keep her memories of him intact? Not destroy them by seeing him as an ill old man. What if he didn't recognise her? What if he told her to go away? Round and round the questions went until she felt dizzy.

'The nurse is with him at the moment, once she's finished, you can see him.' Alain's quiet voice broke her out of her reverie. 'And Helena is not expected until after lunch today.' He held his hand out. 'Come on. I'll take you in.'

Taking a deep breath Belinda stood and reached out for Alain's hand. This was it, now or never. She could choose to walk into the hospice and see her father for the first time in thirty-five years or she could walk away.

A nurse smiled her welcome at Belinda. 'Mrs Marshall? I'll take you through to see your father.'

'Does he know I'm here?' Belinda asked nervously. 'We haven't been in touch for a very long time. I don't want to upset him. If you think it's a bad idea, I can leave.'

'Yes, he knows you're here. I'll come in with you and if I think it's too much, I'll ask you to leave, okay? Here we are,' and she pushed the door open onto a light airy room.

Belinda studied the face of the man who lay in the bed by the window for several seconds, unable to move forward.

The nurse was at his side, speaking gently, 'Enzo, your daughter is here to see you.'

Enzo turned his head to look at Belinda standing at the foot of his bed. 'Blindy.'

Belinda, forcing back the tears that threatened at the sound of the old nickname, smiled. 'Dad,' she said as she cautiously made her way towards the side of the bed and sat on the chair the nurse had placed there.

'Oh, Blindy, I never thought to see you again,' Enzo said, reaching out with his hand for hers.

Belinda gently took the liver-spotted hand with its arthritic swollen knuckles in hers. 'I love you, Dad. I've missed you so much.'

Enzo shook his head. 'I'm so sorry. I've missed you too.'

'Shh. We're together again now, so let's make the best of it. We've a lot of catching up to do.' She sat looking at him, gently stroking his hand and wondering where to begin after all those years of not being in touch.

'Is... is Jean with you?'

Belinda's hand stilled and she bit her lip. He didn't know. She shook her head. 'No. She died three years ago.'

Enzo closed his eyes but couldn't stop the tears sliding down his cheeks. Belinda took a tissue from the packet on the bedside table and gently wiped his face. She sat there not speaking, holding and stroking his hand, waiting for him to come to terms with the sad news.

It was several moments before Belinda saw Enzo's chest heave as he took a deep breath before opening his eyes. 'She was the love of my life and I failed her. Did she ever forgive me?'

'Mum urged me to come to Brittany and lay the ghosts to rest,' Belinda said. 'She told me she was sorry too.' She couldn't in all honesty say whether her mum had forgiven him, she didn't know, but Enzo seemed to accept her answer and squeezed her hand. 'I'm sorry it's taken me so long to come and find you. I wish... I wish I'd come three years ago when I promised Mum.'

She fought back the tears, inwardly berating herself for allowing the feelings of abandonment to overrule her need to have contact with her dad. Seeing him, like this, she knew she would have given anything to turn the clock back and grab whatever extra time with him she could.

'You're here now. That's all that matters.' Enzo closed his eyes again and they both sat in silence for a few moments, Belinda struggling with her emotions and suspecting that Enzo was the same.

The nurse came in, quietly and efficiently checked everything was all right, smiled at Belinda and left the room again.

'You look like your mum,' Enzo said quietly, opening his eyes to watch her. 'Beautiful. Tell me about your life.'

'I have a daughter, Chloe, your granddaughter, and she has twins, Charlie and Aimee, which makes you a great-grandad. I have some photos on my phone. Would you like to see?'

When Enzo nodded, Belinda took her phone out and scrolled through to find a couple of Chloe and the twins. She stood up and angled the phone so that Enzo could see the screen.

'Chloe, she looks like you,' Enzo said. 'I would have liked to meet her.' His words, tinged with regret, were barely audible.

Belinda hesitated, unsure if she was doing the right thing. 'She's actually coming to Brittany in a few days. If the doctor agrees, and you're well enough, would you like me to bring her to see you?'

'That would be wonderful.' Enzo smiled. 'You are married then?'

'Divorced,' she answered briefly. 'Unexpected, but I'm happy about that now.'

'Do you work?'

'Yes. I qualified in hotel management and I work for a chain of three hotels in Devon, but that is about to change. At the moment, I'm helping to renovate Camping dans Le Fôret, a camp-site not a million miles from where we lived.' She smiled at her father. 'I have to admit being back in Brittany feels like coming home.'

'That's good to hear. I never stopped loving you or your mum, you know. I so wish things could have been different for all of us,' Enzo said, his eyes glistening. 'But Helena...' He stopped and shrugged shoulders that Belinda could see were painfully thin under his pyjama top.

'Don't, Dad,' Belinda said. 'I know we'd both change things if we could, but we can't and now is not the time for recriminations. Now is the time to forgive.'

Enzo nodded and closed his eyes and Belinda realised her visit had tired him out and he'd drifted into sleep. Carefully, she stood up and kissed his forehead.

'I promise I'll come again and bring Chloe to see you if I can. Love you.'

The nurse came in as she turned to leave.

'He's fallen asleep,' Belinda whispered. 'I hope my visit hasn't been too much for him.'

The nurse shook her head. 'No, the drugs he's on caused that. Was it a good visit for you both?'

Belinda nodded. 'Yes it was. I'm glad I came and ended our estrangement.' She looked at the nurse. 'I did tell him that if the doctor agrees, I'll come back with his granddaughter. Will that be possible?'

'I'll have a word with the doctor. Telephone me later and I'll tell you what he says.'

'Thank you.' Belinda paused. 'Does my father's wife come at set times to see him?'

'She comes in the afternoon and spends the evening with him,' the nurse said. 'I understand there is something of a family rift, so perhaps it's best if you come late morning, say?' she looked at Belinda.

'I'll ring before I come. Thank you for your understanding.' Belinda looked at the nurse as they walked back to the foyer together. 'How long do you think my father has?' she asked quietly. It was the question she needed to ask but in truth, she didn't want to hear the answer voiced.

'One never can tell, but I doubt it will be long.'

Belinda nodded sadly at the nurse's words. 'If I give you my number,' she said, scrabbling in her bag for a piece of paper and a pencil, 'will you let me know when...'

'Of course I will,' the nurse answered, accepting the piece of paper from Belinda.

'Ah, here is your husband waiting for you. Goodbye.'

Belinda went to protest that Alain wasn't her husband, but the nurse had already turned away.

'Are you all right?' Alain looked at her anxiously.

Belinda nodded and smiled through the tears that were now coursing freely down her cheeks. 'He called me Blindy. The worse part was I had to tell him Mum was dead. He was so upset. Oh, Alain, what a dreadful waste the last thirty-five years have been.'

When Alain pulled her into a fierce hug and held her tight, she didn't protest. She simply gave herself up to the feeling that everything would be all right if only Alain could be around in her life to hug her whenever she needed a hug. Even as she stood in the shelter of his arms Belinda caught her breath at the unexpected thought. Where had that come from? It was just the emotion of the day getting to her – wasn't it?

39

Back at the campsite, Alain said he'd go and check on Marie and collect the lasagna he'd ordered from Fern for their supper while Belinda walked down to Bernie's cabin to collect BB.

Walking through the campsite, thoughts about the visit to her dad were still swirling around in her brain. As she'd said to the nurse, she was happy the estrangement was over, but in reality the visit was too late to talk in-depth about the whys and the wherefores of what had happened to their family all those years ago. So many questions would remain unanswered forever because of Enzo's illness, but she'd be forever glad that she'd kept her promise to her mum. Her dad had always loved her.

Bernie was working in the small garden he'd created in the small strip of land down the side of his cabin. BB was lying on the path watching him and jumped up wagging his tail when Belinda appeared.

Bernie straightened up and smiled at her. 'Ça va?' he said slowly.

Belinda nodded. 'Merci. BB bon?'

Bernie smiled and nodded.

Belinda didn't have the energy to search her brain for Breton words to have a stilted conversation with Bernie, so she simply smiled when he held out BB's lead and said, 'Merci. À demain,' and hoped he'd understand and forgive her for not staying.

She started to walk away but felt a gentle tap on her shoulder. Bernie, with a smile on his face, was holding out three large Marguerite daisies for her. Daisies he'd clearly just picked from the large plant growing at the front of the cabin. Touched, she took them before leaning in towards him and kissing his cheek. 'Merci, Bernie.'

Fighting back the tears at Bernie's unexpected kind gesture, Belinda walked on towards her favourite place: the bench by the river. Ten minutes here would calm her and restore her equilibrium before she returned to the cottage for supper with Alain. She pushed open the gate in the hedge and sank down gratefully on the bench. Her presence disturbed a heron standing on the bank just metres away and she watched as the large bird took off to fly downriver before curving towards the opposite bank and landing on the mud at the water's edge.

Belinda sat there letting her mind wander over the day. The way her father had been so pleased to see her. The way he'd said Jean was the love of his life. The way he'd spoken the name Helena and shrugged.

A question that only he could answer, but one that Belinda knew she could never ask him at this stage of his life, dropped into her mind: Had he been truly happy with Helena? Or had he, like her mum, lived the last thirty-five years with the biggest mistake of his life?

Belinda sighed. She'd never know the whole truth. Neither would she tell him how unhappy Jean had been living her life without him.

Her mobile rang at that moment. Alain.

'Are you okay? Where are you?'

'I'm fine. Sitting down by the river.'

'Supper is ready when you are.'

'Okay. On my way back. And, Alain, thank you. Thank you for today.'

* * *

Belinda sniffed the air appreciatively as she walked into the kitchen. 'Supper smells delicious. Meals like this are going to be so popular in the café. Fern will be the making of it. I hope the new owners will appreciate her.'

Alain glanced up from the salad he was preparing. 'If they've got any sense they will.'

Belinda put the cutlery and glasses on the table and started to tell Alain about the decisions she'd made.

'I haven't told Nigel yet, but I'm not going to work for the new owners. At the end of this month, I'll go home, work a month's notice, clear out the flat, move in with Chloe, start job hunting and hope and pray I have a new job and home before they move to the Vendée.'

Alain poured them both a glass of wine and they clinked glasses before Belinda continued.

'I've also told my friend, Jane, to visit before the end of the month. I don't want the new owners sending me a bill for an unauthorised holiday.'

'That won't happen,' Alain said, laughing.

'You can't be sure; I know what these hard-headed busi-nessmen are like.' Belinda sighed. 'I can't believe how much I'm going to miss this place.'

'Then stay. Work with me. You are good, together we could

make this place really work.' Alain stared at her, waiting for a reply.

Surprised at the way her heart jumped at his offer and filled her with the overwhelming desire to do just that, Belinda knew that it was an impossible dream and pushed the thought away.

'Nice idea, but no. And, just so you know, it's not you, it's them.' Which was the partial truth. She longed to say yes to working with this new gentler Alain, someone whom she was getting to appreciate having in her life, but who knew what the new owners were going to be like?

'Well, if you ever change your mind, let me know. Come on, let's eat,' and Alain took the lasagna out of the oven.

After they'd helped themselves and started to eat, Alain glanced at Belinda curiously.

'Did you ever have a dream when you were younger? Something that you wanted to do so badly it became an obsession?'

'Not really. Although at one stage I desperately wanted to be a rally driver. The summer we left, Dad had bought me a 2CV like yours but...' She shrugged. 'Let's not go there tonight,' and she picked up her wine glass and took several gulps.

'I've had this dream, not since I was a kid, but for a good few years now. Camping dans Le Fôret is at the heart of it.' Alain forked a spoonful of lasagna up. 'You know of Michael Morpurgo, the writer?'

'Yes, I've heard of him. I've even bought a couple of his books. He and his wife are famous for starting Farms for City Children in England.'

Alain nodded. 'All the time I worked for the charity in Africa, I wanted to be back in France, doing something similar with this place. Not a farm, although I always planned to 'ave a small area with animals, just a few chickens, maybe a goat or two, a horse, a cat, definitely a dog. Turning this place into an escape from the city for underprivileged kids. Give them a holiday in the country-side. That was my dream.'

Belinda struggled to keep the look of astonishment off her face. She'd always assumed that Alain was simply being stubborn about bringing the campsite into the twenty-first century. Preferring to keep the site as an homage to his parents.

'Did Nigel know about these plans?'

Alain smiled at her. 'Nigel he 'as always known about, and approved, my plans for the site. Seemed to think through me he would be doing his bit for some underprivileged kids.'

'But now he's sold the site to the new owners who probably won't care a fig about doing anything like that,' Belinda said sadly. 'I'm so sorry, Alain.'

Alain helped himself to some more salad.

'You asked me once why I didn't want you 'ere. Two reasons: One, I didn't want Nigel's troubleshooter 'ere sorting the place out. Me, I could do it on my own. Because I want to give kids from the inner cities a week or two living 'ere, learning about nature, I was determined to keep technology at bay. So, when you arrived and started talking about pods and glamping and going upmarket I couldn't believe it. That wasn't what I'd arranged with Nigel.'

Belinda held her hand up. 'Stop. You had an arrangement with Nigel? I thought it was your parents who'd sold the site to him.'

Alain looked at her. 'Originally, oui. Before I arrived back 'ere, Nigel he 'ad agreed to buy the campsite. Purely I think to 'elp my parents and stop the worry of it all for them. Fortunately, Nigel, he agree to change things for me. He wouldn't buy the campsite, but put up the money to get the place up and running again, I'd keep the costs down, and repay 'im within a maximum of two years.'

Alain picked up his wine glass and raised it in Belinda's direction. 'Bien, the campsite stay in the family and I can start to put my plan for holidays for children into practice. But he insist on sending you over – to troubleshoot and to make sure I keep to my side of the agreement. I think it a perfect arrangement – until you arrived, determined to pull the site into the twenty-first century with lots of technology everywhere and trying to attract the glamping luxury market.'

'So that's why you put up obstacles to the pods, and why he refused to sack you.' Belinda stared at him open-mouthed. 'But what happens now he's sold up? You won't be able to continue.'

'Yes I will. Nigel left our private arrangement with the campsite out of the sale to the new hotel people. We've rearranged things yet again. Now he's going to be a sleeping partner and I've got three years to pay 'im back instead of two.'

Belinda stared at him for a couple of seconds while the truth dawned on her. 'You mean you're the new owner? Or rather you've been the unknown owner all the time.'

'Oui,' Alain said, smiling and nodding at her. 'Mais, now you know. It can be our secret until the first of June when we officially open, oui?' He looked at her anxiously. 'We 'ave a party to tell everyone.'

'Sure,' Belinda said in a daze. 'I won't tell anyone.' She closed her eyes and took a deep breath, trying to clear her thoughts. Could this day get any more bizarre? First the emotional reunion with her father and now it turned out that she'd been working for Alain, not Nigel, all along. Belinda opened her eyes and looked at Alain thoughtfully. 'So what was the other reason you didn't want me here. You said there were two.'

Alain looked at her. 'As troubleshooters go, you weren't what I expected.'

40

The next morning, Belinda, feeling the need to get away from the campsite for an hour or two, slipped BB's lead on and prepared to walk down to the auberge. Maybe a chat with Fern would help sort her thoughts out.

'I'm just walking BB and returning the dish to Fern. Marie's in the office,' she called out to Alain as she saw him in the machinery shed fiddling with a petrol can. She didn't wait for an acknowledgement, just carried on walking down the drive.

To think it was over two months, nearly three in fact, that she'd driven up the road for the first time and the trees lining the route had been waving their bare branches in the wind. Today there was a canopy of green leaves overhead filtering the sunlight down through to the grass-covered verges with their daisies and bee-attracting dandelions.

Belinda remembered how resentful and unhappy she'd felt that first day, wanting to be anywhere but Camping dans Le Fôret. Now she was in a different turmoil with decisions to be made about things she'd never expected to have to give a second's thought to. She couldn't help wondering too, what exactly Alain had meant by his comment she wasn't what he'd expected. Her mobile had rung in the sudden silence that had followed his words with a message from Chloe and the moment had gone before she could ask him.

Yann was busy moving beer barrels as she walked past the village bar and called out a cheerful, 'Bonjour, Belinda,' when he saw her. She waved and called back as she made for the church and the road to the auberge

As she walked up the drive, she heard voices in the back garden, so rather than knock on the door, she made her way to the back of the house. Fern and Anouk were sitting with coffee on the terrace, looking at something on the laptop between them, and they both turned as she called out, 'Coo-ee.'

Lady came bounding over to BB and once Belinda had released him from the lead, the two dogs set off on a mad session of joyful play in the garden.

'I think they've missed each other,' Belinda said, laughing. 'Hi, how are you two?'

'I'm fine thank you,' Anouk said. 'I think the same can be said of Fern too,' she said with a smile, looking at Fern.

'Coffee?' Fern asked, reaching for the cafetière and going to stand up to fetch a cup from the kitchen.

'No thanks. I had one before I left the campsite. Thanks for supper last night, it was delicious.' Belinda put the dish down on the table.

'Grab a chair and sit down,' Fern said. 'I would have collected the dish later today. You didn't have to bring it back.'

Belinda shrugged. 'I fancied a walk and wanted to see you.'

'We thought about you yesterday,' Anouk said. 'How did it go?'

'Better than I thought it would, if I'm honest, but emotional and difficult at times,' Belinda answered. 'I was a bundle of nerves when we got there. Alain took charge and calmed me down.' She took a deep breath. 'Dad told me he'd never expected to see me again.' Belinda sighed. 'I sat with him, held his hand and we talked. We both cried a bit, a lot actually, him while I was there and me when I left. Seeing him so ill and remembering how strong he was years ago...' Belinda shook her head.

'Has anybody given you an idea how long he has?' Fern asked gently.

'No. I asked the nurse, but it's not really a question anyone can answer. She did take my number and promised to let me know as and when.' Belinda looked across at the laptop. 'What were you watching? Anything interesting?'

'I was just reading an email from Scott to Anouk,' Fern said.

'How is he?' Belinda asked.

'He seems to be fine,' Fern said. 'Says he's missing me even though we email and FaceTime.'

'Every night,' Anouk added with a smile.

'I was worried about his real life in America taking over and things between us slowly dying away. Even though he said he wouldn't let it.' Fern fingered the Scotty pendant around her neck.

'Oh ye of little faith,' Anouk said, starting to stand up. 'The man is in love with you. Anyone with a pair of eyes can see that.' Anouk took her cane in her hand and straightened up. 'I've a few things to sort in my room, so I'll leave you two to chat. If you see Enzo again, do please remember me to him.'

'I will,' promised Belinda. She owed Anouk a big thank you. If it hadn't been for her, it was doubtful that the reconciliation with her father would ever have happened.

'How is Scott's cousin?' Belinda asked as Anouk left them.

'She's doing better but it will be a couple more weeks before he'll be free to return.'

'I'll probably have left by then,' Belinda said. 'Once official opening has happened on the first of June, I'll be returning to the UK – jobless and homeless by the end of the month.' As Fern looked at her, shocked, Belinda explained about the hotels being sold and deciding not to work for the new owners. 'Maybe it's the wrong decision given that I have no idea yet of what I'm going to do, but so much has changed in the last few weeks, I feel a new direction – life, even – will be good for me.'

'Will you move to the Vendée to be close to Chloe?'

Belinda shrugged. 'It's an option, although I do feel that Chloe and Max should live their lives without me tagging along. I'll probably help them move and then settle into being a visiting granny.'

'What about coming to live in Brittany? At least you'd be in the same country. Easier to be that visiting granny.'

Belinda nodded thoughtfully. 'It's a thought. Alain wants me to stay working with him... and the new owners,' she added hastily, remembering her promise to Alain.

Fern raised her eyebrows.

Belinda laughed at the look on her friend's face. 'Stop it. Anyway, talking of the campsite, not long now before the café will open. You've organised the staff, the equipment is all in place, and once the kitchen has been inspected, we'll be good to go. As the manager, are you happy with everything? No major crisis or anything we've forgotten?'

'No crisis apart from the fact that I hope I don't let you down,' Fern said quietly.

'Not a chance of that happening. Alain will be there to have your back and give you any help you need.' Belinda stood up. 'I'd better make tracks. Get everything up to date before Chloe arrives and I have some time off. We'll arrange a day for you to come and meet Chloe and the twins.'

Walking back to the campsite, knowing that in a few weeks she would be leaving Brittany again, Belinda sighed. Despite all the upheavals in her life during the weeks since she'd arrived, it was beginning to feel like leaving was the wrong thing to do. But she had no idea as to what was the right thing. At least Chloe was arriving soon and she could talk it through with her.

41

After breakfast the day Chloe and the twins were due to arrive, Belinda gathered together the things she wanted to take down to the cabin situated next to Bernie's where she'd decided Chloe would be staying. As she closed the house door behind her, she could see Alain in the nearby hangar and she wandered over to see what he was up to. Bernie was there with him, helping building what looked suspiciously like a chicken house to Belinda.

'Is that what I think it is?'

Alain gave her a happy smile. 'Oui. Un poulailler for the chickens that arrive soon. I thought for it to go behind our maison. Fresh eggs for breakfast.'

'Your maison. You've forgotten I'm leaving soon,' Belinda said as gently as she could.

'Non. I don't forget.' Alain's happy smile vanished as he looked at her for several seconds before turning back to his work.

Belinda smiled at Bernie before making her way down to the cabin, pushing the look Alain had given her out of her mind.

Once in the cabin, Belinda began to put out the things she'd brought with her, including the welcome basket of local goodies that they planned to place in every cabin for guests and a bunch of flowers in a vase on the table. In addition, she'd brought things especially for the twins: Ribena in the fridge, along with some snacks if they were hungry, a few books, a new soft toy each on the freshly made up single beds, along with a box of biscuits.

Making a mental note to quiz Chloe about how she found the cabin – had they got it right? Had they forgotten anything that guests would want? Were the beds comfortable? – she left and made her way back through the campsite to the office.

* * *

It was mid-afternoon as Belinda was working on the computer in the office alongside Marie when she heard a car arrive and glanced up to see Chloe pulling into a parking slot. She rushed out to meet them and opened the passenger door.

'Hi, darling, let me jump in and show you straight to your cabin. Hi, you two monsters,' she said, looking at the twins strapped into their safety seats in the back.

'Gangan,' they shouted, both holding their arms out.

'Two minutes,' Belinda promised. 'And then lots of cuddles.'

'There aren't enough beds in the house Alain and I share, so I hope you like the cabin,' she said to Chloe as she pointed the way. 'You're a bit of a guinea pig really as I want a full report on how good it is to stay in.'

Belinda lifted the twins out of the car and held on to them as Chloe parked on the hardstanding that each cabin had down one side, before helping her carry the suitcases in.

'How was the crossing?' Belinda asked.

'Good. I'm glad we did a daytime one, there were lots of activities for the kids on board. This all looks lovely, Mum,' Chloe said.

'I've been looking forward so much to this break. Wish Max could have come too, but...' She shrugged.

'Did Charlie and Aimee sleep in the car? If they're not too tired, we can take them down to the river. It's only a short walk. Make sure they sleep tonight.'

'Don't know about them, but I'm tired,' Chloe said. 'Think it might be an early night.'

The next couple of hours flew by as Belinda showed Chloe and the twins the river, introduced the three of them to Fern, walked back through the campsite slowly, giving the twins a go on the newly refurbished tree swings and buying them an ice cream from the shop. There was no sign of Alain anywhere, but Belinda guessed he'd be in the office and didn't want to take the twins there in case they caused havoc. She'd introduce him to Chloe and the twins at supper.

When they got back to the house, Chloe and Belinda kept an eye on the twins while they organised supper. Charlie and Aimee had shrieked with delight on seeing BB again and played ball with him until the dog was panting and Chloe told them to stop. Now the twins were playing a game of their own making, involving stones and sticks in the small garden.

Alain came home just five minutes before the meal was ready and Belinda took him straight out to the terrace to meet Chloe and the twins. Once the introductions were over, Belinda excused herself and went to check on the chicken casserole she'd bought from Fern.

Five minutes later, Alain came back into the kitchen. 'Something smells good,' he said. 'If there's any left when I get back...' He looked at Belinda hopefully.

'Why aren't you eating with us?' Belinda said. It hadn't occurred to her that Alain wouldn't eat with them; they'd had a routine of eating together in the evening since she'd returned from the UK. 'There's more than enough chicken casserole. I didn't make it, if that's what bothers you. It's one of Fern's finest.'

'I didn't want to intrude on your first evening of family time,' Alain answered.

'Don't be silly. If you really have to be somewhere else or if your parents are expecting you, then fine, but if not, you're eating with us this evening. Who else is going to open the wine?' And she handed him the corkscrew with a smile.

With Aimee sat between her and Alain and Charlie next to Chloe, Belinda had the strangest feeling looking around at everyone that they could easily be mistaken for being a unit – a family unit. Chloe and Alain were laughing at something and the twins were managing to eat their food without spreading it everywhere. After everyone had finished, Chloe stood up.

'I think I'd better get these two in bed,' she said.

Belinda stood up too. 'I'll walk down with you and help. I'll clear this away later.'

'Non non.' Alain was already on his feet. 'You go. I do this.'

'Thanks. See you in a bit then,' Belinda said, taking hold of a twin in each hand.

Bernie was outside gardening when they got back to their cabin and Belinda smiled and waved at him.

Once the twins had cleaned their teeth and had a quick wash, they tumbled into bed. 'Story, Gangan.'

Belinda picked up one of the storybooks she'd bought and read them a story each and they were asleep before she finished the second one. She gently kissed them goodnight and went to join Chloe.

Chloe had made herself at home, unpacking her suitcase and, opening the welcome pack she found in the kitchen, was now ready to settle down outside with a bottle of rosé and some nibbles.

'This is going to be a little bit of paradise for the next few days,' she said contentedly. 'The site is lovely.' She picked up the bottle of wine and poured them both a glass. 'I know we had wine with supper, but hey, I'm on holiday. Dad sends his regards by the way.' A remark that Belinda acknowledged with a wave of her wine glass. 'I like your Alain,' Chloe said, raising her eyebrows at Belinda. 'He's lovely. Is that what you wanted to talk to me about?'

'No, and for the record, he's not my Alain,' Belinda answered.

'Judging from the way he looks at you, I think he could be,' Chloe said.

'Don't be daft. He's just a very good friend.' Belinda took a drink of her wine, wondering if that was the whole truth. He'd certainly got under her skin in a good way recently. 'What I need to talk to you about is granny and granddad. Anouk, Fern's ma-in-law, has lived here all her life and was able to tell me the truth about their break-up all those years ago.'

'One or both of them had an affair has always been my guess,' Chloe said, reaching for a handful of crisps.

'It's not quite as straightforward as that.' Belinda took a deep breath. 'They were never actually married. And the reason for that was because granddad already had a wife when he met my mum. A wife who had left him six years earlier.'

'Why didn't he just divorce her?' Chloe, ever pragmatic, asked.

'Because back in the day it wasn't that easy and also no one had heard from her or knew where she was in all that time. So when she turned up, eighteen years after granny and grandad got together, it was a shock and caused a huge scandal. Helena told all and sundry that she was still Mrs Belrose and she had no intention of divorcing.'

'Poor Granny. No wonder she was so bitter.'

'It explains a lot,' Belinda said. 'I wish though she'd told me the truth years ago.' She helped herself to a few crisps, glancing at

Chloe as she did. 'The other thing I have to tell you is that Granddad is here in Brittany and still alive. Very ill but alive.'

'Seriously?' Chloe gave a shocked gasp. 'He's here in Brittany? Are you going to see him?'

'He's been living in my old family home with his wife but a few days ago he was moved into a hospice where I've already been to see him. Nobody can say how long he has to live, could be a few days or a couple of weeks.' To her own ears, the words sounded automatic, unemotional, when the truth was she felt like a limp rag from all the emotion of the past few days.

'Can I see him? Meet him at least once?' Chloe asked quietly.

'I've shown him a photo of you and the twins and I've promised him, if the doctor allows it, I will take you to see him.'

'Thanks.'

The two of them sat silently for several moments, both lost in their own thoughts, before Belinda spoke again.

'I thought maybe one day while you're here we could go for a drive around. You said once I'd never told you about where I grew up.'

'Yes, I'd like that.' Chloe stifled a yawn.

Belinda stood up. 'I'll leave you to go to bed. I guess the twins will wake early as usual?'

'Oh yes. Six thirty, if I'm lucky,' Chloe said.

'I'll walk down with breakfast croissants for you in the morning. Sleep well.'

'Thanks, Mum. See you tomorrow then.'

Walking back through the campsite, Belinda passed a few people sitting outside their caravans enjoying the lengthening shadows and the bats that were flitting around. Too early for the owls to be calling, but Belinda knew she'd hear them later on. It was a sound she loved and one she'd miss when she left.

Alain was sitting out on the terrace reading when she got back to the cottage. 'Chloe settled in all right?'

Belinda nodded. 'Twins are fast asleep too.' She sank down on the chair next to him. 'You done your last patrol?'

Alain nodded. 'Oui. You like a nightcap?'

'One of your hot chocolates? Mmm, please. That would be lovely.'

Alain disappeared to the kitchen and Belinda closed her eyes. It seemed only seconds before he was back with two mugs of hot chocolate, one of which he handed Belinda.

'Thank you. And thank you for clearing up after supper.' Belinda smiled at him before taking an appreciative sip of her drink. 'Any idea what the forecast is for the next few days?'

'Cloudy with sunshine.'

'I've promised I'll give Chloe a short guided tour of where I grew up while she's here.'

'It is a good thing for you to do?' Alain asked. 'It won't upset you?'

'No, I don't think it will,' Belinda said thoughtfully. 'Having the twins with us will ensure that the memories don't get out of hand.'

42

The next morning when Belinda collected a bag of croissants from the shop and walked down to the cabin, the twins were already outside playing ball with Bernie, while Chloe watched. Belinda called out her usual Breton greeting to Bernie and he waved at her.

'I tried my schoolgirl French out, but I'm not sure he totally understood me,' Chloe said. 'He seems a lovely man.'

'He is, but he only speaks Breton, although I know he does understand some basic French.'

Five minutes later, coffee had been made and the croissants distributed, with a happy Bernie accepting one and sitting down at his own table in the next garden, where the twins and BB promptly joined him.

'Anything special you want to do today?' Belinda asked.

Chloe shook her head. 'I think a quiet day here ambling around. Maybe a picnic lunch down by the river on that bit of sandy beach? I've brought several of their favourite toys, so the twins will be happy playing here in the cabin's garden. I'll go for a walk with them later, find those tree swings again. I just want to relax really while I'm here. Do nothing for a few days.'

'Are you sure? I had lots of places lined up for a visit,' Belinda said.

'Quite sure. It's lovely here and, to be honest, the thought of dragging the twins around to see the sights...' Chloe gave a mock shudder.

'I suppose they are a bit young to do the touristy thing. But we must have one day out at least,' Belinda said. 'If only to go to one of the local markets.'

'Yes, I'd like that. Otherwise I'd rather spend some time here all together, although I would like to see where you grew up and visit the hospice, but right now I'm happy just to relax here with you.'

And so, for the next few days, they stayed on the campsite playing with the twins and having some mother and daughter bonding time. Thoughts of her father were never far away from Belinda's mind and she wondered about visiting again, taking Chloe with her. She rang the hospice every day when the nurse merely told her there was no real change and yes, his wife was there often. When the twins had their afternoon naps, Belinda caught up with office work. Alain joined them for meals and both he and Bernie played ball with them. Fern and Anouk came for lunch one day. On the fourth day, the hospice rang.

Belinda took the call when they were down by the river with a picnic tea. As soon as she realised who was calling, she wandered a little away upriver for some privacy, in case it was bad news. After the call ended, Belinda walked slowly back to the others.

Chloe looked at her anxiously. 'Granddad?'

Belinda nodded. 'The nurse rang to say if you hoped to see him while he's well enough to receive visitors we should try and visit within the next twenty-four hours. I said we'd go tomorrow morning.' She tried to not let Chloe see how emotional she felt at the thought of what would probably be the last visit.

Alain, when she told him about the phone call later, immediately said he'd take them. 'The twins also. I look after them.'

'I was going to ask Fern if she and Anouk would mind babysitting them,' Belinda said.

Alain shook his head. 'It will be a short visit, I think. I look after them. We take my car and leave at nine o'clock. D'accord?'

'Thank you,' Belinda said.

* * *

The next day, once the twins' safety seats, as well as their buggy, had been transferred to Alain's 4 x 4 and BB had been handed over to Bernie, they left for the hospice. Chloe, in the back with the twins, quietly reading them their favourite story. Belinda, sitting in the front next to Alain, wondered whether Enzo would be compos mentis enough to know they were there, or whether the drugs would have dulled his mind too much.

Less than an hour later, she was surprised when Alain turned into the hospice grounds. The quiet journey had passed quicker than she'd expected.

Alain parked and turned the engine off. 'Right. You two, go. The twins and I will walk while we wait.' He touched Belinda's arm gently. 'I hope it is not too difficult for you.'

Belinda gave him a wan smile before she and Chloe got out of the car and walked towards the hospice. Belinda, relieved to see the nurse she knew in the foyer, went straight over to her.

'Ah, Mrs Marshall, and your daughter. Enzo is more disorientated today than the day you saw him. I think perhaps one person at a time standing by his bedside. If you come first to see him, I'll fetch her afterwards.'

Belinda nodded and followed her as Chloe went to sit on one of the chairs in the waiting area.

The nurse stayed at the back of the room as Belinda went to stand by the side of her father's bed and gently took his hand in hers. 'Dad, it's me Belinda.'

At her words, his eyes opened briefly and she felt a slight squeeze of her hand before his eyes closed again and he drifted away. Belinda bit her lip as she looked at him. He was definitely weaker today.

The nurse touched her arm. 'I'll fetch your daughter.'

Belinda glanced at her and nodded. She sensed that her father was struggling to cope with any interaction. She didn't want to tire him out. Better to cut her time with him short so that he could meet Chloe.

'Dad, Chloe, your granddaughter, has come with me today. The nurse will bring her to you.' She bent and kissed him gently on the forehead. 'Bye, Dad. God bless.' Instinct told her she was unlikely to see him again.

Belinda turned as the nurse ushered Chloe into the room and spoke quietly to her.

'Your granddad is heavily sedated and he's drifting in and out of consciousness. Hold his hand as you talk to him quietly, tell him who you are, but don't expect a huge response, if any. Your mother and I will stay at the back of the room. Are you comfortable with that?' Chloe nodded and walked slowly towards her grandfather.

Standing at the back of the room, watching Chloe as she carefully picked up her grandfather's hand and gently stroked it, Belinda bit her lip. If only the two of them could have known each other properly.

'I know you don't know me, but I'm Chloe, your granddaughter.' Chloe's voice, filled with emotion, was barely audible. Belinda could tell she was struggling to hold back the tears.

Several seconds passed as she stood there, looking down at him before Enzo's eyes fluttered open and he saw his granddaughter for the first time.

'Hello, ma petite, thank you for coming. You look like my Jean,' he whispered, giving her a weak smile before his eyes closed again.

Chloe stayed where she was for several more moments, but Enzo didn't open his eyes again, and she glanced towards Belinda and the nurse.

It was the nurse who moved forward. 'I think it best if we leave him to sleep,' and she ushered them out of the room.

Chloe frantically searched for a tissue in her bag as the tears started to fall.

The nurse gave her a sympathetic glance. 'I know it's been hard for the two of you, but I think Enzo will pass the happier for seeing you both.'

Belinda exhaled a deep breath. 'He won't be alone will he when... the time comes.'

The nurse shook his head. 'No. I promise someone will be with him. His wife is planning on spending the next few nights here.'

'And you'll let me know?'

The nurse nodded. 'Of course. Goodbye.'

As they left the hospice building, a woman leaning heavily on a cane and walking with difficulty, her eyes downcast watching every step she took, was about to enter. Belinda politely held the door open for her and both she and Chloe stood to one side.

The woman lifted her head to look at them and mutter 'Merci' as she drew level. The thank you died on her lips as she faltered and looked at Belinda before visibly pulling herself together and moving forward again.

Belinda stared after her. She didn't need the confirmation of hearing the nurse greet the woman with the words, 'How are you today, Madame Belrose?' She'd known the moment the two of them had locked eyes seconds ago it was her father's wife.

43

'Are you all right?' Chloe asked, looking at Belinda through her still glistening eyes. 'You've gone pale, like you've seen a ghost.'

'Not a ghost exactly. That woman who just passed? That was Helena. I sort of realised it before I heard the nurse call her Madame Belrose. She doesn't look too healthy herself.'

'What?' Chloe looked back towards the hospice. 'It was? Do you want to go and... not sure what, talk to her maybe?'

Belinda shook her head.

'It's best left. I wouldn't know what to say to her, to be honest. Ah, good. Here's Alain and the twins. Did they behave?'

Alain nodded. 'Yes. I bribed them with promises of treats. How was Enzo?' he asked gently.

'Not good. It was emotional, to say the least,' Belinda said. 'Helena arrived too as we were leaving. I dread to think what would have happened if we'd still been in Dad's room.' She took a deep breath. 'You all right, Chloe? I'm sorry it was all a bit of an anticlimax with Granddad being so sleepy with the drugs.'

'I'm glad we came though,' Chloe said.

'Come on then, let's get the twins in the car and get going,'

Belinda said, feeling a sudden need to be as far away as possible from the hospice.

Alain drove out onto the main road, turned right and before long they were bowling along the dual carriageway in a homeward direction. When twenty kilometres later he indicated and took off along a slip road, Belinda glanced at him.

'Not going straight back to the campsite?'

'I promised Charlie and Aimee a surprise and this is the way,' Alain answered. 'We don't 'ave the need to rush back. Marie is in the office, Bernie has BB, Fern is at the café for deliveries. We 'ave some hours free. Une petite diversion.'

Five minutes later as they passed an official destination board on the side of the road, Belinda realised where they were heading. 'We're going to Lac de Guerlédan, aren't we?'

Alain nodded. 'You like?'

'It will be interesting to see it again,' Belinda said quietly. 'It's bound to have changed in the last thirty-five years. I remember trekking round it with the school on an environmental trip. Lots of trees and wild flowers.'

'These days, it's popular with tourists. This time of year, not so busy,' Alain explained. 'Lots of space everywhere.'

The lake was glistening in the midday sunshine as Alain parked in a gravelled area near a restaurant with picnic tables overlooking the lake.

'It's beautiful,' Chloe said, taking her sunglasses out of her bag and slipping them on.

Alain quickly found a table for them, ordered three coffees and a couple of soft drinks for Charlie and Aimee. 'We 'ave lunch here, oui?' he said. 'I promise the twins frites and 'ere they are très bons.'

'Sounds like a plan,' Belinda said, grateful that Alain had

taken charge. She suddenly felt tired and incapable of making any rational decisions. Coffee and food were definitely needed.

Alain looked at Chloe. 'I think today is not a day for lingering at lunch. I order frites and chicken goujons for us all? With salad for three and half a carafe of wine for you two, d'accord?'

Chloe smiled at him. 'You're right. The twins will want to be off playing as soon they've eaten. Thanks. Chicken goujons will be great.'

Sitting there in the sunshine watching the activity on the lake as she drank her coffee, Belinda tried to address the emotional feelings that had been threatening to swamp her since leaving the hospice. Feelings of guilt for not returning immediately to Brittany like her mother had urged were mixed in with anger at the way in which her relationship with her father had been torn apart.

The sane part of her brain wanted to believe nothing that had happened in the past was her fault, that she couldn't be blamed for the actions of her parents. But another part screamed 'you're feeble and pathetic' into her conscience for not facing up to things years ago when it would have been possible for her, if not her mum, to heal the rift with her dad. It added up to one indisputable thing. She could have had a relationship with her father if she'd been brave enough. There was no hope of rekindling her relationship with him now, as much as she would have liked to – a fact which made her feel bereft. Belinda smothered a sigh. Somehow she was going to have to learn to live with the knowledge that she'd simply given up on him all those years ago. And that realisation hurt. She'd failed someone who had once been the world to her.

Their food arrived at that moment, along with the half carafe of wine and while Alain tucked in and Chloe made sure the twins could manage before starting her own meal, Belinda quickly poured Chloe and herself a glass. 'Santé,' she said, raising her glass before taking a mouthful. When she did pick up her cutlery, she discovered the frites and goujons of chicken were delicious and that she was in fact hungry.

Charlie and Aimee ate all their chips and most of the chicken pieces before starting to fidget while the grown-ups finished their meals. While Alain went to the bar to pay, Chloe took the twins to the toilet and Belinda wandered down onto the path to wait for everyone. When Alain joined her, she smiled at him.

'Thank you. I'll settle up with you later for the meals.'

'Non. My treat. Are you okay? The visit today, it upset you?'

Belinda nodded. 'But I'm better now. Here come Chloe and the twins.'

Alain held out his hands to Charlie and Aimee and they both ran and grabbed a hand. 'Ice cream time,' he said. 'But first we 'ave to walk a little way to the best ice cream shop.'

Watching him walk along the path, a twin on either side holding his hand, Belinda smiled. The campsite visits he planned for disadvantaged children would be a huge success because he seemed to know instinctively how to deal with them and what they needed. What the twins needed right now apparently was a large ice cream cone covered in sparkles and, reaching the beach shop, they joined the queue to buy them.

Belinda and Chloe settled for a modest coffee-flavoured ice cream with a flake, but Alain had the same as the twins. Clutching their ice creams tightly, they made their way along a small deserted jetty and sat dangling their legs and feet in the water as they enjoyed them.

'Is this still the largest man-made lake in Brittany?' Belinda asked. 'I remember the teacher being inordinately proud of that fact when we came.'

Alain nodded. 'Oui. A few years back, they drained it to work on the dam itself. It was fascinating to see the ruins but sad in a way, knowing how many hamlets and how much land had been sacrificed. And now, it is full again. No one remembers what lies under the water.'

'It's a beautiful spot,' Chloe said. 'I'd loved to go sailing here. Maybe when the twins are about eight, we'll come back and spend a holiday on the campsite, teach them to sail. You up for that, Mum, coming back?'

'Who knows where we'll all be in five years,' Belinda answered. 'But yes, in theory, I'll come with you.'

After their ice creams were finished, they walked slowly back to the car for the rest of the drive home. Within minutes, the twins were asleep and everybody was lost in their own thoughts. It was after Alain had turned off the main road and was driving along the country lanes towards the campsite that Belinda recognised where they were.

'If you could pull over in the lay-by just past the next crossroads, I can point out the cottage where I used to live to Chloe,' she said quietly to Alain. 'The entrance drive is about twenty metres along the road, but you won't be able to see the cottage from there as the drive has a curve in it.' As Alain slowed the car before stopping in the lay-by, Belinda said, 'There you go, Chloe, that's the cottage where I grew up.'

Sitting there, looking across a field at her old home, Belinda felt a flood of emotions flow through her. The cottage itself was a typical Breton building, with gabled dormer windows, red shutters fixed to the wall downstairs and a red wooden front door. The field at the side where she used to ride Lucky was bright yellow with rapeseed flowers and the tall trees in the copse seemed to have been cut down.

Closing her eyes, in her mind she could still visualise the layout inside the cottage. A room on either side of the hallway, her bedroom next to the large kitchen at the back, and stairs leading to the main bedroom and bathroom on the first floor were hidden behind a door in the kitchen. Unbidden, a memory of her and her parents in the kitchen leaped into her mind. It was summer and they'd spent the day collecting and stacking enough bales of hay in the barn to feed their animals through winter and now the three of them were enjoying their supper sitting at the pine table. Belinda couldn't remember the food they ate but she knew there had been wine and a can of lemonade for her. What she could still remember all these years later though, was that both she and her parents had been a happy family that evening. She wished with all her heart that things had never changed.

Belinda opened her eyes and came to with a small start as Chloe spoke.

'It looks lovely, Mum,' Chloe said. 'Typically French. Which sounds silly, I know, but some of the cottages I've seen would look at home in England.'

The rest of the drive passed quickly and once back at the campsite, Chloe had to wake the twins up. Both Aimee and Charlie woke up grumpy, so Chloe said she'd walk them down to the cabin and see if playing with BB and Bernie would cheer them up.

Before Belinda and Alain went to the office to check that all was well, they took the baby seats and the buggy out of the car and took them into the cottage, where Belinda thanked Alain for the day.

'Lac de Guerlédan was a great idea,' Belinda said. 'Just what was needed to lift Chloe's and my spirits after the hospice.' Belinda ran her hands through her hair. 'Seeing my dad for what I know will be the last time was harder than I thought.'

'Come here,' and Alain pulled her into his arms for a hug. For several seconds, Belinda stayed there savouring the closeness and knowing Alain felt concerned for her.

'I could get used to these comfort hugs you keep giving me,' she said softly.

Alain looked at her wordlessly before giving her a gentle kiss on her head and releasing her.

44

Fern, busy fine tuning things in the café to her satisfaction before the impending dreaded hygiene inspection, hummed happily to herself as she worked. It had felt strange today arriving at the campsite without Belinda or Alain being there to greet her. She hoped that their visit to the hospice was not proving too traumatic for Chloe or Belinda. At least they were in good hands with Alain.

Fern smiled to herself. As much as Belinda might deny it, the telltale signs of their growing closeness were there for all to see. The evening they'd come for supper before Scott left, she'd detected a softness in Alain's eyes as he'd looked at Belinda. The solicitous way he'd silently watched her, ready to shield her from anything that might upset her when Anouk had mentioned her family, well that spoke volumes. She could only hope that things had progressed between them before Belinda left.

As she cleaned the café windows it struck Fern how much her own life had changed in the last few months since she'd met Belinda. Anouk moving in with her was, she supposed, the biggest change of all so far, closely followed by this job – something which would never have happened she suspected without meeting Belinda. She was so looking forward to summer and earning some extra money. Extra money that she could save towards recuperating the money invested in the auberge. And then there was Scott.

The café door opened at that moment and Fern, expecting it to be a hopeful camper looking for food, opened her mouth to apologise for the café not being open, but it was Fabian. She looked at him in surprise.

'Hi. What are you doing here? Anouk said she was expecting to see you this morning. Oh,' her hand flew to her mouth, 'has something happened to her?'

'Non. Anouk is fine,' Fabian quickly reassured her. 'I wanted to see you. You look well. Are you 'appier too?'

'Yes I'm happy,' Fern said, smiling at him. 'How are you all settling in at the Huelgoat house?'

'It is wonderful. Carole she too is 'appy,' Fabian said. 'Anouk tells me you are the manager here for the season.' He hesitated. 'She also tell me you have met a man?'

Ah, so this is where the conversation was headed, Fern thought and waited for Fabian to continue.

'An American?'

'Yes Scott is American.' Fabian, she could tell, was having difficulty in finding the right words to say what he wanted. Was he about to accuse her of being disloyal to his father? Tell her that it was too soon after Laurent? Well, she wasn't going to help him out, put words in his mouth, so she waited patiently.

'I am very 'appy for you,' Fabian said, taking a deep breath before continuing. 'But you tell this Scott please, that if he 'urts my step-mama he will regret. I will be on his case.'

Fern stared at him in astonishment. Fabian was concerned about her new relationship but not for the reasons she'd been expecting. He could have no idea how much his words had moved her. How much he'd reminded her of how protective Laurent had always been of her. Anouk had been right when she'd said Fabian was more like his father than he realised. Impulsively Fern leaned in and kissed Fabian's cheek.

'Thank you. I'm really touched by your concern. Scott will be back here in a few weeks and you'll meet him then. Anouk likes him and I'm sure you will too.'

'Good.' Fabian exhaled a deep breath, clearly relieved he'd said his piece. 'This place it looks good, you will 'ave a busy summer 'ere when people learn about your cooking. I 'ave to go.' A quick hug and he was gone, leaving Fern with a happy smile on her face.

She finished cleaning the windows, putting everything away tidily in the designated cupboards before standing and looking out of the now sparkling windows, deep in thought. She might have blithely told Fabian that he would meet Scott soon but in truth she had no idea of when that would happen. Every day when they spoke Fern hoped Scott would give her a return date she could write on the calendar and begin to cross the days off but so far all he'd been able to tell her was that things with his cousin were improving.

Thoughtfully she fingered the Scotty dog pendant that permanently hung around her neck these days. As much as she longed for his return, and she'd surprised herself when she'd inwardly acknowledged just how much she longed for that, there was nothing she could do except wait. Scott had promised he'd be back as soon as possible and she believed him. She could tell when they spoke on FaceTime that he was hating the separation as much as she was.

Absence makes the heart grow fonder might be a true saying but it was a difficult one to accept and live with. Fern sighed. All either of them could do was to knuckle down in their different countries, keep busy and the time would eventually pass. At least with summer fast approaching, Fern knew she'd soon be busy with the auberge and now the café.

She couldn't help wishing though, that as well as Scott returning so they could be a proper couple and enjoy the summer together, that Belinda wasn't leaving. The first real girlfriend she'd made in years, Fern knew Belinda was really going to leave a gap in her life when she left.

45

The next day when Belinda went down to the cabin with the usual breakfast croissants, Chloe greeted her with a sad smile. Charlie and Aimee took their croissants and went to sit with Bernie and BB as usual and Belinda glanced up at her daughter as she placed a cup of coffee in front of her.

'What's wrong?'

Chloe shook her head. 'Nothing anyone can do anything about.' She pulled her croissant apart and spread some marmalade over it. 'It's just I can't stop thinking about Granddad. I've thought more about him in the last twenty-four hours than I have done in twenty-three years.'

'Given the circumstances,' Belinda said gently, 'I'm not surprised. He'd been written out of our lives, but suddenly being here, he was pushed to the front of mine too.' She took a sip of coffee. 'Would you rather I hadn't said anything to you? Not told you he was here in Brittany; that he was ill? Maybe it was unfair of me to burden you with both a first and final memory of him.'

'No, I'm glad you told me. Granny keeping family secrets was bad enough, so don't you start.' Chloe sighed. 'Sorry, that sounded harsh, I didn't mean it to.'

Belinda was silent for a few moments. 'I honestly don't know what to say or how to tell you to stop overthinking things. I'm struggling with that myself.' She gave a rueful smile. 'I guess once you get back to Max and start packing up for your new life in the Vendée, memories of yesterday's visit will start to fade and merge into being something that touched you deeply but didn't in the end have a detrimental effect on your life. I hope so anyway.'

'But what about you?' Chloe asked quietly. 'It's not going to be easy for you to forget what you've learnt and seen since you've been here.'

Belinda was quiet for several seconds before she took a deep breath. 'I think, and this applies to both of us, it's impossible to turn the clock back and there's nothing we can do to change things, so we have to accept and try to move on. You will focus on a happy life with Max and the twins and I'll concentrate on you all.'

'Does that mean you'll come to the Vendée?'

Belinda rubbed her face and eyes. 'I still haven't decided, to be honest. Give me a bit more time to think about it, okay?' She finished her coffee. 'Right, it's your last full day. What do you want to do? Alain has suggested we have a barbecue this evening. Invite Fern, Anouk, and Bernie of course, and any of the campers who want to join us. What do you think?'

'Sounds good. The twins and I met up with another family by the swings. I'll find their caravan and invite them.'

'That's the evening sorted then. What about the rest of the day? There's probably a market on somewhere.'

Chloe shook her head. 'I'd just like to pootle about the camp-site, if that's all right with you. I might wander down to the shop and pick up a few bottles of wine and some cheese to take home for Max. And a final picnic lunch by the river again would be good.'

'Okay, I'll leave you to it and go and do an hour or two in the office. See you later for lunch.'

* * *

Belinda was on the phone taking a booking for a camper van for three weeks in August when Alain opened the office door and came in with a smiling Fern. Once she'd finished taking the details down and promised to send a confirming email, Belinda ended the call and turned to Fern.

'We passed. We can open the café whenever we like,' Fern said excitedly.

Belinda partially covered her face with her hand. 'The kitchen inspection this morning. I'd completely forgotten about it. I'm so sorry.' How could she have forgotten something so important? Having a lot on her mind was no real excuse.

'It is okay,' Alain said. 'Now we make plans for the official opening party.'

'We can celebrate a little tonight as well, can't we?' Belinda said. 'Chloe likes the idea of a barbecue for her last night. You and Anouk will come, won't you?' she said to Fern.

'Love to.'

* * *

Alain fired up the barbecue down on the entertainment area for the evening and news spread like wildfire through the campsite that the invitation was open to everyone. Still early in the season, there were only three or four camper vans and three caravans currently on site and nobody booked into the cabins. The family Chloe had mentioned arrived early with their two boys and were soon involved with Charlie and Aimee playing ball.

Watching Alain cooking at the barbecue, Bernie cheerfully helping him and handing out the food, Belinda found herself thinking again about the future when her time here was over. So far, the only decision she'd taken was to leave Milton Hotels when Nigel completed the sale. It was the first step in her new life and she should have felt happier about it than she did. It was not knowing the direction of her second step that was bothering her.

'Penny for them? You look miles away.' Fern wandered over to her side with two glasses of Prosecco and handed her one. 'Cheers. I've settled Anouk down with some new camper-van friends and she waved me away, told me to find you, so talk to me.'

'Not worth a penny or even a centime. How's Scott?'

'He's fine. Hoping to have a return date fairly soon.'

'I bet you're looking forward to that.'

Fern nodded. 'I still can't quite believe I've met someone else who I really like. Or the fact that he seems to like me too.'

'Believe it. You know, I'm really going to miss this place,' Belinda said, watching Alain as he turned to smile at something Chloe said.

Fern followed her gaze. 'Place or person?'

'Place... oh hell, all right, person as well,' Belinda admitted.

'Then stay,' Fern said.

'It's not that easy.' Belinda said automatically. Could she really pack up her old life in the UK and come back here and work for Alain like he'd suggested? Was she brave enough to take the leap?

'It's not that difficult either. Try turning it on its head and think of it as an opportunity. Once you've packed up your flat, given up your job, you can be footloose and fancy free for a few months. You've got the chance to do whatever you want, to go wherever you want.' Fern gave her a quizzical look. 'And I think you know deep down what you want.'

46

Both Belinda and Chloe were subdued the next morning at breakfast in the cabin.

'Even though parts of your week have been unexpectedly traumatic for you, I'm glad you came and I hope you are too,' Belinda said, glancing at her daughter.

'It's lovely here and most of the time has been great,' Chloe answered. 'As for the traumatic part, well...' She sighed. 'Yes, it was upsetting, but I'm glad I was here. I hoped it helped you to have me here?'

'More than you'll ever know,' Belinda said.

'You'll let me know when Granddad dies?'

Belinda nodded. 'Of course. Now, what time do you plan to leave for the ferry?'

'I thought about half eleven? I can take my time driving up to Roscoff and have a bite to eat in the restaurant at the ferry terminal before we board.'

'Want a hand packing the car?'

Chloe shook her head. 'No, I'm an expert at it these days.'

'In that case, I'll take Charlie and Aimee for a last walk down to the river. Keep them out of your way.'

'Thanks.'

The twins were happy to hold her hand as they walked along the river path and stood enthralled to watch a young deer cross the path, making its way into the field adjoining the campsite.

'Its tail bobbed up and down like a rabbit,' Aimee said, delighted.

By the time they returned, Chloe had packed the car, moved it up to the forecourt by the office and was standing talking to Alain. The twins promptly let go of Belinda's hand and ran up to Alain, who picked them both up and swung them around.

'Say goodbye and thank you to Alain,' Chloe said.

Belinda watched as both Charlie and Aimee hugged and kissed him goodbye before running over to her.

'Bye bye, Gangan.'

'Bye bye, you two. I'll see you soon,' Belinda said, watching as Chloe strapped them both into their seats. She gave Chloe a hug. 'Travel safe. Let me know when you're home.'

'Will do,' and Chloe gave Alain a goodbye hug before getting in the car and starting the engine. She wound the window down and beckoned Belinda over.

Puzzled, Belinda said, 'What is it? Have you forgotten something?'

'No. I just wanted to say, I don't think you should come to the Vendée with Max and me. Love you.' Giving her mum a mischievous smile, she drove off, leaving a speechless Belinda staring after the car. What was that all about?

Standing next to Alain, stood waving as Chloe disappeared out of sight, Belinda's mobile buzzed. Absently, she pulled the phone out of her pocket and, not looking at the caller ID, pressed the receive button.

'Hello?'

'Madame Marshall?'

The moment she heard the measured tone of the hospice nurse, Belinda knew what she'd phoned to tell her.

'I'm sorry to have to tell you that your father, Enzo Belrose, passed away early this morning.'

'Thank you...' Belinda couldn't get any more words out and collapsed against Alain as he put his arm around her, took the phone and spoke in rapid French to the nurse.

Ending the call, he put the phone in his own pocket and pulled Belinda's shaking body against him in a tight embrace, and let her cry her heart out.

* * *

Later that evening, Belinda and Alain were sitting in the cottage garden after supper, although Belinda had played with most of her food rather than eating it. Whatever she'd expected to feel when the end came for her dad, it hadn't been this huge sense of loss that made her feel even guiltier for all the wasted years.

When Belinda's mobile rang, she looked at Alain in surprise.

'My phone sounds as though it's ringing from your pocket. I expect that is Chloe saying she's home.'

Alain smiled. 'I forgot I still had it,' and he handed it to her. But it was Anouk, not Chloe.

'Belinda, ma cherie. Sad news today, I'm so sorry.'

'Thank you.'

'I have to tell you what I have just heard from a relative of Enzo's.'

Belinda stilled and waited.

'There will be no religious ceremony, just a private burial at the cemetery the day after tomorrow, but she, Helena, is not telling anyone what time. Says she doesn't want anyone there. I 'ave to tell you, this is not normal in France. We like to say a final farewell to our loved ones.'

'Thank you for telling me,' Belinda said, switching off the phone and turning to Alain. 'Dad is being buried privately the day after tomorrow apparently, but Helena doesn't want anyone there. No service. No nothing.' Belinda rubbed her eyes. The news had upset her, but she was all cried out. 'Isn't that quick for a funeral?'

Alain shook his head. 'Not here in France. By law, they 'ave to 'appen within six days of a death.' He looked at her. 'Would you 'ave gone?'

'I'm not sure. I wouldn't have wanted my presence to cause a scene or gossip, so probably not. I would like to pay my last respects though. Will you take me to the cemetery someday?'

'Yes,' Alain replied. 'Whenever you're ready and want to go, I take you.'

47

For the next few days, Belinda lost herself in work. With the official opening day getting closer, there was a lot of promotional work to do. Belinda updated the website booking form, wrote a press release and sent it out to as many journalists as she could find, both in England and in France. The local paper contacted her when they received theirs and said they'd send a photographer on the day. She created a Facebook page, a Twitter account and an Instagram profile where she uploaded photo after photo of Camping dans Le Fôret.

In addition to all this, she was working with Alain with the preparations for the party he wanted to throw before the official opening when he planned on telling everyone he was the new owner.

Fern was going to open the café a day or two before the official opening. 'Need to iron out any possible snags without being pressured by a long queue getting impatient,' she explained to Belinda. 'And as I'm in charge of the food for the party, it will give me a chance to use the kitchen and also put the staff to work.'

* * *

The evening before the party when Alain was out with Bernie putting a slide up in the children's park area, Belinda phoned Jane.

'You are still coming tomorrow? I forgot to tell you earlier to bring some party togs with you. We're having a "before we are open" party tomorrow night.'

'I'll throw something floaty and revealing into the case,' Jane said. 'Something to catch the eye of the sexy-looking Serge Gainsbourg type you work with.'

'Behave yourself. Jeans and a sparkly top will be fine,' Belinda said, laughing. 'It's a campsite.'

'Have you decided what you're going to do after you leave Milton Hotels?' Jane asked.

Belinda hesitated. She had yet to tell Jane about everything else that had happened recently. 'A lot has happened over here and I haven't had time to give it much thought,' which wasn't strictly true, but her time and thoughts had been swallowed up by her dad, the hospice and Chloe's visit.

'Ooh, sounds intriguing,' Jane said. 'Tell me more.'

'Too much to tell for now. We'll have a good catch-up when you're here,' Belinda promised. 'I'll tell you everything then.'

Thoughtfully, Belinda put her phone down. She had made a decision, but she wasn't going to share it with anyone until she knew for certain it was the right one. And she wouldn't have the answer to that until the night of the party.

* * *

The campsite was a hive of activity the next day, with bunting and lights being hung and draped around trees and buildings. The tall oak trees and the silver birches that lined some of the paths had coloured uplighters placed at the base of their trunks, ready to throw purple and green lights up into the branches as evening fell. The restaurant had fairy lights hung around its takeaway serving hatch that was acting as the bar for the evening. Tables had been dragged out of the restaurant and covered with white cloths ready for the buffet-style food and crockery to be placed on them. Alain had arranged a couple of speakers around the entertainment area and set up a sound system using the electricity from the restaurant.

It was late afternoon when Jane and Brett arrived, later than expected because of roadwork delays. Belinda took them down to their cabin to settle in, apologised for not being able to stay and chat, but she had to go and change for the party. 'Just follow the music when you're ready and you'll find the party. I'll see you in a bit.'

Back at the cottage, Alain was already dressed for the party and about to leave.

'You're looking... good,' Belinda said. She'd been about to say hot but couldn't be sure how Alain would react to her saying that. Maybe later when she'd talked to him and asked him a certain question, maybe then she'd tell him how good he looked tonight. Or maybe not.

'Merci. The bathroom's all yours. I go collect my parents,' and he was gone.

Belinda decided a shower would have to do – as much as she longed to soak in a perfumed bath, there wasn't time. Half an hour later, she was showered, hair and make-up done. She took a favourite dress off its hanger, slipped her arms into it and did up the buttons that ran down the front from the sweetheart neckline to the hem. A rich blue in colour and ethnic in style with raised embroidery, she knew the slightly fitted waist and flared skirt suited her.

There was already quite a crowd of people as she walked through the campsite down to the entertainment area. Fern was fussing around the food tables and Anouk was sat holding court with some friends from the village.

Fern gave Belinda a big happy smile as she saw her and Belinda could tell she was bursting with some news.

'Scott sends you and Alain his best wishes and he'll be back at the end of June. He's booked his ticket.'

'Oh, Fern, I'm so pleased for you,' and she gave her friend a hug. 'Any idea where I'll find Alain?'

'He was just showing a couple into a cabin,' Fern said. 'Why don't you go and find him. It's his party and he should be circulating.'

'True. I didn't think anyone was booked in for a cabin tonight.' Belinda turned and began to walk towards the first of the cabins, wondering which one had been booked. She had her answer when she saw two people sitting around a table, and Alain pouring them a glass of champagne each. Must be his parents, although they looked familiar.

One of them must have seen her coming because Alain turned and smiled at her, at that very moment she recognised Nigel and Molly and began to run towards them.

'I don't believe this. Why didn't you tell me you were coming?'

'Because it was a surprise,' Nigel said.

Belinda turned to Molly. 'How are you? Aren't you supposed to be resting still? Not travelling.'

'I'm much better. A change of scenery is good for me,' Molly said. 'This place is looking a lot better.'

'Alain has worked wonders,' Belinda said.

'You, of course, didn't do anything.' Alain laughed and shook his head at her.

'How long are you staying?' Belinda asked.

'Definitely a week. Maybe longer,' Molly said. 'Alain was telling us you've had a difficult few weeks?'

Belinda nodded. 'Emotional, that's for sure. But I understand why Mum did what she did better now.'

Molly patted her arm. 'Your mum was wracked with guilt over the way things affected you.'

Belinda took a deep breath. 'All in the past now, Molly.'

Nigel stood up and held his hand out to Molly. 'Come on then. Let's join the party and find some food. I'm starving.'

Alain walked alongside Belinda as they made their way back down to the restaurant. 'You look beautiful tonight. Lovely dress.'

'Thank you,' Belinda said, suddenly feeling shy and uncertain, remembering the decision she'd made. A decision that involved asking Alain a certain question. The answer to which would decide her future. She took a deep breath. She had planned to wait until later but now seemed as good a time as any.

'I've been thinking, as you're the new owner of the campsite, and I quite like working with you, and I'm going to be unemployed and homeless in a few weeks...' She paused. 'That maybe, if you wanted me to, I could come back for the rest of the season and work for you.' She deliberately kept her voice light and didn't look at him as she spoke. 'The only problem is, I don't know where I'd live.'

She heard Alain's sharp intake of breath before he caught hold of her hand and held it tightly. 'Pas de problème. You stay with me, in the house,' Alain said. 'And I do my best to persuade you that that's where you belong.' As he took her in his arms and bent his head to kiss her, Belinda knew she'd made the right decision. She belonged not only in Brittany but also in Alain's arms.

EPILOGUE

A YEAR LATER

Belinda returned to Devon the week after the party and official reopening of Camping dans Le Fôret. Before she left, Alain took her as promised to the cemetery and she said her goodbyes to her dad. As well as placing two white potted roses on his grave, one from her and one from Chloe, she also put a pot of daisies in the middle for her mami. Now Belinda lives in Brittany, she visits the grave once a month and tends the flowers.

Nigel told her not to worry about working a month's notice, just empty her flat and get organised for her new life in Brittany with Alain.

Chloe received the news that her mum was returning to Brittany and Alain with a grin. 'I knew that was going to happen. You looked so right together when I was there. I'm so pleased for you. And when we get to the Vendée, you'll both be just up the road.' Belinda didn't point out that it was in fact a couple of hundred miles up the road, but at least it would be the same country.

Alain had the first group of children to stay at the campsite in September at the end of the season. This year, there are plans for at least six group visits.

Bernie still lives on the campsite and there are no plans for him to move. In fact he is helping Belinda with her Breton language skills.

Enzo's cottage now belongs to Belinda. Currently it was standing empty. The plan was for Belinda and Alain to renovate and decorate it during the coming winter when the campsite closes, and live there out of season. A plan Belinda is surprisingly happy about.

Helena died within nine months of Enzo. Just a week before she passed away, Belinda was surprised to receive a short letter from Helena asking her to visit. 'There are things that need to be said' was the cryptic sentence at the end of the letter.

Belinda agonised for hours over whether she should go to see Helena. What could it possibly achieve? In the end she'd gone out of the kindness of her heart not knowing what to expect. It had been a strange feeling driving up the lane to the smallholding and parking outside her former home.

The door had simply been pulled to and Belinda pushed it open and walked in, calling out 'Hello'. Helena had been sitting at the kitchen table waiting for her.

'Good of you to come,' she'd said, indicating a chair. 'I wasn't sure you would.'

Belinda had sat and waited for Helena to speak.

'Although he knew he was dying, Enzo was a happy man for the last weeks of his life,' Helena had told her. 'Your mother was the love of his life, not me, and he adored you. Seeing you again meant everything to him.' She'd taken a deep breath then. 'I'm ashamed to say it was me who kept the two of you apart. I was the one who lied and convinced him you didn't want to have any contact with him.'

Belinda had nodded. 'I'd finally worked that out for myself. Sadly your actions made three people desperately unhappy and

I'm not sure you were particularly happy either. Life could have been so different. I hope you aren't asking me to forgive you, because I can't.' She'd given Helena a compassionate look before she stood up to leave. 'But I do feel truly sorry for you.'

There was nothing more she could bring herself to say to Helena, who was clearly an ill woman, and she'd quietly left, closing the door behind her.

BREAKING NEWS:

Earlier today, Belinda and Alain, with Chloe, Max and the twins, joined Fern's daughters and their families, Anouk, and four cousins of Scott, to celebrate the marriage of Fern and Scott in the village Mairie.

Their reception is now underway in the newly refurbished campsite restaurant. Fern insisted it was the only place she wanted to hold it. Fabian, Carole and their family have joined them with other local friends.

Scott is soon going to whisk Fern away on a secret honeymoon, and Anouk and Lady are going to stay in the cabin next to Bernie so that Alain and Belinda can keep an eye on them both. The newly-weds have had their first dance together and are now planning on slipping away and leaving everyone to party, but first Fern is determined to throw her bouquet.

Her aim is good and Belinda catches it easily. Alain leans in and whispers something in her ear. She turns and is heard to say, 'Maybe next year.'

ACKNOWLEDGMENTS

As always my huge thanks go to the team at Boldwood Books: Caroline my patient astute editor, Nia and Amanda, Jade the copy editor and proofreader, Shirley – you are all ace and thank you for making my books the best they can be.

Thanks to my online writing friends and fellow Boldwood authors, who boost me up and keep me sane when I have a bit of a wobble!

Huge thanks to my husband who has taken over the kitchen while I write and produces the most delicious meals and naughty treats just when I need them.

My heartfelt thanks also go to you, the reader – without you buying and liking my books I wouldn't be able to do the best job in the world. Receiving an email from someone who has read one of my books and has not only enjoyed it but says it took her away from all her problems for a couple of hours is a wonderful and rewarding feeling.

Jennie x

MORE FROM JENNIFER BOHNET

We hope you enjoyed reading *A French Affair*. If you did, please leave a review.

If you'd like to gift a copy, this book is also available as an ebook, digital audio download and audiobook CD.

Sign up to Jennifer Bohnet's mailing list for news, competitions and updates on future books.

http://bit.ly/JenniferBohnetNewsletter

Villa of Sun and Secrets, another gloriously escapist read from Jennifer Bohnet, is available to buy now.

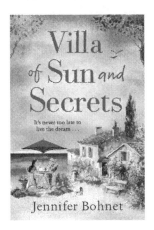

ABOUT THE AUTHOR

Jennifer Bohnet is the bestselling author of over 10 women's fiction novels, including *Villa of Sun and Secrets* and *The Little Kiosk By The Sea*. She is originally from the West Country but now lives in the wilds of rural Brittany, France.

Visit Jennifer's website: http://www.jenniferbohnet.com/

Follow Jennifer on social media:

[f] facebook.com/Jennifer-Bohnet-170217789709356

[twitter] twitter.com/jenniewriter

[instagram] instagram.com/jenniebohnet

[BB] bookbub.com/authors/jennifer-bohnet

ABOUT BOLDWOOD BOOKS

Boldwood Books is a fiction publishing company seeking out the best stories from around the world.

Find out more at www.boldwoodbooks.com

Sign up to the Book and Tonic newsletter for news, offers and competitions from Boldwood Books!

http://www.bit.ly/bookandtonic

We'd love to hear from you, follow us on social media:

facebook.com/BookandTonic

twitter.com/BoldwoodBooks

instagram.com/BookandTonic

Made in the USA
Columbia, SC
21 November 2020